Bachelor Swap

A Bachelor Tower Series World Novel

Lacey Black

Lacey Black

Bachelor Swap

A Bachelor Tower Series World Novel

Copyright © 2021 Lacey Black

Cover Design by Melissa Gill Designs
Cover Photo – Deposit Photo

Editing by Kara Hildebrand

Proofreading by Joanne Thompson & Karen Hrdlicka

Format by Brenda Wright, Formatting Done Wright

ISBN-13: 978-1-951829-10-0

Welcome to the Bachelor Tower Series World

Ruth Cardello's Bachelor Tower is now a World where every apartment is occupied by a hot bachelor. Garry F. Brockton created an all-male haven for ambitious men who want to live like kings and play by their own rules. Casino nights, a fully equipped gym and lap pool, cigar and Scotch bar, and a media room with screens the size of the average movie theater. The list is endless. Men use the connections they make there to launch their careers or stay on top. It's impossible to get into and even harder now that Brockton's niece inherited the building after his death. She's trying to shake the place up, but for now it remains a haven for ambitious men. The best part: the tower attracts women, beautiful women who hang out in the lobby bar and vie for an invite upstairs.

Under new management, the place has a bit of a curse: Lately, even the most diehard of the bachelors have been falling in love. . .

Welcome to the Bachelor Tower Series World.

Chapter One

Mason

"Last call for Flight 2455 to Boston."

My palms are clammy, and I almost turn around. I *should* turn around. Yet my feet carry me toward the gate.

I hold out my cell phone and scan my ticket. "Thank you, sir. Have a pleasant flight," the attendant says with a beaming smile and too-white teeth.

I mumble something somewhat polite in return, reposition my worn duffel bag over my shoulder, and head down the walkway, which is backed up with passengers waiting to board the plane. Before I can turn and make a mad dash out of the tunnel, the door is closed behind me. The only way out is forward.

Onto the plane.

I don't have a fear of flying. Don't get the wrong idea here. I'm fine flying and have done so a dozen times. It's the destination that has me dragging my feet and sweating profusely in my flannel shirt. A city I've never visited and am dreading with everything I am.

Boston.

It only takes a few minutes before I'm boarding the plane. "Good afternoon, sir. There aren't many seats left open. Please take whatever you can find," the flight attendant greets when I step inside.

"I'm in first class," I inform her, showing my phone with the seat number.

"Oh, then if you'll follow me," she replies, turning to the left and walking to the front. "Seat 4B. May I take your bag?" she offers when we reach my seat.

"No, thanks. I've got it," I reply, shoving my bag against a garment bag in the overhead bin and probably wrinkling the suit or dress inside. Oh well.

"Something to drink?" she politely asks, as I drop into my seat.

"Water, please." I should order scotch.

She nods and heads the few feet to the front of the plane.

"Surely this isn't your first time flying," the man beside me states. I glance over, instantly recognizing money. He's wearing a three-piece suit in crisp black with a blood red tie. His aged face is freshly shaved, and his blue eyes sparkle with mischief.

"No," I state, buckling my seat belt and relaxing in the plush first-class seat.

"I fly almost weekly nowadays for work."

"That's nice," I mumble, closing my eyes and hoping the suit takes the hint.

"Morris Thompson, Mr. Wilder," he says.

When I crack open my eyes, I see his hand extended toward me. "Have we met?" I ask, hesitantly placing my hand in his.

Morris chuckles. "A few times, but never in the boardroom. I believe the last time I saw you, you were soaking in the sauna. I almost didn't recognize you so...casual."

I glance down at my faded Wranglers and dusty ol' boots. My flannel is untucked and mostly clean, if not a little wrinkled. The start of a beard spreads across my face, since I have no clue when the last time I shaved was. Hell, I probably even smell a bit like the cattle I fed right before I jumped into my truck to head for the airport.

Realization hits me like a Mack truck. Morris here thinks I'm Matthew.

My twin brother.

As far back as I can remember, we've been mistaken for each other. That happens a lot when you're an identical twin, especially with those who don't know you well enough to recognize the subtle differences that do exist. Hell, back in junior high, we used to switch places with each other when deemed necessary. You know, like when I had a math test and Matthew was above average in mathematics, or when it was time for the science fair and my brother had to present his project on bridge building. We both have our strengths and weaknesses and learned early on how to play them in our favor.

Until one day, it bit us in the ass...

"What brought you to Montana? Business or pleasure?" he asks, as the attendants go over their pre-flight instructions.

"Both," I reply, looking over his right shoulder to see us taxiing to our runway.

"Me too," Morris says before diving into his tale of business takeovers and corporate mergers. I start to zone out after the first ten seconds, and it isn't until we're in the air and the flight attendant is delivering more drinks, do I realize I should probably be paying attention.

This will be my life for the next thirty days.

Even though Matthew and I haven't spoken much in the last few years, I'm headed to Boston to meet up with my brother. The one who vowed to get me out of my latest pickle if I do just one little thing for him. Something we agreed to never do again.

Switch places.

***

Turns out, Morris lives in the same building as Matthew. I figured that out quickly as we flew across the Midwest and he wouldn't shut up about the place. The older man has a serious hard-on for what's known as the Bachelor Tower. Every amenity you can imagine at your fingertips. Women in the bar just waiting for an invitation to join you upstairs. More business contacts than a man knows what to do with.

Except, apparently, it's not just men anymore.

Morris bitched for thirty minutes straight about the fact there's now at least one female living within the confines of the men-only apartment complex. Something about the niece of the previous owner and how she wrecked the empire her late uncle built. I wanted to ask who gives a shit, but apparently, it's a bigger deal than I thought. Women don't belong in the Bachelor Tower, according to Morris.

When the plane finally lands, I'm more than ready to get the hell away from Morris Thompson. I quickly unbuckle and stand, stretching my lower back. I open the overhead compartment and grab my duffel bag, anxious to get the hell out of this tin can. Away from Morris and his nonstop jabbering.

Since luck hasn't been on my side in the last year, at least, I'm stuck exiting the plane with the man right behind me. When we make it inside the airport, I try to speed up, but surprisingly, Morris keeps pace. Even with his suitcase and garment bag, he remains by my side as we maneuver through the crowded airport.

When I reach the front entrance, I start to look for the driver my brother was sending. I have no idea what he looks like, but since I'm the spitting image of the guy's boss, I figured it'd be no problem for him to pick me out of a lineup.

"Ahh, I see George is here, Mr. Wilder. Pity I didn't message Frank to cancel my ride so we could ride together," the man who has been my talking shadow since the moment I boarded the plane says.

"Yes, pity," I reply, heading toward the man I assume is George.

"See you soon," Morris announces before turning and heading toward his own driver.

"How was your flight?" George asks as I approach, reaching for my bag.

"Fine," I mumble, slipping through the open door and sinking onto the soft as butter seats.

George closes the door behind me and deposits my bag into the trunk. I sigh, relaxing for the first time in more than forty-eight hours. Hell, probably even before that. Life has been...*stressful* lately.

I'm not usually this much of an asshole, I swear. In fact, I'm the fun, easygoing twin. Matthew has always been the focused, driven brother, the one who rules the boardroom and closes any deal, not caring who he fucks over along the way.

I'm the other brother. The one who jumps in with both feet without weighing the odds, who rarely listens to the advice of anyone around him, and who usually skates through life by the skin of his teeth.

Well, my teeth weren't able to save me this time.

I'm in deep water with no raft in sight.

That was, until Matthew called me.

I should be surprised he found out about the shit back in Montana, yet I wasn't. His laser-focused attention to detail and keen eye picked up on the fact my ranch was in trouble. That or he knows the bankers in town, which wouldn't surprise me in the least.

Matthew has contacts all over the world, why not in Casper, Montana?

The ride to where my brother lives isn't too bad, despite being midafternoon on a Saturday. Even as we move steadily through the city, this place is nothing compared to Casper. Two stoplights and a Walmart are all we have back in the southern Montana town, which suits me just fine. The less populated, the better, in my book.

Eventually the car stops in front of a big building. It's large and regal with floor-to-ceiling windows and a view from just about any angle. I can already see why my brother loves it. It's better than Park Avenue in New York City. When the door opens, George is standing there.

The first thing I notice when I step outside is the sky is as gray as my mood, and the fact it looks almost odd against the pristine building laid out in front of me. I can't help but stare up at it, as if it were a painting in a museum.

"Good afternoon, sir. If you'll follow me," a gentleman in a uniform says, opening the front entrance.

"Thanks," I reply, stepping through the doorway and into the spacious lobby.

Then I notice is a large bar. There are a handful of men sitting around, but it's the women who catch my attention. There's almost twice as many women as men in the room, all dressed to the nines with their *assets* on full display. Yeah, this place is nothing like the Smoky Saloon back home.

Sighing, I follow the doorman to the elevator. "Mr. Wilder is expecting you, sir." As soon as the car door opens, I step in and wait, not sure where I'm going. The doorman makes it easy though and presses the button for the twelfth floor. "Twelve oh four, sir. Have a good day."

Then the door closes behind him and I'm left in silence.

Sagging against the back wall, I close my eyes and contemplate all my options once more. Yeah, I've already been over them a million times, which is why I'm actually here—in Boston—and riding the elevator to my brother's apartment.

The bottom line is I don't have any options.

Not if I want to keep my ranch.

The damn beef prices dropped and have been down too long. The cost of feed isn't helping either, and over the last year, I've gotten behind. I've let all of my farmhands go in an effort to save money, but it's not enough. The bank is breathing down my neck, threatening to take what I've built if I don't come up with half the back mortgage now, and the other half in three months. It's not like I can just snap my fingers and produce one hundred and fifty thousand bucks, dammit.

That's when my brother called.

Convenient, isn't it?

I'm saved from having to speculate into the whys and hows of my brother's timing when the door opens for the twelfth floor. I step out and glance down the long hall, finding a handful of other doors, all spaced pretty far apart. I have a feeling this place isn't some small apartment with minimal closet space.

Just as I approach door numbered 1204, it opens, revealing my twin. Even though we haven't seen each other in well over two years, Matthew looks exactly the same. Hell, he looks exactly like me, if I were to shave my face and put on clothes that probably cost more than my work truck back at home.

"Mason," Matthew states in way of greeting. He steps back to allow me to enter and glances down the hallway before closing the door behind me. "How was your flight?"

I shrug and glance around the apartment. "It was fine."

"Good."

We stand there awkwardly for several long seconds, each taking the other one in. My brother and I have always been more different than one would expect. Our similarities stopped in the looks department, that's for sure.

Matthew is well-dressed and regal. He's wearing suit pants and a button-down shirt, even while at home in the middle of a Saturday. He no doubt has a standing appointment to get his hair cut at a salon and his nails manicured. The leather shoes on his feet probably were flown in from Italy or Paris, where fashion reigns supreme and money is no object.

Me? I have cowshit on the bottom of my dusty ol' work boots.

"Why don't we head into my office and we'll discuss the reason I brought you here," Matthew states, his tone flat, as if he were making a business transaction instead of visiting with a brother he hasn't seen in a while.

But I guess that's what this is.

A business deal.

As I follow behind my twin brother, I can't help but notice how clinical this place is. Not a splash of color anywhere. White carpet, tan leather furniture—that looks like it just rolled off the showroom—and boring black-and-white art that looks like it was done by a kindergartener. And the kitchen? From what I can tell, it looks like it hasn't actually ever had a meal cooked in there.

The room my brother uses as an office, however, is a night and day contrast to the rest of the home. Old, worn leather chairs and a large desk with character. A large shelving unit with books, no doubt collector editions. Matthew only collects things he can make financial gain from in the long run.

"Have a seat," he says, walking over to a small bar and pouring a finger of golden liquid into two glasses.

When he rejoins me, he hands me a glass. "Thanks."

Matthew takes his seat behind the desk and quietly observes, scrutinizing my presence as he sips his bourbon. I take a hearty drink of my own and relax back into the chair. "So, you're the one who brought me here. What's up?"

My brother grins wickedly before finishing off his drink. He doesn't answer my question, just shuffles around a few papers before settling on a manila folder. He moves everything else in the vicinity of his folder and slips a pair of glasses on to his face. I'm not sure when he started wearing glasses, but it doesn't help soften his appearance.

Matthew slides into business mode. He's tense and completely serious, scanning the documents in front of him with a keen, sharp eye. If I were a lesser man, I'd be a little unnerved sitting across from him right now, especially when he focuses those sharp dark eyes on me.

He leans forward, turning the document and sliding the open folder across the desk. I mimic his movement and lean forward, my own gaze dropping down to what he's showing me. My eyes widen as I scan the contract; the one with my name on it. There's also no missing the dollar amount displayed at the bottom.

When I glance up, I see him relax for the first time. He hitches an ankle over his knee and leans into his seat, a triumphant grin on his face. "I have a business deal for you."

Chapter Two

Kyla

"How are the animals?" my best friend, Amalee, asks between bites of her chef salad.

"Really good." I set my fork down, excitement racing through my veins. "We got in a new Belgian horse yesterday. She comes from a farm just outside of town. She's in her twenties already and such a sweetheart. It took me a few tries, but I got her to eat an apple out of my hand."

Amalee rolls her eyes, but smiles. "You and those animals."

Those animals have been my life for nearly four years. I've always had a soft spot for animals of all kinds. I used to rescue birds and small squirrels regularly when I was younger, much to my parents' and housekeeper's dismay. She'd always find the shoebox or small crate I'd stash somewhere in my room and insist they be removed immediately. *"Rabies,"* she used to bellow as she'd cart them off, never to be seen again.

"This one was well cared for, but the owner recently passed, and the family didn't want her. They donated her to the shelter," I tell her, referring to the Boston Cares Shelter. "We shouldn't have any problems connecting her with a new home."

BCS is a volunteer based, donation-funded animal shelter, connecting mistreated or unwanted pets with their forever homes. Most of them are cats and dogs, but we do have a large barn for other animals. I'm my four years of volunteering, I've seen goats, horses, a llama, cattle, and even a few donkeys. Sure, they're unusual for a city like Boston, but Boston's a growing, unique place, especially in the suburbs.

Amalee grins her red, glossy lips at me. "I can already see your wheels spinning. Need I remind you, you live in a condo?"

I scoff, but don't dispute her statement. I do, in fact, live in a condo. The penthouse, actually. But it's the fact she's able to read me like a book. She knows me well enough to understand that if I had a place to keep Dolly, the horse, I'd take her in a heartbeat.

"You should just move, Kyla."

Startled by her statement, all I can do is stare at my oldest friend.

She sets her fork down and leans in. "I'm being serious. You hate that condo and hate the city. You're only still here because of your dad, whether you want to admit it or not."

I open my mouth to reply, but nothing comes out. She's not wrong. I'm not a huge fan of the city, and the condo looks more like a museum than a home. But what really got me was the part about my dad. My throat tightens, mostly because I know she's right. I can't leave my dad. Not now.

"Listen, Ky, I'm not trying to make you feel bad. I know your situation isn't ideal, but I wish you'd just put yourself first every once in a while. It's okay to want what you want and actually go after it." A look of sadness crosses her exotic features as she picks her fork back up. "Anyway, let's not spoil our lunch. Heaven knows when the next time our schedules will jibe again."

I pick at my salad, but don't really eat any of it. Instead, I push it around to give the appearance, something I perfected as a child. "How is work going?"

"Excellent. Busy, and I love it," Amalee beams with pride from across the table. She's a corporate lawyer, recently promoted to junior partner. She works her tail off seven days a week, eighteen hours a day, in hopes of someday having her name added to the marble sign in front of her firm's building.

We chitchat through the rest of lunch before the one subject I've been waiting for finally comes up. Just as the waiter removes our plates, she asks, "So, how are things with Matthew?" She waggles her eyebrows suggestively, earning her an eye-roll in return.

"Fine."

"Fine? New relationships are never supposed to be *fine*, Kyla."

I shrug and glance around. "He's very busy."

My friend doesn't reply right away, but I feel her eyes on me, observing and judging. "A man who owns his own company is busy, yes. When was the last time you went out?"

I stop and think back. "Two weeks ago?"

Amalee just blinks at me. "Seriously? You guys have only been seeing each other for what, two months? And you haven't seen him in two weeks?"

I open my mouth, but nothing comes out. I know it sounds bad, and I guess, in reality, it is. At first, Matthew was attentive. He pursued me hard, stopping by the animal shelter and sending me random thinking of you gifts. But the moment we actually started seeing each other, he became distant. We do the typical dinners out at fancy restaurants, but there is no intimate contact. No hand-holding and the kisses are rare and chaste. Nothing I'd expect dating a man like Matthew Wilder would be.

"The sex must be pretty damn good for you to date someone who puts that sour look on your face." Something must cross my features, because her mouth drops open and she gapes at me in shock. "Seriously?"

I smooth out my used napkin on the table in front of me and avoid eye contact. "We haven't gotten to that part in our relationship yet."

"After two months? Is he saving himself for marriage?"

That comment gives me pause. I already know the answer to her question. Matthew Wilder has a reputation, in the boardroom and in the bedroom. I've heard many comments over the years from other socialites, all vying for a chance at being invited back to his place. Heck, many have already been and their stories are legendary in small circles.

What I don't understand is why he chased me so hard and then nothing. And I admit, I was a hard sell. I didn't make it easy. I wasn't interested in being another notch on his bedpost. At thirty years old, my goal is more about long term and settling down than a quick romp in the sack. Yet, once I actually agreed to his insistent requests for a date, it was nothing like I imagined.

"I don't think so," I finally confirm. Leaning forward to keep nosy neighbors around our table from overhearing, I add, "I just don't think we're clicking, Amalee. I can appreciate his desire and drive for work, but it's like I'm not even an afterthought when he gets home at night. The times I've texted him, he rarely replies, and when he does, it's polite, yet curt."

"So what are you thinking?"

Sighing, I try to verbalize what I've been contemplating for a few days now. "I think I'm going to go over there and see what's up. If he gives me the brush-off, I'm going to end it with him."

"Wow, I'm so proud of you. Kyla Morgan breaking up with the great Matthew Wilder. It's poetic, actually. Do you think he's ever been the one to be broken up with?"

I scoff, but don't answer her. We both know the answer would be no.

"Anyway, I thought of showing up with dinner tonight. We usually go out on Saturday evenings, but I'd rather stay in. Maybe if we're out of the fancy restaurant scene, he'll be different," I suggest, though I doubt it. Matthew's more of the take what you get kind of man, and I'm sure the setting isn't going to change that.

"I think you should do it. Send him a message now that you're coming over for dinner. Don't give him a chance to back out. And if he does, well, show up anyway. Kiss him and see if there are any sparks that lead to an inferno in the bedroom. If not, you know what to do."

She makes it sound so simple.

But in reality, it is. If there's nothing between us, then why are we dating?

Grabbing my phone, I pull up his name. First thing I notice is it's been two days since I've even heard from him. There's a slight tremble to my fingers when I start to type my message.

Me: *I'd like to come over for dinner tonight. Six o'clock. There's something we need to discuss.*

I exhale loudly as I set my phone down on the table. Usually it takes upwards of an hour or two for him to reply, so when I see the bubbles appear almost instantaneously, I'm pleasantly surprised.

Matthew: *Sounds great. I'll order Thai from that little restaurant you like.*

My eyes widen when I read his message.

"What?" Amalee asks.

"He's, uh, well, he's ordering dinner for us."

"See? Maybe he's just been busy and not trying to be standoffish. You said he was closing a deal, right?"

Setting my phone back down, I murmur, "Yeah. He mentioned it's almost complete."

"I bet that's the problem. A hundred bucks says you two are naked and doing the nasty before dinner is even delivered," she replies with a giggle.

"Maybe," I mutter, not quite so sure I agree.

"But if not, then you're already prepared for what to do. Kiss him and see what happens. At least if you have to break up, you won't be blindsided."

Very true. The last serious boyfriend I had broke up with me at dinner on our two-year anniversary. I was expecting the diamond earrings I saw a receipt for but was given the boot instead. Turns out, those earrings were for someone else, and he had another reservation with her later that evening.

When the check arrives, I pull out my credit card faster than she does. Amalee knows better than to argue with me in these instances. She knows I have the money, not that it's actually mine, in the way that I actually earned it. It's my mother's money, plain and simple.

My mother passed away three years ago from a brain aneurysm. Worse than losing your mother at the age of twenty-seven was being the person who found her. We were supposed to have lunch, but I was running late. To this day, I wish I would have called instead of texting her. Or maybe reached out to Beula, their housekeeper, to check on her. But no, I went on with my morning, completely oblivious to the fact my mother was dying across town.

Margaret Morgan came from money. Her father was a New York senator for more than three decades and had his name attached to several businesses throughout the state. When he passed, his fortune went to her, his only daughter, and when my mother died, it went to me, her only heir. Honestly, I don't want the money. It's more than I'll spend in this lifetime, but it does afford me a few luxuries and freedoms, like volunteering my time at the animal shelter.

I'm their number one donor.

After the waiter delivers my card and I sign the slip, we exit the restaurant and stop on the sidewalk.

"I'm so glad we got together," my friend says, pulling me into her arms and hugging me tightly.

"Me too," I reply, honestly.

"Remember, if he isn't going to produce the goods, then give him the boot," she says, leaning in and adding, "and hopefully those goods are at least eight inches."

I bark out a very unladylike laugh and shake my head. "You're bad."

Amalee winks and grins. "Oh, I know. I'm working so many hours I have to live vicariously through you."

"That's not a good thing, Am."

She stands up straight. "I've been flirting with one of the men down in finance. He's not bad looking. I'm thinking of letting him slip his hotdog in my bun."

My eyes widen. "Amalee!"

"What? It's been a long time since I've gotten some meat, Kyla. A really long time. I'm desperate, hence the guy down in finance. I'm pretty sure he wears a toupee, but I don't care. He can just take me from behind, so I don't accidentally pull it off his head."

I cover my mouth with my hand to suppress my giggle, but it doesn't work. "That's way more information than I needed or wanted to know."

She just shrugs. "I've gotta go back to the office. Text me later tonight after you either break up with him or shag him into oblivion."

Shaking my head, I turn and head in the opposite direction, praying no one heard her crude comment. Though, I'll admit, it does hold a bit of merit. I don't necessarily need the oblivion part, but a little shagging would be nice.

As I slip into my car, my phone rings. I already know who's calling, and I'm smiling as I answer. "Hi, Daddy."

"Kyla, how are you?"

"Just wrapping up lunch with Amalee."

"Ahh, how is Miss Dawson?"

"She's fine. Busy working. How are you?" I ask, as I start the car and the phone switches over to my Bluetooth.

"I'm all right," he replies, yet I hear the hesitation in his voice.

"What's wrong?" I ask, dread filling my body. I'm so dang grateful I didn't pull out of the parking garage yet.

"Nothing," he insists before sighing. "I've been doing some thinking, honey."

"Uh oh, that's worrisome," I tease, though it doesn't ease the anxiety.

"I'm ready to take a step back."

If I'd been standing, my knees would have buckled.

"What? From Evolution Technologies?"

Dad chuckles. "Yes, honey, from Evolution Technologies."

"But..."

I'm so floored by my dad's statement, I'm unable to speak. Dad started this company when he and mom were first married, and the technology industry was starting to boom. Dad's business grew leaps and bounds when he was able to secure government contracts. In fact, he's had offers over the years that contain so many zeroes, it would make your head explode. He's always turned them down, though, so it begs the question: why now?

"Why?"

"Well, honey, I want to improve my golf game," he states with a chuckle. "I want to sit in the backyard, listen to the birds chirp, and watch the sunset. I want to travel. Someday, I'd like to watch my grandkids grow, and I can't do that when I'm working seven days a week. You don't want the company. It's not in your blood, and that's fine. I want you to do whatever you want with your life, and I know that doesn't involve Evolution."

"But, Dad, you love that place."

"Yeah, I do, but it's time to pass the torch, Kyla. I'm not getting any younger."

"You're barely sixty," I remind him. My parents didn't meet until their late twenties and were both my age now when they married. A year later, I was born.

"Yes, but most days I'm feeling seventy, and I don't want to let all my good years pass me by. We don't know how much time we have on this earth, honey, and I don't want to spend all of mine at the office."

A soft smile spreads across my face. "I'm happy for you, Daddy."

"Me too, but it's not final yet. I've had a few offers, but one in particular I'm drawn to. They've made a more than generous offer, and I've signed the letter of intent to sell. It's another technology firm here in Boston with some big hotshot at the helm."

I snort. "Sounds like you."

Dad barks out a laugh. "Maybe back in the day, but I'm content with just being your father for now."

And that right there is why I'll never leave.

I'm all he has left in this world. With Mother passing, he's all alone in that big house.

"All right, I need to go. My next appointment is here."

"Let's do lunch soon," I suggest.

"Sounds good. You could bring that fella you've been dating, you know."

I think back to Matthew and his recent standoffish behavior. "We'll see. He's been busy with work."

"Bring him by anytime. I'd like to meet the man my daughter is interested in."

"We're still pretty new and casual, Daddy."

"Humor your old man, will you?"

Smiling, I reply, "Okay, I'll bring him by." I have no intention of doing so.

"Love you, Kyla."

"Love you too, Daddy."

I press the end button on the screen and back out of my parking spot. With a quick glance at my dash, I realize I have a little free time to stop by the shelter and visit with the animals before I need to head home to prepare for my dinner with Matthew. I have no idea how tonight will transpire, but I'm hoping to have the answers I need by the end of it. The truth is, we're missing that spark.

That sizzle.

Sure, he's handsome in a domineering, brooding way, but the few times we've kissed, my toes haven't exactly curled. In fact, it was more reminiscent of kissing a cousin, if I had one to compare it to.

My point is I have a decision to make where Matthew is concerned, and I'm hoping tonight will help me decide one way or the other.

Do we move forward or do I move on without him?

Chapter Three

Mason

I scan the document in front of me, with a critical eye. When I get to the bottom, I glance at my twin. "Are you serious?"

Matthew doesn't so much as flinch. "You need the money, and I have it."

"But...you want me to be *you*?"

He nods once. "For three weeks. It should be a walk in the park."

"A walk in the park? Seriously? I know nothing about running a business like yours, Matthew," I argue, reaching for the glass, only to find I've already emptied it.

"Or any business, if your financial situation is any indication," he retorts, hitting directly below the belt.

"Fuck you."

He just gives me a half grin and relaxes farther into his chair. "Do you have another way of securing one hundred and fifty thousand dollars, Mason? I don't see another bank anywhere in the United States touching this with a ten-foot pole. The beef market is shit right now, which means you have cattle you can't sell for profit. How long has this been going on?"

I refuse to answer, mostly because he already knows the answer. If my brother has found out about the lack of loans and the debt already incurred, he knows more than he's letting on. So instead of pacifying him, I just return his stare.

"I'm told the market projection is on the upturn, but in the meantime, you have a debt owed and no way of paying it."

The bastard gets even more comfy, as if he's not talking about *my* livelihood. I'm well aware the market tanked and is expected to rebound this fall, but the damage is already done. I've cut costs wherever I can. My only help is a seventeen-year-old kid who lives a few miles away. He comes over and helps whenever I need it, which I try to keep to a minimum. I manage the day-to-day aspects of maintaining the fifteen-hundred head herd, but everything else has gone to shit. I've sold off everything I could, including the horses and other small animals I had. The barns are in need of some TLC, but the money isn't there yet to maintain them. It's been a rough year, to say the least.

When my brother realizes I'm not going to answer, he sits up and rests his elbows on the desk. "You need one hundred and fifty K. I have it. I'm willing to throw in an extra fifty if you help me out."

"By pretending to be you for three weeks." It's not a question.

"Yes."

I sigh and rub my thumb between my eyes. I have a massive headache starting, and it has nothing do to with traveling today and everything to do with the weight on my shoulders. It has followed me to Boston and is staring me straight in the face in the form of my twin. "What exactly do I have to do?"

My brother gives me the full wattage of his smile now. He knows he has me. Hell, he knew the moment I boarded the plane.

"I've lived in this building for almost a year. The contacts I've made and secured because of it were exactly the reasons I fought so hard to get into this place."

"What's so special about it?" I ask, recalling the sterile environment I walked into.

Now, his grin turns wolfish. "The Tower. It was originally owned by Garry F. Brockton. I was personally invited to live here after we met last year. Unfortunately, he passed away recently, and now the building is owned by his niece. She's making...*changes*."

"What kind of changes?" I ask, curiously.

"Until recently, no women live here."

I blink once, twice, three times, while processing this information. "Until recently?"

"Yes. She allowed the first woman to move into the building not too long ago, and it's been nothing short of troublesome since. All of the tenants here are male, with money, and all looking to make connections and more money."

"But I saw a dozen women in the bar when I entered this place," I tell him.

Matthew just smiles. "And none of them live here. They're here for the sole purpose of being invited upstairs."

"Meaning to an apartment."

Matthew nods.

"Okay," I start, rubbing the sides of my forehead now. "So what do you want me to do?"

"I want you to oversee the redecorating of my home. It's too...white. I have a decorator coming in next week to update the furnishings. We've been communicating through email, and she's fully aware of what I'd like to see here."

"Oversee it? That's it?"

Again, he smiles. "I've spent the better part of six months working on a new business deal. The last two months have been pivotal, and I recently found out the company is as good as mine. The financing is secured and the final contract all but signed. I've spent long nights working out the terms of this merger, and it's finally complete. I'm supposed to receive the paperwork in two weeks, signed, sealed, and delivered. The company is mine."

"Congratulations," I mumble. "How does this involve me?"

He shrugs. "It doesn't really. The contract will be submitted electronically, the signed document couriered the same day. I just need you here to accept the package."

"That's it?"

"That's it, unless he requires a dinner meeting to help grease the wheels."

My heart stops beating. "Matthew, I can't pretend to be you and talk business," I counter, anxiety building in my chest.

"You won't have to talk business. That part is already done. The old bastard seems to like me, for whatever reason, and the last two times we've met, under the guise of discussing business, we've merely talked about life, his family, and the travels we've done."

Great, so now I have to entertain a lonely rich guy, like a call girl. Jeezus.

"So, let me get this straight. You'll pay off the one hundred and fifty thousand I owe in back mortgage, taxes, and bills, as well as throw in an extra fifty thousand, and all I have to do is oversee some remodel of your bachelor pad and maybe have dinner with some old guy you're buying a business from?"

"Well, there is just one more task."

I raise my eyebrows in question.

"I need you to break up with my girlfriend."

That causes me to pause.

"Say what?"

Matthew goes back to his casual, relaxed demeanor, kicking his leg back up, as if not a care in the world. "Kyla Morgan. I'm done with her."

I think my jaw unhinges. "You're *done with her?*"

He shrugs. "Pretty much. Beautiful girl, decent rack, but not what I'm looking for in life."

"And that is?"

"She wants a future. Family. Kids. The whole shebang."

"And you do not."

He taps the tip of his nose in response and smiles. His phone chimes with a text message, and he quickly pulls it from his pocket. Matthew reads the message, an absent grin on his face, and types back a message, setting his phone down when he's done. "Speak of the devil, you're having dinner tonight."

"What?"

"Relax, Mason. It's dinner here. She wants to talk. I told her I'd order Thai food."

Like a fish out of water, my mouth just opens and closes repeatedly, while my brother slides a pen across the desk. "So that's it? Just break up with the poor girl?"

He shrugs and stands. "She's of no use to me anymore."

My stomach twists. Is this the man my brother has become? I knew he was ruthless in the boardroom, but this? He's not even breaking up with her in person. The asshole is relying on me to do it.

Sighing, I glance down at the paperwork in front of me. "Is a contract necessary?"

Matthew places his dirty glass over by the decanter and leans against the cabinet. "I use NDAs in pretty much all of my dealings, Mason, and I wanted the terms clearly stated."

Realizing I'm out of options, I flip the paper over to the last page and grab the pen. "So dinner with the old guy, redecorate, and break up with the woman you're finished playing with. That it?"

"That's it."

29

Pen poised, I finally scribble my name on the line and toss the packet onto the desk, already knowing I'm going to regret this.

"Great," he says, gathering the document and sticking it into a folder before locking it in a cabinet drawer behind his desk.

"Now what?"

"Now? Now you enjoy everything my lifestyle can offer. Break up with Kyla and take advantage of the building. There's a spa, lap pool, full gym, cigar lounge, and even a movie theatre. Hell, invite as many ladies from the bar up to the apartment as you want while you're here. Hilda changes the sheets daily," he states bluntly, as he pulls another folder out of his desk drawer. "This is everything you need to know about The Tower and Wilder Group."

I set the new folder down and follow behind my brother as he leaves the room. He heads into a large bedroom, where I find three large suitcases stacked beside the bed. "What's this?"

"I'm headed to Fiji, Mason. I'm tired and need a break. You're handling everything here, so I'm off to the island for three weeks."

"You're leaving the country?" I demand, crossing my arms over my chest and blocking the exit.

"I am," he says, grabbing the bags and pulling them to the doorway where I stand. "I'll be in touch."

My mouth drops open. I don't know what I thought, but this wasn't it. I guess I hadn't really thought this far ahead as to where my brother would actually be in this equation. "What if I need you?"

"Email me."

"This is bullshit."

Matthew shrugs and advances. "This is what you agreed to do. You want to back out now? Good luck getting the money you need by the deadline."

My shoulders slump in defeat as I step aside, allowing him to exit the room. I trail behind as he heads to the front door. When he pulls it open, George is standing there, holding my bag. "Good afternoon, sirs. Your bag, Mr. Mason," he says, holding it out. The moment I grab it, George reaches for the luggage my brother is taking.

"George is taking me to the airport. His contact information is in the folder I gave you. He'll be available to take you wherever you need to go," Matthew states, stepping through the open door. "Take care, brother."

"Yeah. You too," I mumble, feeling a little shellshocked.

"George is the only one who knows you're not me. Make sure you keep it that way as to not break the terms of the contract, Mase. I'd hate for you to do all this work and walk away with nothing."

With that, my brother heads for the elevator, his driver hot on his heels, leaving me alone in his fancy freaking apartment.

I glance around the space, the white-and-black sterile environment, my mind trying to wrap around what the hell just happened. Actually, I do know what just happened. My brother played on my weaknesses to get what he wanted or needed. Just like he used to. Worse, I'm in no position to tell him to get fucked. The fact remains I need him, or at least his money, and if pretending to be him for a few weeks is going to get me that, I guess that's what I need to do.

Sighing, I head back to his office to retrieve that folder of information. Overseeing the remodel shouldn't be a problem. In fact, maybe I'll add my own flare to the design and tell her to incorporate a steer head and a bear skin rug. Making sure the contract with the old man shouldn't be a problem either, as long as the deal is as good as signed like Matthew said. And breaking up with his girlfriend? Not exactly my forte, but I'll do it for two hundred thousand dollars. He

31

didn't give me a timeline for that part, so as long as it's complete by the end of the twenty-one days, I'll be in the clear.

Shouldn't be too hard, right?

***

By the time I've read the contents of Matthew's folder—twice—it's nearing six o'clock. Annoyance and anxiety bubbles in my chest as I recall what I have to do. It's not the actual break-up that has me upset, but the fact it's my brother's. *He's* the one who should be calling things off with this woman, not me. Now here I am, meeting her for the first time over curry noodles and about to send her packing. Just my luck.

I just pray she's not a clinger.

I fire off a large order to the little Thai place down the street. Not only did he leave me the takeout menu but also his credit card. Since I don't know what Kyla likes, I decide to go big on the order and cover just about anything. Plus, I'll have leftovers for a few days too. Even though Matthew left me his card doesn't mean I should rack up the unnecessary charges.

Although I really should.

At five until six, the phone rings. I almost don't answer it—habit back home, since it was always the bank calling—but recall seeing details about the front desk calling up for guests. "Hello?"

"Mr. Wilder, Miss Morgan is here. Shall I escort her up?"

"That would be great, thank you," I reply before replacing the phone receiver. I read visitors and guests of tenants aren't allowed to roam the building freely. They must be accompanied by a tenant or building personnel at all times. Seems like an odd rule, but this whole building is weird as hell. It's just a bunch of rich assholes trying to see whose dick's bigger.

I can't help but wonder when I'll break the news to the woman on her way up to the apartment. I mean, the polite thing to do is to at least feed her. Matthew did invite her up here for dinner. So as much as I'd rather just meet her at the door and give her the boot on behalf of my thoughtless brother, I won't do it. She deserves more than what he's giving her, so the least I can do is buy her some spicy noodles.

Funny, when I think back to the information my brother left me, there are pages and pages of details in regard to the building. Another page on the business deal I'm to help finalize, as well as computer printouts on the new design concept for the apartment. Yet, there was only half a page of details regarding Kyla. Three sad little paragraphs. That tells me one thing: he didn't even take the time to get to know the woman he was dating.

It actually pisses me off on her behalf.

My brother has always been a selfish asshole, but this might be a new low, even for him. Matthew loves women. Hell, in college he went through them like Kleenexes. When I kept up with him early in his career, he had a new one on his arm every other night. He swore they always knew the score, and none of them seemed to care.

But this? This is new.

Why date her if he wasn't even going to bother to find out what her favorite drink was or if she preferred staying in or going out? None of those details were in her information. But do you know what was?

Her bra size.

A knock sounds at the door. Like a man walking to the electric chair, I drag my feet and move slowly until I'm finally standing directly in front of the large piece of mahogany. When I glance through the peephole, I only see the man from downstairs. He's directly in front of the me, blocking the view of the woman accompanying him.

Reluctantly, I disengage the lock and turn the knob. "Good evening, Mr. Wilder. Your guest is here," he states, stepping aside and revealing the woman behind him.

The very beautiful woman.

"Thank you," I croak, my throat suddenly extremely dry.

Kyla glances up, her hazel eyes look almost espresso under the dim hallway lighting. The moment our gazes meet, the earth moves. I actually have to grab onto the doorjamb to keep myself upright. In fact, I wonder for a brief moment if we're experiencing an earthquake. I must be the only one feeling it though, because she doesn't move to the doorjamb with me.

"Hello, Matthew." The sweetest sound, the voice of an angel.

"Kyla."

Her smile is slow and…endearing. Adorable, even. It's not seductive, brimmed with red, harlot lipstick, as I would expect. There's an innocence to it. Purity mixed with goodness and light. I realize Matthew is way out of his league here, and frankly, so am I.

I'm so screwed.

Chapter Four

Kyla

There's something in his eyes that pulls my attention and holds it firmly in place. I'm not sure what exactly, but I'm drawn to those chocolate eyes more so than ever before, and I can't place why. I've always been attracted to Matthew—I wouldn't be dating him if I wasn't—but there's something different about him. Something softer and, dare I say, friendly about him.

In the short time I've known him, Matthew's always been a passionate man. No, not with me, per se, but in business. I've read enough articles and heard enough talk to know he's ruthless in the boardroom. He wants what he wants now and isn't above doing what's necessary to get it. I've come to admire his desire and drive, even if it's not exactly directed toward me.

"Come in," he states, stepping back to allow me entrance. He thanks the doorman who accompanied me to the apartment and closes the door softly behind me. "Can I get you something to drink?" he asks, stepping around me and walking toward the expansive kitchen.

"Oh, sure. A glass of red wine?" I ask, setting my bag and jacket down on the edge of the couch.

Matthew seems to stumble around the kitchen, which strikes me as odd. It's almost like he's nervous or something. Maybe he senses that our time together is drawing to a close. I mean, he didn't even kiss me hello. He rarely takes my lips, but there's usually a chaste kiss on the cheek in greeting.

Sighing, I head for the kitchen and pull out the closest barstool. I watch as he opens the wine fridge and glances down at the bottles. What is he doing? I observe in complete fascination as he pulls a few bottles from the top rack, glancing at the contents, before sliding them back into place. A small smile breaks out on my lips as he struggles. I should feel horrible at finding humor in his difficulties, but the fact that the Great Matthew Wilder isn't perfect is all I can focus on.

Taking pity on the man who seems to always have it together, I stand up and move toward the glass-front cabinet beside the small refrigerator. I feel his eyes on me as I pull the door open and retrieve a bottle of my favorite wine.

"Oh. I must have misunderstood you," he mumbles quietly, reaching for the bottle.

As his warm, rough fingers graze against mine, I jolt of electricity slides through my veins, landing squarely between my legs. A small gasp slips from my lips, but I quickly cover it with a cough. Glancing up, I find his dark, intense eyes focused solely on me, but he remains quiet. If he felt anything from our touch, he doesn't say a word, which only makes me wonder if I possibly imagined it all along.

I retrieve the corkscrew and two glasses from the same cabinet and set them on the counter. Matthew makes quick work of opening the wine, though he does seem to fumble a touch when removing the cork. Maybe he's had a long, trying day.

"Thank you," I murmur, taking the glass he sets in front of me. The liquid is cool and tart, a rich woodsy scent filtering from the glass. I've always preferred the dry red over the sweeter whites, even as a younger woman. My friends always tease me about my preference, but it doesn't bother me any.

"Food will be here soon," he says, taking a sip of his own glass and grimacing. Another grin breaks out on my lips as I watch in complete fascination as he takes another tentative sip before setting the glass down and pushing it aside. Apparently, Matthew isn't a fan of red anymore.

"How was your afternoon?" I ask, noticing for the first time his outfit.

"What?" he asks, following my eyes and glancing down.

"I've just never seen you so...casual before. And in jeans? I didn't think you owned any," I state, realizing how well those jeans fit him. They're not too tight, but definitely accentuate his lean hips and tight thighs. Not to mention the...*bulge* in the front. It's not so formfitting that I'd be concerned about the discomfort, but more highlights certain areas. Suddenly, all I want to do is check out the back view to see if that angle is as delicious as the front.

Shocked by my own thoughts, I look away quickly and take a hearty drink of wine. At this rate, I'm going to be half drunk before the food arrives.

"Oh, yeah, I guess I don't usually wear them much, but I do own a few pairs," he replies. Matthew heads to the refrigerator and pulls it open. For such a large unit, I notice it's awfully bare. He does find a bottle of imported beer and pulls it out, twisting off the cap and chugging half the contents.

I'm about to ask him to elaborate on his day when the phone rings. He practically runs over to the receiver and answers it. "Hello?" He pauses for a few seconds before replying, "Please send it up. Thank you." When he replaces the handheld receiver, he glances at me over his shoulder. "Food's on its way up."

I nod and watch him walk to the door.

Yep. The back view is definitely as firm and fit as the front.

Feeling a flush spread up my cheeks, I jump up and retrieve some utensils and plates for dinner. It takes me a few tries to find the correct cabinet, but by the time Matthew returns with our food, I have two place settings prepared. He sets several bags on top of the counter in front of me, the glorious scents of the contents tickling my nose and causing my stomach to growl.

"Hungry?" he asks, a crooked smile on his full lips.

My word, those lips. They look positively edible.

Maybe that kiss I plan to lay on him later won't be so bad after all.

"Yes, I guess I haven't eaten since my earlier lunch with Amalee," I state, as he pulls container after container from the bags and sets them out in front of the plates. "Wow, are you hungry?" I ask, noticing we have enough food to feed half the building.

"Oh, uh, yeah. Long day. Haven't eaten," he replies, handing me the first opened container.

Eventually, we sit side by side, eating our food. It's really good, and frankly, I enjoy sitting in his apartment more than a restaurant. It does feel slightly uncomfortable, but that's nothing new. Most dinners were a little stiff when you think about it. The only time I truly saw Matthew relaxed was when he was discussing business, whether with me or someone at a table nearby.

"So, how was your afternoon?" I ask again, realizing he really didn't answer my earlier question.

"Oh, good. I talked to my brother," he states casually, taking a big bite of his food.

My fork halts on its way to my mouth. "Your brother?" I whisper. "I didn't realize you had one," I add, hating that I really know nothing

38

about this man other than what's on the surface. We've never really discussed family, though I've tried. Actually, we've talked more about my family in the last two months than anything else. Come to think of it, not only did I not know he has a brother, I'm not sure I've heard mention of his parents.

That thought is so depressing and validates my decision to potentially move on from this relationship.

I can feel Matthew's eyes on me, but I keep my gaze on my food, as if it were the most interesting pile of noodles and pork I've ever seen. Does he feel this complete disconnect too? He has to. There's no way he could miss it. It's awkward and painful, at best, and basically a third party to dinner.

"Yeah, he's my twin," Matthew replies, his comment completely shocking me.

I glance up, my eyes probably bigger than the plates we're eating off. "Twin?"

Matthew sets his fork down. The look on his face I'm unable to decipher, but that's nothing new. I've learned early on he holds his cards very close to his chest. "I didn't tell you that?" he asks, as he reaches for his beer bottle and drinks most of the contents. "I thought I had."

"No," I reply with an uncomfortable chuckle. "I'm pretty sure I would have remembered something like that."

"Oh, sorry," he says, picking at his food. "We aren't particularly close."

Feeling overwhelmed and a little ticked off, I ask, "And your parents?"

He meets my gaze, the muscles in his neck working hard as he swallows. "They're in Pennsylvania. When Mason and I graduated high school, he went out west, while I went to Cornell. Our lives took two different paths."

I feel my face squinting a little as I try to comprehend his words. "You're not that far from your parents though. Do you see them often?"

Matthew shrugs. "Probably not as often as I should."

Grabbing my fork, I play around with my food before taking a small bite. "Any other brothers or sisters I should know about?" I can't help the bite in my tone.

He shakes his head. "No way were my parents going to have more after me and Mason," he says with the slightest grin. "We were...wild when we were young."

It's then I notice the slight stubble on his face, as if he hasn't shaved in a few days. Matthew is always so clean-cut and put together, but this version is...hot. Very hot, actually. The combination of jeans, flannel shirt, and stubble is enough to set my heart racing. I've only seen him in suits or trousers and sweaters, which still makes for a sexy man, but this casual, laid-back version of Matthew is almost better. It seems more real, if that's possible.

"Hmm," I reply to his statement.

As we finish up our meal, Matthew finally speaks again. "How's the shelter?"

I blink a few times, surprised by his question. In the two months I've dated Matthew, he's rarely asked about it. In fact, I've always felt he finds my volunteering there silly. No, he's never said that, but it's in the way his eyes glaze over with boredom when I start to tell him about a rescue we received that day or an adoption we sent to its forever home.

Pushing my plate away, I turn slightly toward him on the stool. "Going well. We received a Belgian horse earlier in the week. She's the most beautiful animal I've ever seen. Her coloring is simply gorgeous and her stance so regal. Her owner passed away, and his family didn't want the responsibility of raising her. It can be hard to find homes for large animals in the city," I tell him, leaving off the part about wishing I could take her home.

"My brother used to own a few horses in Montana. They're splendid animals," he replies, the smallest smile on his lips, as if he's recalling a visit out that way.

"They are. I always wished my parents would have built a small barn in our backyard when I was growing up, but they never did. I took riding lessons from a woman for a year or so, but it never went any further than that. It's a commitment to raise, breed, train, or compete with larger breed animals, and my parents weren't really ready for it. Well, my mother wasn't. I'm sure I could have easily talked my dad into getting me a horse or two," I state, grinning at how easily I could manipulate my dad to get what I wanted back then. However, Mother put her foot down when it came to animals, claiming to be allergic.

After another few long seconds, he asks, "Would you like another drink?"

Liquid courage? Yes, please!

"That would be great. Maybe we could take the drinks into the living room and talk?"

When he nods in reply, I collect the plates and set them by the sink while he tops off my wine glass and grabs himself another beer. I slip the lids back onto the to-go containers and set them in the fridge, all while Matthew watches me. I wish I could read his mind sometimes. He's so hard to figure out.

"Ready?" he asks, taking my glass and his bottle and heading for the living room.

41

The room is very formal, and not at all what I'd picture Matthew having in his living room. In fact, it almost feels like a showroom. Even the décor doesn't scream Matthew Wilder. Not that I really know that much about him, as proven by the missing family details, but this is definitely not how I'd picture him living.

"This room is getting redone next week," he says out of the blue. When I look his way, I realize he must have been watching me.

"Oh?"

"Yeah, this room pretty much sucks," he says bluntly, making me laugh.

"It's very nice," I reply, only slightly lying. It is actually a pretty great room, just not the style I'd go for.

He snorts and shakes his head. "It's too formal for my taste. I'm thinking of adding a big elk head above the mantel."

I look from the location he indicated back to him, trying to figure out if he's joking or not, finding just the slightest touch of humor in his eyes. "Really?"

He sits down on the couch and kicks his feet up on the coffee table. The sound of his boots—Holy cow, he's wearing work boots—scraping against the ornate, dark wood echoes through the room. "Really. I think it would look nice. Don't you?"

I take a seat beside him, keeping a comfortable six-inch space between his body and my own, and look at the mantel. "Well, I think it will depend on what else you're going to do with the room, but if elk heads are what you want, then I think you should definitely do it."

Reaching for my wine glass, I take a hearty drink. I'm not sure if it's for liquid courage or to try to calm my racing heart, but the familiar taste does help relax me.

That is, until I set it down and turn to face him.

Positioning myself on the edge of the couch, I focus on Matthew, who's lounging, looking all comfy. "I was hoping we could talk."

"Sure," he says, mimicking my position on the couch and angling to face me.

I'm not really sure how to begin. Do I just blurt out my questions about our relationship or ease into them? Matthew's always been blunter with little patience when it came to waiting for anything, so I assume blunt is better. But when I look up at him, he seems to just study me, as if he's taking me in. There's something in his gaze that causes me to relax, even though my anxiety is sky high.

I end up standing. I need to move, so I pace back and forth in front of where he sits. To my surprise, Matthew doesn't say anything. It's as if I truly have something on my mind, and he's waiting for me to say it.

"So, I've been doing some thinking," I finally spit out in a rush.

"Yeah?"

"Yes. About you and me." I stop pacing and turn to look at him. He's standing up now, directly behind me, towering over me with his large presence. I have to look up to meet his gaze, and when I do, I'm not exactly sure what I see. Apprehension? Relief?

"Okay," he replies, shoving his hands in his pockets and rocking back on his heels. "Hit me with it."

So I do.

I basically throw myself at him, wrapping my arms around his neck and pulling him down toward my mouth. Matthew stumbles a bit, but rights us quickly so we don't go down. One minute he's ripping his hands from his pockets to steady me and the next they're threaded in my hair, his hot mouth plastered to mine. Holy cow, what a kiss.

His tongue glides along the seam of my lips, coaxing it open and delving deep inside. I hear a moan of pleasure, and it takes a few seconds to realize it came from me. My hands work up the back of his neck and glide into his hair. It's a touch longer than it was the last time I saw him and oh so silky and soft.

I can feel his entire body pressed against mine, hard and unforgiving. Oh and I do mean *hard* in places I've never felt before. At least not from Matthew. My entire body feels alive and on fire as I wiggle against him, seeking out more contact, more *everything*. Each time I rub against his erection, a surge of moisture gathers between my legs. It's the first time I've ever experienced anything so...*animalistic* from just a kiss.

But this isn't *just a kiss*.

This is like holding a grenade and pulling the pin.

It's terrifying yet thrilling at the same time.

And I want more.

Matthew is the first one to pull back, releasing my lips and gasping for oxygen. "Holy shit," he mumbles, as he tries to come to terms with what just happened.

"Wow," I whisper, placing a shaky hand over my rapidly beating heart. My body still tingles with desire, a foreign feeling I've never experienced when kissing Matthew before.

He brings his thumb up and traces my swollen lips. "You were saying?" When I give him a look of question, he adds, "About you and me."

Oh.

That.

I think the burning question about whether or not there's any spark between us was just answered. Not only did it flicker, it combusted magnificently. There's definitely something there, and now I have to decide if I want to continue exploring it or not.

Who am I kidding?

If there are more kisses like that, I'd be game for not only exploring it but dropping my clothes and exploring other things too.

"Oh, that. It was nothing. Nothing at all."

Chapter Five

Mason

What the hell was that?

I just kissed my brother's girlfriend...and liked it.

A lot.

So much so, I'm standing in front of her with a hard-on, my lips burning for one more taste.

I take a step back to give myself some much-needed air, but it doesn't help. I'm drawn to her heavily lidded hazel eyes. They're a gorgeous combination of brown and green with gold flecks, and so expressive. I can see every emotion swirling within. I don't think I've ever been so attracted to a pair of eyes before in my life.

"I, uh, should probably go," she mutters, taking her own step back and glancing around the room. When her eyes land on the small clutch she arrived with, she hurries over to retrieve it and holds it closely beneath her elbow. "Thank you for dinner."

"You're welcome." I open my mouth, not sure if I want to invite her to stay or blurt out the words I'm supposed to speak. There's only one reason my brother accepted her dinner invitation, and that's to check off one of the three items on his list of demands. Only, I'm not sure I can do it.

At least not right now.

He just told me I had to break up with her before he gets back. He didn't say it had to be done tonight, even though the opportunity may have presented itself well. It just doesn't feel right in this moment.

"Do you have big plans tomorrow?" I ask, escorting her to the front door.

We step into the hallway and head for the elevator. "I'm going to stop in and check on Dolly and see if we've had any adoption requests. Maybe even take her for a ride. One of the other volunteers is taking care of the cats and dogs, so I volunteered for barn duty."

As the elevator descends, it stops on one of the lower floors, the doors revealing two older gentlemen. The first thing I notice is the way their eyes peruse Kyla head to toe. The taller of the two catches me glaring and quickly averts his gaze. The other man doesn't seem to notice I'm even inside the car with them but could probably tell me exactly what size bra cup Kyla wears.

I pull her into my arms and kiss her once more. I wish I could say it was solely for their benefit, but that would be a lie. I want to kiss her again just as much as I want to show these assholes she's with me.

"How about I meet you there? I'd love to meet Dolly," I whisper, sliding my thumb over the apple of her cheek.

Her eyes light up. "Really? You'd want to spend your Sunday morning checking on a horse?" She seems truly surprised by my suggestion, and I realize my mistake. I want to meet the horse. My brother would rather work on his latest deal. But there's no going back now.

Shrugging, I reply, "Sure. I can work in the afternoon."

The elevator dings, signaling our arrival on the bottom floor. The two men file out and head straight for the bar, the room much fuller than it was a few hours ago. With her fingers entwined with mine, I step off the elevator behind her and slowly make our way to the front entrance.

"I was going to go around ten. Does that work for you?"

"Ten is fine," I state as we approach the door. I notice the doorman scurrying off to retrieve Kyla's car, which means we only have a few minutes left of our time together.

"Great. I'll meet you there?"

"Yep," I reply, catching movement out of the corner of my eye. It's the first time I see the action of The Tower firsthand. There are people milling around the lobby, chatting about their next business deal or how successful they were this past week. Women flood the bar area, all dressed to the nines in their most revealing designer dresses and sparkly diamond jewelry. A few are even led to the bank of elevators, clearly invited up to an apartment to continue their evening on a more one-on-one basis.

I can see the appeal of the place and why my brother loves it so damn much, but at the same time it does nothing for me. This may be a bachelor's paradise, but it's not mine. I'd rather be in the middle of a barn, knee-deep in cowshit, with a shovel in my hand. I'd prefer taking a mare for a ride around the field and feeling the breeze against my skin. Quiet. Peaceful. Solitude.

Just the way I like it.

"Well, my car is here," Kyla says, breaking me out of my thoughts. "Again, thank you for dinner."

"My pleasure," I reply, and realize how true that statement is. I really did enjoy having her there. Even if it was slightly awkward at first, that shared kiss broke any ice we may have experienced in the beginning.

"See you at ten?" she asks, as if seeking one more confirmation that I won't ditch her. Something tells me my brother wasn't too attentive where she's concerned.

"I'll be there." I move to kiss her cheek, wishing we were somewhere a little more private. Her skin is warm against my lips and makes my fingers itch to touch, but I refrain.

Kyla gives me a little wave and moves through the door to her awaiting car. I watch as she slips into the driver's seat and slowly pulls away from the valet drive.

"Still dating the Morgan girl, huh?" The man who asked is tall, wearing a three-piece suit and reeking of expensive cigars. His light blue eyes are a little glassy, as if he might have spent a little too much time in the lounge.

I'm sure I should know who he is, but don't have a clue. Opting to put on my best Matthew face, I turn away from him and head for the elevator without so much as a glance back. Sometimes, there's a plus to pretending to be the asshole brother. Smiling, I slip inside the car and head back up to the apartment.

With Kyla front and center on my mind.

***

The ringing of my cell phone wakes me with a start. I reach blindly for the device, even though there's a little light flooding through the edges of the room-darkening shades. "Hello?" I mumble.

"Why are you still in bed?" my brother's curt voice breaks through the line.

I glance at the alarm clock and do quick math. "It's three in the morning, Matthew."

"No, it's six in the morning in Boston. It's three in Montana."

49

I groan and flop onto my back, my head swimming with fog and my stomach not too happy at the moment.

"What's wrong with you?"

"Nothing. I couldn't sleep last night so I drank some of that bourbon in your office," I groan, wishing I hadn't had the second glass. But by that point, as the clock hands ticked past midnight, I needed the second to try to stop replaying that fucking kiss so I could get some sleep.

Matthew laughs like the asshole he is. "John Fitzgerald Special. That baby is twenty years old and about three grand a bottle. It was a gift from the president of Google for a business venture I sent his way. I bet that second glass snuck up on you like a prom dress in the back seat of a Buick."

I suck in a deep breath. "Jesus. Wait. What time is it in Fiji?"

"Just after eleven. I was just getting ready to go to bed, and imagine my surprise, I get an early morning text from Kyla."

Shit.

"I take it by the fact she was confirming my visit to the shelter at ten, you didn't break things off with her last night."

My mouth opens, but nothing comes out.

"Doesn't matter, I guess. Just as long as it's done by the time I get back. You might as well have a little fun with her while you're there. Maybe it'll loosen her up a bit," he states so matter-of-factly that I almost miss the entire point of his comment.

Have fun with her? Like she's a disposable toy? What the hell is wrong with him?

And loosen her up? Ha! If my brother could only have seen her last night, throwing herself at me and kissing me like there was no tomorrow. I still feel the impact of those hot, passionate lips twelve hours later.

"Anyway, I texted her back and told her my phone was going to be out of commission for a bit and have a temporary number. This way she'll bother you at six in the morning and not me."

"Fine," I bite out through a tense jaw. "Anything else?"

"No. I'm off to bed. I'm snorkeling tomorrow morning with Nihola, a local woman who promised to give me an up close and personal tour of the island." I can hear the smile in his voice and envision the wicked gleam in his eye.

"Talk to you later," I mumble, clicking off my phone before he can even reply.

Tossing the phone onto the bed, I pull one of the pillows over my face and groan. My head is heavy, a sign of too much alcohol the night before. Couple that with only a little more than five hours of sleep and you have the makings of a hellacious headache.

In desperate need of some pain meds for my head, I crawl out of bed and shuffle to the en suite bathroom. The room is massive, with some fancy toilet that shoots water at your ass and tile shower big enough for a cheer squad to join you. Not that that'll be happening anytime soon, but you get my point.

I open the closet and start rummaging through a basket of over-the-counter medicine until I find extra-strength acetaminophen. I pop two into my mouth and guzzle cold water straight from the tap to help me swallow the pills. I wipe off my mouth with a fancy hand towel and head for the massive shower. It takes me a few seconds to figure out how to turn it on. What the hell happened to a dial you turn? This thing has buttons and jets and more technology than a microwave.

When I finally have it on and the water temp set as hot as I can stand, I shove my boxers down to my ankles and step inside. The steam instantly starts to soothe my aching body and clear my head.

I let the near-scalding water beat against my skin from all four angles, thanks to the fancy jets, propping my forearms against the cold tile and inhaling a few deep breaths. My mind automatically goes to Kyla and those swollen pink lips.

And just like that, my cock's getting hard.

I ignore it, though. Technically, she's not mine to be getting all excited about.

Instead, I reach for my brother's too-expensive shampoo and body wash and finish up my shower. By the time I shut off the water and reach for the towel, I'm feeling dramatically better than before. My headache is nearly gone, and my stomach has settled enough to remind me it's time to eat something.

After wrapping the towel around my waist, I head for the mirror and use the same fancy hand towel to wipe away the steam. I give myself a good once-over. Stubble a few days old, bags under my eyes, and the wariness of the unknown reflected under them. I ignore it all though and reach for my toothbrush.

When my teeth are clean and my hair finger combed, I head back to the bedroom to get dressed. Since I'm heading to the shelter today, I opt for a pair of blue jeans and another flannel shirt. Both items I'm assuming I won't find in my brother's massive closet anywhere. I throw on my worn boots and grab my wallet and keys before heading off to the kitchen in search of food.

Unfortunately, I come up practically empty. Not even coffee grounds for the fancy single-cup machine sitting on the counter.

"Well, since I'm pretending to be you, Matthew, it looks like you're buying me breakfast. Hope there's someplace close I can charge your card for breakfast," I mumble, making my way to the front door.

Gratefully, the elevator ride is solo, but my reprieve is short lived. I follow behind as a small group of three men in suits heads through the front door and makes a right on the sidewalk. I follow behind, but not too close, knowing there has to be a place to get breakfast nearby. I'm in luck. There is a fancy little restaurant two doors down with a lighted open sign in the window. The three men head inside in front of me, but I make sure to hang back just enough to not be confused as a member of their group.

The moment I step into the restaurant, I find two dozen men sitting around, eating various breakfast options, drinking Bloody Marys, and talking to whoever is at the table beside them.

I hold back my groan, but barely. I could easily slip out of here, find a nearby overpriced coffee shop, and grab some breakfast, but instead, I make my way to the back corner of the restaurant and keep my eyes down. Settling on a table for two, a cup of coffee is delivered almost immediately by a young, energetic brunette. "Good morning, Mr. Wilder," she coos, sliding a small menu in front of me, proving that my brother has been here a time or two. "I'll be back in a few minutes."

After a quick scan of the menu, I settle on a hearty breakfast of eggs and biscuits with gravy, something I'm sure my brother wouldn't approve of. But in my line of work, I'd burn those calories off by noon.

My mind goes back to my ranch, to the cattle in the field and the outbuildings falling down. In my head, I've already spent most of the money my brother is paying me to cover the back mortgage and taxes owed and will use the rest around the property. Once the beef market goes back up, I'll be able to recoup my recent losses and hopefully make the ranch profitable again.

I have to.

It's the only thing I've ever wanted to do with my life.

"Did you make a decision?" the server asks, offering me a flirty grin.

"Biscuits and gravy skillet, eggs over easy, gravy on the hash browns, and wheat toast."

She seems startled by my order and doesn't immediately write it down. Matthew probably orders eggs benedict or yogurt and granola. "Coming right up, sir."

I don't even notice when she scurries off to place my order because I'm already focusing on my cell phone. I mean to shoot my former farmhand, Anthony, a quick text to check on things, but don't get very far. Instead, I find a message sent an hour ago from an unknown number and quickly discover it's from Kyla.

Kyla: *Sorry to hear about your phone troubles. Looking forward to seeing you at ten.*

Me: *Me too. See you then.*

And I realize I am. Sure, I'm anxious to see the Belgian she mentioned, but it's more than that. I'm excited to see Kyla again, to get to know her a little better. I've never been so damn eager to see someone before, which should probably be a little alarming, but it's not. Well, not as bad as I thought it'd be.

Guilt sweeps in almost immediately. I hate lying to her. I hate the deception of leading her to believe I'm someone else, especially for money. I hate that my brother is so callous when it comes to her, treating her like some nameless, meaningless business transaction he can walk all over at his whim.

54

Most of all, I hate the sound of my brother's name on her sweet lips.

The server returns with my food. It's a massive plate full of comfort food. "Thank you," I mumble before she slips away, leaving me with a big breakfast and my conscience.

Fortunately, I'm saved from having to deal with the guilt of lying to Kyla when a shadow falls over my plate. "Good morning, Matthew. Worked up an appetite last night, I see," the man states, a coy grin on his face.

Before I can reply to his comment, he takes the empty seat across from me. "May I help you?" I ask, cutting into my biscuits and gravy and taking a hearty bite.

The man just grins, bringing his cup to his lips and sipping the hot liquid inside. The sound instantly grates on my nerves. I fucking hate listening to someone sip or slurp. "I was just discussing with Darnell Masterson about your big business venture."

I mentally roll my eyes. "Yeah? What do you know about it?" I ask, taking a big bite of eggs and hash browns.

"Well, I heard they were entertaining another very generous offer."

That makes me pause. Setting my fork down, I lean back in the chair and take in the man across from me. He appears to be a few years older than me, with the start of gray hair coming in around his ears. He's freshly shaved and reeks of expensive cologne. "I'm sure you're mistaken," I finally reply, reaching for my coffee.

The man shrugs. "Possibly. Though, Masterson is usually spot-on when it comes to hearsay in the business world. He seems to have more contacts than any one person can have. Hopefully he's mistaken."

I grunt in reply, taking too big of a drink of hot liquid and scalding my tongue in the process.

"Anyway, I thought I'd just mention it to you. Something to keep an eye on," he replies, slurping from his coffee cup once more. "I heard Miss Morgan was here last evening."

I snort. "You've heard a lot already this morning."

He lifts a single shoulder, getting comfy in the chair and waiting for me to comment. I don't indulge, however. I go back to my breakfast, pretending he's not there. I have no clue if these guys are my brother's friends or not, and even though I should probably play nice, I just don't have it in me. Not when these guys are sitting around gossiping like teenage girls in a schoolyard.

"Well, I can see you're busy. I'll let you enjoy your breakfast. Maybe we'll see you in the sauna later today," the man says, getting up and taking his coffee with him.

I'm left with my mind flopping between the mention of the business deal that's supposedly all but signed and of Kyla. I realize how small this community is, even if it's a huge building. Everyone knows everyone and everything and I'm not a fan. I much more prefer the small rural town I've become used to in the last decade.

Sighing, I drop my napkin on the table, breakfast forgotten.

I'm stuck here for twenty days, and this is going to be a big challenge.

Good thing I have Kyla to help pass the time.

Chapter Six

Kyla

"Look at you, pretty girl," I greet the horse in the paddock behind the shelter.

Dolly whinnies, as if she knows how gorgeous she truly is, and nudges my hand with her muzzle. I take a few minutes to pet her, loving the feel of her soft hair under my palm. Longing sweeps in as I give the mare a small smile. Out of all the animals I've seen come through the shelter, this is the one I'd keep in a heartbeat. From the moment I saw her, I wanted her. I just wish I had somewhere to keep her.

"How about a good workout today?" I ask, reaching into my back pocket for the brush. We don't have a ton of room around the yard, but enough I could get her up to a trot for a few laps.

"This must be Dolly."

The deep voice startles me, but I know who it is. Matthew made it.

I quickly turn around and smile. "Hi."

"Hey," he replies, giving me a quick grin before turning his attention to Dolly. "Wow, what a gorgeous mare." Matthew steps up beside me and pets Dolly's back with long strokes.

"Isn't she? I was just telling her we're going for a ride today."

"Oh, I'm going to have to take her out too," he says, patting her side. I get a good look at the man as he leans against the fencing. He's wearing another pair of well-worn jeans and a flannel shirt.

Boots adorn his feet that look like they've seen a few horseback rides in their day. This casual, rugged version of Matthew is almost better than the suit and tie.

Actually, I think I like it more.

"Let's take her into the barn and get her saddled up. The family of the original owner sent everything with her: bridles and bits, a few reins, lead ropes, and a stunning leather saddle with pads."

He's already moving toward the gate, leaving me trailing behind and practically running to catch up. Matthew holds the large gate open for me, latching it after we're both inside. For the next ten minutes, I don't do a thing but watch as Matthew prepares Dolly for a ride. He talks to her almost the entire time, getting to know the big, beautiful horse in a way I've never seen before.

"Tell me about the owner," he says, as he secures the saddle around her abdomen.

I go through the story, everything from the time we got the call about the Belgian mare through today, and even though Matthew continues to prep the animal for a ride, I know he's paying attention to me. I'm also surprised I'm not asked to help, but he clearly knows what he's doing around a horse.

When there's nothing left to say, he turns and gives me a crooked grin. "You ready?"

I nod anxiously, stepping forward and reaching for the saddle horn. I place my foot in the stirrup just as I feel two large, warm hands wrap around my waist. I'm being hoisted into the air before I can even push off myself. A loud gasp echoes throughout the barn, and it takes me a few seconds before I'm settled into the saddle to realize the noise came from me.

"I could have done it," I tell him, annoyance laced in my words.

Matthew just smirks at me, his stubbled jaw even more pronounced in natural lighting. "I know you could have, but I'm not about to pass up an opportunity to assist a pretty lady," he replies, handing me the reins. "Ready?"

"Yes, but you could have hurt yourself," I chastise, even though he didn't so much as break a sweat from lifting me up.

Matthew snorts. "I've wrangled bulls a lot bigger and more aggressive than you."

His statement strikes me as odd, but when Dolly suddenly steps forward and follows Matthew around the paddock, I forget about his unusual statement and focus on the ride. We don't have a lot of space behind the shelter, but it's enough for Dolly to get a little exercise. She's a beautiful, regal animal who's well trained. She never tries to trot faster than I'm allowing and follows my lead expertly. She'll be an amazing addition to someone's home.

After a solid twenty-minute ride, Matthew glances at me, an eager look in his eyes. "Mind if I take her around?"

"Of course not," I reply, steering the horse over to the side of the paddock. The moment my foot is positioned and I'm turning my body to dismount, those big hands return to my waist and help me down. I reach up and stroke Dolly's neck while he mounts her in one fluid motion.

Yeah, he's definitely done this before.

"Why don't you step outside the fence, darlin'?"

The term of endearment catches me off guard and my feet stumble slightly, but I eventually make it to the gate, ensuring it's secured behind me. With one foot propped up on the fencing, I watch in rapture as Matthew quietly talks to Dolly and runs a hand over the side of her neck. I can't hear what he's saying, but I can tell Dolly is paying attention.

Then, suddenly, he sits up straight, holds the reins tightly in his hands, and kicks her belly. The horse jumps forward, and a startled holler spills from my lips. I'm just about to run for the gate, to tell him to stop, when I see her slow right before the fence and turn. Dolly races along the fencing, her long legs falling into an easy stride.

My mouth is agape as I watch them together. Matthew handles her as if he's been on horses his entire life, and Dolly hangs on his every command. He runs her harder than I did but is always in control. It makes me wish they had a larger area to really stretch her legs. As I relax against the fence, a smile spreads across my lips and I wouldn't turn away from them even if I could.

"Wow, someone knows how to ride," Edith states, stepping beside me. She's the only paid employee the shelter has. She manages it, finalizing all paperwork and adoptions that go through our doors, as well as handling the grants and donations. She's exceptional at her job, one of the most caring individuals I've ever met.

"Yeah," I mumble, my eyes glued to the man on top of the horse.

We stand there for several minutes, watching Dolly get a good workout. When Matthew finally slows her down to a trot, she places her hand on my shoulder and says, "He looking for a horse? There are places you can board them around Boston."

With that, she turns and heads for the shelter once more.

I'm lost in my thoughts of Dolly and boarding locations when they step up beside me. My hand automatically goes to her nose as she snorts in excitement. "Did you have fun, girl?"

"I think we both needed that," Matthew says, pulling my gaze up to him. He sits proudly on top of the animal, so comfortably and confidently, a happy smile on his lips.

"I think you've spent more time on a horse than you led me to believe, Cowboy."

Those dark eyes seem to brighten just a little bit. "Oh, uh, yeah, I rode my brother's horses any time I was visiting. He had a few when he first bought the ranch, but slowly sold them off." A look crosses his face, but before I can dissect it, he quickly shuts it down. "So, Cowboy?" he asks, replacing the scowl from moments ago with a big, gorgeous smile.

I shrug and watch him dismount Dolly. "It seemed fitting at the moment."

With the reins in his hands, he stops directly in front of me. I have to look up to meet his gaze, but when I do, I suck in a deep breath. He's so dang handsome with the sunlight shining over his large, muscular frame and his brown eyes twinkling with delight. "I like it," he finally says, swiping a strand of hair off my forehead. His fingers are calloused and rough, but still sends a shiver down my spine.

"Me calling you Cowboy?" I whisper, my throat suddenly very dry.

He shrugs. "Yeah."

I give him a small smile and nod, vowing to use the new nickname whenever I can. If it makes him that happy, I'll gladly call him the silly name over and over again.

"What do you say we get this girl into the barn, brush her down, and give her some food?" he suggests, leading the horse—and me—into the small structure.

We work side by side for several minutes without saying a word, as if we've been doing this together for years. Matthew removes the bridle and bit before moving on to the saddle, while I brush Dolly's gorgeous coat. Actually, I find myself watching more than helping, but he doesn't seem to notice. He just works silently, making sure the animal is taken care of the way any animal lover would do.

I'll admit, I've never pictured Matthew as an animal lover. In fact, he's never once asked about the shelter, other than in a general, conversational setting, and mostly when we're at dinner or in a business meeting setting. And even then, I've never felt like he was truly listening to me.

As I finish brushing Dolly, Matthew goes to retrieve a bale of hay. I watch him carry it into the open stall, pull out a pocketknife, and cut the cording. *Pocketknife?*

He glances up and gives me a sheepish grin. "Never leave home without it." Clearly, I spoke that out loud.

When he has the hay tossed into the feeder, he grabs the hose, filling up the water bucket with fresh, cold water. Only then does he come back out to where I stand with Dolly and help lead her back to the stall. She goes straight to the food, while Matthew makes sure the door is secure and she's set for the day.

"Well, now that she's taken care of, how about some lunch?" he asks, keeping his eyes trained on the animal in front of us.

"Oh, uh, that sounds lovely. I'll just need to run home and freshen up." I glance down at my blue jeans and boots and wince, knowing I probably even smell like horse.

"No need. We can go as we are."

My eyes widen as I look his way.

"What?" he asks, setting his boot on the bottom rung of the wooden gate.

"I've just never known you to go out looking so...casual."

Matthew takes in his own appearance before shrugging his broad shoulders. "Sometimes, you just have to go with the flow and live your life on your own terms." He gazes into the stall, watching

Dolly move from her food to the water, but doesn't elaborate. Something tells me there's much more to Matthew Wilder than anyone—myself included—suspected.

"I know of a great little café not too far from here. We've ordered sandwiches and soup from there many times," I suggest.

"Sounds great," he replies, pushing off the gate and turning to face me. He shoves his hands in his pockets, the action pulling the groin of his jeans even tighter. I avert my gaze before he can see me ogling him, but barely.

"Let's go, Cowboy," I state playfully, heading out of the barn, Matthew hot on my heels.

***

"This place is pretty great," Matthew says between bites of his grilled ham and cheese sandwich.

"Isn't it? Whenever anyone suggests we place an order, I'm the first one to write down what I want," I tell him, taking a small bite of my homemade tomato and basil soup. It pairs perfectly with the grilled cheese on wheat with a slice of tomato.

"I can see why," he replies, wiping his mouth with a napkin. After he eats a few potato chips, he asks, "So, why don't you have a place with a dozen cats and dogs and a horse?"

I swallow the food in my mouth and reach for my lemonade, trying to find the right words to give him. The last thing I want is to sound ungrateful for what I have. "My penthouse was a gift from my father. The building has a strict no-pets policy." I leave out the part about feeling obligated to stay there, since I'm all my father has left.

He cocks his head to the side, as if considering my words. Instead of asking more questions I'm not sure I want to answer, he switches gears. "Well, if you could have animals, what would you have?"

A small smile instantly plays on my lips. "Easy. I'd adopt Ringo the cat and Archie the mixed bulldog and golden retriever. And if I had a barn, I'd take Dolly in a heartbeat."

Now it's Matthew's turn to grin. "A mixed bulldog and retriever? How'd that happen?"

"I hope that's a rhetorical question, and I don't really have to explain the birds and the bees to you," I tease.

His brown eyes seem to smolder and darken almost instantly as he holds my gaze. "No, I'm very well versed in the birds and the bees."

My throat is suddenly too dry, and the apex of my legs is...well, not.

"I just meant that's an unusual mixed breed," he says, pulling my focus from how my body responded to his statement.

"It is, but not completely uncommon. We've seen a lot of strange combinations in the last few years," I state with a small shrug. "I mean, animals aren't nearly as picky as humans when it comes to...that."

Matthew snorts a laugh. "I've known my fair share of humans who aren't nearly as picky as they should be when it comes to...that."

I glance down at the remains of my lunch to hide the light burn on my cheeks. Just the thought of sex has my mind on the man across from me. Even though we've never gotten to that part in our relationship, I can't stop thinking about his hands, how big and strong they are. About his arms and the way the shirts he wears hugs them. Then there's the thickness I saw in his jeans last night when we finished our kiss. Suddenly, all I can think about is what it would be like to take things to the next level with Matthew.

Considering I wasn't even sure about the status of our relationship yesterday at lunch, the one-eighty I've experienced in my own head is shocking.

Clearing my throat, I place my napkin on the table. "I suppose you're right. I've known a few people who think more with their bodies than their heads when it comes to the opposite sex."

I don't tell him I've always heard that very sentiment more often than not when it comes to the man sitting across from me. However, in less than twenty-four hours, I've come to learn there's a lot more to Matthew Wilder than meets the eye.

And frankly, I really like it.

I like him.

After lunch, we start walking toward the shelter and my hand slips within his. It's so very foreign to me, to hold his hand, but so natural and comforting at the same time. Comforting. Funny, that's not a word I would have ever thought I'd use when it comes to the man beside me, but it's the only adjective that is fitting in the moment.

The light breeze helps cool my flushed skin. When we reach the block that houses the animal shelter, Matthew turns his attention to his left. Across the street is a large park with walking paths, basketball courts, and jungle gyms for kids to play on. Over the years, I've witnessed many families partaking in picnics and play dates, friends gathering to shoot hoops, and women walking and talking on the paths. It's a great place, one of the few in this part of the city.

When he stops, we both watch the activity going on across the street for several minutes. We pay no attention to the people walking around us, their mutters of frustration as we take up a large section of real estate on the sidewalk. Usually, I'd insist on moving, to not block the walkway for others, but for some reason, I stay where I am. I focus on the smiling mom, pushing her young daughter on the swing. At the taunting and teasing of the boys playing basketball on the court. At the couple sitting on a blanket under the tree, feeding each other grapes from a small plastic container. Suddenly, I'm smiling at their jovialness, too. At the little slice of heaven they've all created, even for just a short period of time.

"Do you have to go back right away?" Matthew asks, glancing down and meeting my gaze.

"No. I'm not volunteering anymore today."

The ghost of a smile plays on his lips. "Would you take a walk with me across the street?"

I feel the grin spread across my lips almost immediately. "I'd love to," I reply, squeezing his hand.

He nods and turns, leading me through the crosswalk when we have the right of way and toward the grassy area before us. I'm not exactly sure why I'm so giddy about walking with Matthew, but all I know is I am. In fact, I'm more content with spending time with him in a park than I've ever been.

I'm just not sure how long it will last.

How long until Boardroom Matthew returns, leaving this calmer, more authentic version behind?

I might as well hold on to it while it lasts.

Chapter Seven

Mason

Do you know how long it's been since I've been to a park? Yeah, me neither. When Matthew and I were growing up, we'd go mostly to play basketball or baseball with friends. We'd play until the streetlights came on, which was our cue to get home for dinner.

As I was watching the kids play across the street, the memories came flooding back. That was when Matthew and I still had common interests. When you're young, you can find mutual ground with Legos and a ball and glove. It was as we got into high school, our differences really started to show. No, not in appearance. We were still as identical as you could get, but in our personalities and interests. Matthew had always been better academically, but I won hand over fist in things like science club and shop class. I thrived in FFA, or Future Farmers of America, while Matthew was better suited at leading the debate team and student council.

By the time high school ended, we knew he was destined for bigger and better things. With his 4.0 grade point average and his stats on the baseball team, Matthew was receiving offers left and right for schools that cost more per year than most cars. Me, I was headed for full-time employment with a local construction company a town over.

My parents always did what they could to be fair between my brother and me, but we all knew that post-high school assistance was going to be limited, especially with Matthew eyeing Ivy League schools. The day I told them I wasn't going to college and choosing to work full time, I saw the relief in their eyes. Both of my parents worked hard, but in a small town of two thousand in Pennsylvania, there's only so much they could do. Mom worked at the local laundromat and dry cleaners, while Dad spent all his days pouring concrete for a small outfit in town.

When the weather would turn shitty and he'd get laid off from pouring concrete, Dad helped as a farmhand at a large dairy and beef operation just outside of town. That's actually how I got the taste for raising animals. I used to beg him to take me with him to work on Saturdays and holidays, preferring the dirt and grit of taking care of animals over gaming consoles like my friends. By that point, Matthew was knee-deep in his studies or one of his many girlfriends and didn't have time for the breakout basketball games or playing catch in the backyard like he used to.

I wish I could say that was when our relationship changed, but I know that'd be a lie. We had always been able to play off each other's differences and weaknesses, but by that point in high school, the distance was too far. Our bond was broken, and it was both of our faults. So, we both went our separate ways after we graduated high school, making lives of our own without the brotherhood we always had.

"You're thinking awfully hard over there," Kyla says, pulling me from the memories of my past.

I feel her hand give mine a little squeeze as we slowly stroll toward the walking path. "I was just thinking about how my brother and I used to play basketball with friends in a park like this growing up."

"Mason, right?" When I glance down at her, she gives me a small grin and adds, "You mentioned his name last night."

"Yeah, Mason. We're identical twins and used to play ball with friends as much as possible. It was better than being stuck inside all the damn time, that's for sure."

Feeling her gaze return to me, I glance her way and meet her eyes. "Do you get outside much now? You seem pretty content to be inside working. In fact, besides my father, I don't know anyone who's happier to be working around the clock like you." I know she means it in a teasing manner, but there's no missing the slight hurt that flits through her eyes.

"I get outside when I'm heading to the office," I tease. I can picture my brother in his stuck-up suit, talking on the phone, and paying absolutely no attention to the world around him, while he's headed to the office in his chauffeured car. For someone who spends all of his time outside or in a barn, that concept is foreign and sad to me.

"You're funny," she whispers, a smile playing on her lips. Confusion flits across her face, almost like she doesn't know what to do with that realization. She's probably never thought Matthew to be funny. Oh, he used to be a hoot, back when we were younger, but as he aged, he became more focused, more about grades, service organizations that would look good on college applications, and eventually business.

"Tell me more about you. More about your past," I encourage, leading her to a park bench and taking a seat. Even though I read her bio in the packet of bullshit my brother left me, I feel like it didn't even scratch the surface of what makes Kyla tick.

"Well, you already know my mother passed away three years ago. My dad told me he's ready to retire, which makes me happy and sad."

"Why?" I ask, leaning back against the bench, my focus solely on her.

"Well, I'm glad he'll finally have some free time to do the things he wants to do, like more traveling and maybe even finding a hobby that doesn't involve work," she states, giving me a small smile. "But sad because that company has been a big part of our lives. He built it from the ground up, working his butt off for so many years. I'm sad to see it turned over to someone else when he sells it."

"There's no one in the company who wants to buy it?" I ask.

She shakes her head. "No. I don't think anyone on his executive team could afford it," she says with a smirk.

"You?" I ask, but she's already shaking her head no again.

"Heck no. I've never been interested in business like that. I enjoyed going there when I was younger, but not so I could learn the ins and outs of the business. I went there to watch him work and spend time with him. Running his business was never my passion, and he's always known that."

Extending my legs out, I watch as a wisp of her hair blows in the slight breeze. It makes my fingers itch to hold it in my hand and feel the softness of the strands. "So what is your passion? If you could be doing anything, what would it be?"

Kyla smiles instantly. "I'd do something with animals. I've been volunteering at the rescue for several years now, and I'd love to do more. I don't know what, but something. Maybe start my own rescue that offers discounted spay and neuter options. We get so many strays dropped off that are pregnant. I'd also focus my resources on adopting out those older dogs and cats. The kittens and puppies always go first. Someone looking for a first pet usually goes for something young and cuddly, while the older animals sit until the right person comes along. I'd push for those adoptions more."

I don't even realize I'm smiling until she gives me a hesitant grin back and asks, "What?"

"Nothing," I reply, shaking my head. "It sounds like you've already given this some thought."

She shrugs and turns her attention to the basketball game playing out in front of us. "Maybe. I've always said *someday* I'd own a huge house out in the country somewhere with a barn and tons of room for plenty of animals in need of love to run and play."

I can tell there's something more she wants to say, but doesn't, and I don't push. Instead, I focus on the fact her dream sounds awfully damn similar to my own. In fact, images of Kyla heading to my barn to feed the horses, a big Labrador retriever trailing behind her, plays through my mind. Considering I've known her for a matter of twenty-four hours, that picture is startling. I tell myself it's just because she painted such a vivid picture and stick with it, ignoring the niggling alarm in the back of my mind calling me a liar.

We end up sitting on that bench for fifteen minutes, both of us lost in our own thoughts, but the crazy part about it is I can't get over how content I am. Again, with that word. *Content.*

"So this week is the big renovation, right?"

"Yep," I reply, recalling one of the three tasks my brother left for me to complete. "Sounds like a big project, but it should be complete by the end of the week."

"I bet it'll be nice to have a little personality in the space," she says, the corner of her lip curling up.

"You mean you don't approve of the sterile museum vibe?"

Kyla shrugs her delicate shoulders. "Well, I guess it's nice, but I don't know. It doesn't really feel like you. When I met you yes, but as I continue to get to know you, it doesn't quite feel right."

A fresh wave of guilt sweeps through my body, rendering me completely speechless. I shift where I sit, trying to ease the tightness in my neck and chest, but it doesn't help. Instead, it just feels like I'm carrying an extra forty-pound weight on my shoulders.

"Come on, Cowboy," she says, jumping up, a broad grin on her face.

I follow, a little too quickly, and stand beside her, eagerness and excitement in my veins. "Where are we going?"

The smile she gives me steals my breath. Her entire face lights up, her eyes a dazzling mixture of green and brown shine with utter delight. I realize I want to make her smile like this a thousand times over. I want to forever see this look on her face.

But I know I won't.

"We're going to my second favorite place," she proclaims, taking my hand and practically tugging me toward the shelter. As we approach, she asks, "Can we just take one car?"

"That's fine. I'll drive," I state, pulling a set of keys from my pocket. Turns out, even though my brother uses a driver for most of his transportation, he actually owns a second vehicle. I found the keys to an Aston Martin DBS Superleggera in his office, and even though he left it out of his packet of information—accidentally, I'm sure—I figured, since I'm pretending to be Matthew, I might as well enjoy all the perks that go along with it.

"Wow, have you had this thing all along?" Kyla asks, stopping short beside the fancy sports car.

Since I don't really know the answer to her question, I go with a quick, "Yes."

I unlock the doors, which deactivates the high-tech security system, and open the passenger door. It may have been a while since

I've dated, but there are a few things that have stuck with me, like always opening a door for a lady.

When I get into the driver's seat, Kyla is looking around, gently—and carefully—touching the dash. "Okay, this car is beautiful, and I'm pretty sure I've never said that about a car before."

I snort a laugh. "Yeah, she's okay."

"Does she have a name?" she asks, her eyes brightening with mischief.

"A name?"

"Yeah, don't all guys name their cars and trucks?"

Her comment makes me laugh—hard—because she's not too far off base. My old Chevy back home was named Peggy Sue. She isn't a new truck, but she is dependable and exactly what I need to get around the ranch and roads of Montana. "You're funny," I state, deflecting.

She sets her small wrist purse down on the floor. "Don't think I didn't notice how you completely avoided my question. Someday, you'll tell me the name of your fancy car."

Clearing my throat, I ask, "So where are we going?"

"It's a surprise."

I can't help but smile. "How exactly will we get there then, if you won't tell me where we're going?"

Kyla seems to think a few moments before reaching out and touching the computer screen on the dash. I watch as she inputs an address into the navigation system. If she noticed the shelter's address was the last used location in the system, she doesn't say anything. The truth is I have no clue where anything is in Boston. Perhaps using George was a better idea after all.

Fortunately, I'm saved from having to explain why I don't know where anything is by the computer telling me to pull out of the lot and head to the right. I follow the directions, moving through downtown Boston, not too far from the complex my brother lives in. It takes nearly twenty minutes to get where we're going, but the moment we reach it, I can't help but grin.

This is one of her favorite places?

Of course it is.

I pull into Franklin Park Zoo and am lucky to find a parking spot about halfway across the lot. It's a gorgeous Sunday afternoon, which means this place is going to be packed with families. A big part of me wants to pull right back out and not deal with all the kids and the crowds, but when I spot the smile on her lips and hear the sigh of contentment, I pull into the parking spot and shut off the car. I should be worried about leaving my brother's car in the middle of busy lot, but I really don't care. If he gets a few door dings, it would serve him right.

"Come here often?" I ask, following her gaze to the front entrance of the zoo.

She nods a little shyly and averts her eyes. Her wholesome, sweet demeaner does something to me. I can't pinpoint it exactly, but I know I like it. Way more than I should.

"Well, come on. Let's go see the animals," I state, opening my door and moving around to open hers as well.

Kyla slips her hand in of mine, and together we walk to the entrance of the zoo. Definitely not how I pictured I'd spend a Sunday afternoon, but I think I like it just the same. First the park, and now the zoo. Matthew would have hated all this, and probably would have refused to come, but not me. Animals are right up my alley.

Then there's Kyla.

It feels too right to soak up every ounce of her light and goodness. Despite the darkness that surrounds me and the deal I made with my brother, I'll hold on to each and every sliver of her grace and elegance I can. She's like a ray of sunshine in a dark tunnel, warm and inviting, and fuck if I don't want to grab a hold of it for dear life.

Chapter Eight

Kyla

I'm still smiling.

Three days later, I catch a glimpse of my reflection in a window or a mirror, and I'm still wearing this big goofy grin. Sunday was the perfect day. First, with the visit to the animal shelter and riding Dolly, but then lunch, the park, and the impromptu trip to the zoo. I thought for sure Matthew was going to throw a fit, but he did the exact opposite of what I expected. He did what I had hoped.

He rolled with the punches and seemed to enjoy himself doing it.

I even snapped a picture of him leaning against the fencing, watching a giraffe eat tree leaves. He looked so casual, so relaxed, as he gazed up and just observed the big animal eat. I couldn't help but take the photo to document the moment.

After we spent the rest of the afternoon strolling around the massive zoo, we enjoyed corn dogs and an elephant ear before we caught the final dolphin show of the day. When it was time to go, he drove me back to the shelter to retrieve my car. Even though I had hoped he would invite me over to his place for a drink, I knew it wasn't in the cards. It was getting late and we both had to work tomorrow. He'd never so much as hinted an invite for me to stay over, or even come upstairs for a nightcap.

Unfortunately.

Up until Sunday night, I've been content with a chaste kiss on the cheek goodnight, or so I had thought. But after I experienced that toe-curling kiss on Saturday, I realized I could never be happy with just a few chaste kisses. I wanted more of the mind-blowing ones from earlier in the weekend.

When he helped me to my car, he leaned in, clearly planning to kiss my cheek once again, but the moment his lips hovered over my skin, I moved. Those full, warm lips changed course and landed smack-dab square on mine. I could feel the electricity slide all the way down my body, as he coaxed my mouth open and slid his tongue inside. Just as I moved my hands to his back, he broke the kiss, seemingly a little dazed by how quickly the kiss moved from zero to sixty.

After that, he quickly bid me goodnight, promising to be in touch soon. In the last three days, I've only received a quick text to check in, but haven't been able to connect with him further. I'm hoping to change that tonight. I know his apartment is being remodeled and redecorated, so I want to invite him to dinner at my place. He's never been there, always opting for public dinners in restaurants, but I'm hoping he'll consider something low-key for this evening.

I step into the conference room at the shelter and grab my phone. We use this room for families who are here to adopt one of the pets. It gives them privacy to fill out the necessary paperwork and spend a little time with their potential new pet before they take him or her home. I'm meeting Edith in a few minutes to go over the final details on the Fur-ever Home Gala coming in just two weeks.

Me: *Hey, Cowboy. Plans for dinner?*

He doesn't reply right away, but that doesn't surprise me. Matthew is always busy with work, so I set my phone down on the tabletop and take one of the hard plastic seats.

"So sorry I'm a few minutes late. I had someone call about Shadow, and I didn't want to miss the opportunity to potentially adopt him," Edith announces as she steps into the conference room, another volunteer, Debbie, hot on her heels.

Shadow is an eight-year-old black Labrador Retriever who was brought to us a year ago. When he was rescued, he was chained to a tree outside, malnourished, and scared to death. It took us a few months to even see any sort of trust in those dark eyes. Now, he's a little less timid, though you can still see the hint of wariness reflecting in those soulful orbs. The fact that someone is interested in the dog is wonderful, and I'm hoping it works out.

"That's such good news," I tell her, a smile instantly spreading across my face.

"Agreed. They're a young couple with a small boy. They're coming in later this afternoon to meet him," Edith adds, returning my grin with relief in her eyes. "It was because of the boosted Facebook post that they saw his cute face and wanted to give him a home."

"That's why this fundraiser is so important," Debbie notes, taking a seat beside me.

"Most definitely. Not only does it fund the shelter for the year, but it helps with vital advertising and promoting our adoption services. Putting the animals directly in view definitely helps tug on those heartstrings a little more."

"So we're just over two weeks away from the Fur-ever Home Gala. What do we still need to do?" I ask, anxious to get down to business.

The idea of the gala was actually mine. After I had started volunteering at the shelter, I saw how important donations were. I made several contributions myself, but after attending a fundraiser for a local not-for-profit youth sports center, the idea of a formal gala came to mind. I pitched the idea to Edith, who agreed it could be highly beneficial to the shelter. The first event brought in almost one hundred thousand dollars, between the per-plate dinner and the silent auction. The second annual event last year, we doubled our proceeds. We have big hopes for this year's event.

"I've been in contact with the caterers and the band. Both are set. Deadline to purchase tickets is this Friday, and so far, we're sitting at just over three-hundred and fifty."

"I'll give it another push on our social media pages, but that's not really the demographic we're targeting to sell tickets," Debbie adds, and she's absolutely right. Most people can't afford a five-thousand-dollar plate dinner. Our targeted audience is more of the business world. Those who want to see their names associated with a charity and their photos in the papers. My father was a big help in filling tables last year and has been nothing short of amazing in helping promote again this year.

I smile at Debbie, the older grandmotherly woman with a big heart for shelter animals. Debbie lives in a small duplex not too far from here and isn't in a financial position to purchase a dinner plate for her and her husband. When I approached Edith with the idea of the gala, it was with the stipulation that all volunteers and significant others could attend at no cost to them. I have the money just sitting in several accounts, accruing more interest than I could possibly spend, so I donate the cost of their plates anonymously. Only Edith and I know who pays for their plates, and I'd like to keep it that way.

"Do you have your dress?" I ask the woman sitting beside me.

Debbie beams a wide grin my way. "Yes, I found a hell of a deal at Nordstrom's last weekend. It was on their clearance rack, and I was able to even get a new pair of pumps too. Charlie's renting a tux again, and it's supposed to be in the Thursday before the gala."

When I glance across the table to Edith, she gives me a shy smile. "I found one too. It's silver and dips a little lower in the front than I've ever worn," she starts before Debbie interrupts her.

"But it was too gorgeous to pass up! She's going to knock Frank's socks off when he sees her in it," Debbie adds, referring to Edith's husband. Edith and Debbie went shopping together last weekend after they closed the shelter. I've been meaning to ask how their little excursion went and am pleased they were both able to secure new dresses to this year's event.

"What about you?" Edith asks.

I shrug my shoulders, recalling the red dress I found a few weeks back. It has a halter top and dips dangerously low in the back. Like Edith, it's a little flashier than I usually go for, but on a whim, I tried it on and fell in love. I found a pair of gold strappy shoes that will probably kill my feet before the first course is served, but the sales associate made a compelling case in favor of the gold Jimmy Choo shoes. "I found something, yes."

"You're being mysterious. I can't wait to see it," Debbie coos.

"And what about Matthew? Is he attending with you?" Edith asks.

"Oh, uh, well, I'm not sure yet. He's so busy," I reply, casually trying to brush off the fact I'm not sure if he's attending or not. When I brought it up about a month ago, he wouldn't commit, claiming to not know where he'd be with the business deal he's been working on. I was disappointed with his response and haven't brought it up since. I suppose I could mention it tonight under the guise of needing confirmation for his dinner plate. The truth is, I've already secured his ticket when I purchased my own, in hopes of him attending with me.

"Well, I hope he can make it. I've heard he fills out a tuxedo pretty nicely." The comment came from Debbie, and a bubble of shocked laughter spills from my throat.

"Debbie! I can't believe you said that," I tease, grinning like a loon, mostly because I'm just as curious to see him in a tux. I imagine the photos online don't do him justice.

The older woman shrugs as she giggles. "Well, it's true. Rumor has it, he has a nice rear end."

"You're married," I proclaim, trying to hide my blush behind my hand.

"But not dead, sweetheart. I've heard all the rumors about your Matthew Wilder," she whispers with a wink. "You're a lucky, lucky woman."

"Anyway," I jump in, clearing my throat. "What is left on the gala?"

Edith is just sitting there, grinning. "Not much. Are you still available to oversee the set-up process?" she asks.

I volunteer for this job every year. I love organizing and overseeing the transformation from empty ballroom to gala ready. "I'm looking forward to it. I'm meeting with the hotel's event manager that morning at ten."

"Sounds great. I'm so grateful for your assistance," Edith says.

"Absolutely my pleasure." And it is. She'll work the shelter that day, while I'm at the hotel ballroom.

Edith slips a few printed photos out of the folder in front of her, sliding them across the table. "All right, there are only a few final decisions to make. Let's choose the floral centerpieces."

***

The meeting wraps up when the family arrives to meet Shadow. Not wanting to overwhelm the young boy and his parents, or Shadow, I head out back to the barn. Dolly's standing outside, watching me approach. "Hey, girl," I say as I reach the fence.

Dolly moves my way when I extend my hand and allows me to rub her nose. "You sure are a pretty one."

She whinnies and nods her head, as if agreeing with my statement.

Smiling, I mentally run through the list of last-minute details we discussed in the meeting earlier. The color scheme is gold and navy blue, and the centerpieces are going to be stunning with the décor the ballroom has. Crisp white pillars, gold twinkle lights, and greenery with navy blue ribbons throughout will really tie it all together. And then there's the favors I commissioned through a local chocolatier. She's making gourmet chocolates in the shapes of dogs and cats for attendees to take home at the end of the evening. The band is from Boston too and comes highly recommended by the hotel. The lead singer sounds like a younger version of Whitney Houston. And throw in tons of donations for the silent auction, including trips, spa services, gift baskets, and, I believe the event is going to be as successful, if not more so, than last year.

Edith will speak again about the importance of donations and what they go toward. We've even been working on a slideshow presentation, showcasing this year's adoptions, along with the animals still waiting for their fur-ever homes. Nothing tugs at the heartstrings—and the wallets—like photos of shelter animals.

I feel my phone vibrate in my pocket and grab it. My small smile widens when I see a reply from Matthew.

Matthew: *No plans.*

I quickly type out my reply, not knowing how busy he is. If I wait too long, it may be another hour or two before I catch him again.

Me: *I was thinking of making you dinner at my place tonight.*

Matthew: *Dinner I don't have to order from downstairs and listen to boring*
conversations about who makes more money? Count me in. I have a few things to wrap up, but could be there around seven, if that works.

Me: *Perfect. See you then, Cowboy.*

Matthew: *I'll be there.*

With a quick check of the clock, I slip my phone back into my pocket. It's nearing three thirty, which gives me just enough time to stop by the market and grab a few things to make the spinach and cream cheese stuffed chicken breast recipe I found online. I screenshotted it months ago, but never had a reason to make it. Until now. I can stop by the store and grab what I need, take a quick shower, and have dinner ready by seven with no rush at all.

But first, a quick ride on Dolly.

Chapter Nine

Mason

For the second time, I give George the night off and opt to drive my brother's car. The thought of him either waiting for me, while I'm at Kyla's, or having to call him to pick me up, like a teenager calling Mom for a ride home, doesn't sit well with me. Instead, I input the address Matthew left me in his paperwork in the GPS and drive myself to Kyla's place.

When I pull up in front, I'm left awestruck at the magnificent building standing before me. In a way, it reminds me of my brother's residence, but more ornate. Doormen and valet services, gold-etched window trim and deep burgundy coverings.

"Good evening, sir. Are you visiting?" a young man in a valet uniform asks as he approaches the driver's door.

"Yes, Kyla Morgan. I'm Mas—Matthew Wilder."

Fuck. I almost screwed that up by giving the wrong name.

The man doesn't seem to notice my blunder and gives me a polite nod. "She's expecting you, sir. Corbin is right inside and will assist you with the elevator," the younger man says, his white-gloved hand extended for the keys.

After handing them over, I head for the front entrance. "Good evening, sir," the man at the door says.

"Good evening," I repeat, shoving my hands into the pockets of my jeans and stepping through the doorway. I tried to put on a pair of khaki slacks before heading over here but hated them the moment I buttoned them. I kept the blue button-down but traded the pants for a pair of blue jeans.

"This way, Mr. Wilder," he states politely, leading me toward a bank of elevators.

Glancing around as we walk, I'm impressed. The building she lives in, while a tad over the top with their chandeliers and ornate architecture, seems relatively secure, with extra safety measures in place, including a doorman. It gives me a sense of relief, knowing she's in a place that values her safety and that of those around her.

We stop in front of a bank of elevators, the man using a key card and his palm to open the one on the far right. "This elevator will take you straight to the penthouse, sir. If you need anything, let me know. I'm Corbin, and I'll be here until eleven. Miss Morgan can call down to let us know when you're departing, and valet will have your car brought around. Enjoy your visit, sir."

And then I'm left alone inside the elevator, being whisked up to the penthouse floor.

I almost canceled tonight's dinner, but I was being honest with her earlier in my text. After three days of going down to the bar and listening to the rich assholes comparing dick sizes, I was more than ready for a change of scenery. If I hadn't received her text, I would have ordered something from a local restaurant or diner. A big juicy cheeseburger and fries or maybe baked lasagna with garlic Texas toast. You know, comfort food. Things the diner back home in Montana is famous for.

The door opens and I step directly into Kyla's apartment. It's massive. Two floors with a wide staircase, a formal sitting area, and a view of Boston Harbor. As much as I'd like to check out the water, I catch a whiff of something mouthwatering.

"Oh, hey. I didn't hear the elevator."

I turn around and find Kyla standing at the threshold between the sitting area and the kitchen. She's wearing a light blue and green striped apron with an embroidered hand mixer on the chest and a welcoming grin. "I just got here," I reassure her, my legs carrying me toward her all on their own.

The second she's within reaching distance, I wrap my hand around her waist. My intention is to place a kiss on her cheek, but that's not what happens. Instead, the moment my fingers grip her side, my mouth finds hers. She seems taken by surprise, but only for an instant. Her mouth quickly opens, allowing my tongue to slip inside. Blood swooshes in my ears, and fire races through my veins.

When I feel her fingers slide up my chest and grasp my shirt, I rip my lips from hers. We're both breathing hard, her eyes a little unfocused and dilated. "Well, hello to you too," she whispers.

All I can do is stare at her swollen lips, and fuck, if I don't want to kiss her again.

Yeah, this is definitely not how tonight was supposed to play out.

I clear my throat. "Sorry," I mumble, guilt replacing the fire once coursing through me.

Kyla giggles. Fuck, she giggles the sweetest sound I've ever heard. "Please don't apologize for kissing me. I kind of liked it." A blush sweeps up her neck and stains her cheeks.

"Me too," I confess. More than I should, all things considered.

She clears her throat and adds, "Dinner will be ready in a few minutes. Would you like some white or red wine? I think I have some scotch, whiskey, and possibly brandy in the liquor cabinet. Or there's a little beer in the fridge." My eyebrows draw together in question, causing her to grin. "Sometimes I prefer a beer at the end of the day over a glass of wine."

"A woman after my own heart," I tease, following behind her as she heads to the kitchen.

Kyla moves easily to the massive refrigerator, pulling two bottles of light beer from within. I've never understood the necessity for an appliance that big, especially those fancy ovens that cook all sorts of different things at the same time. Of course, I'm a simple man. As long as I have a stovetop, a microwave, and a small refrigerator freezer that keeps my stuff cold, I'm good.

She pulls a bottle opener out of a drawer and pops the tops off. When she slides one my way, I take a long drink. The beer isn't my usual brand, but it's not bad. Kyla takes a small gulp before setting her beer down on the counter. "I guess I should have asked if there was anything you didn't like, but I recall you mentioning a shellfish allergy," she states, pulling a pan of something mouthwatering from the oven.

I almost reply to her comment. I love fish, actually. Whitefish and crab are one of my favorites to splurge on at one of the restaurants back home. But not Matthew. He's allergic, something we found out the hard way when we were on vacation down in Florida around the age of five. He used to carry an EpiPen, just in case, but since I haven't spoken to him much in the last handful of years, I'm not sure if he still does.

"Whatever you decided on smells amazing," I state, leaning against the counter and watching her finish preparing dinner.

She stops and gives me a soft smile.

"What?" I ask, feeling a little uncomfortable under her gaze.

"I've just can't get over seeing you so casual," she says, returning her attention to the oven and pulling a second pan from within. She closes the door and turns off the unit, tossing the hot potholders onto the counter. "Jeans and boots? Not to mention the stubble. I never would have thought I'd see the day," she adds, averting her gaze, but not before I see the blush return. "I think I like it."

I take another drink of my beer to hide my smirk and watch her uncover the second pan. "Are those Brussels sprouts?"

She hesitates. "They are. I wasn't sure if you'd eat them or not, but I can whip up another vegetable if you'd prefer. These just looked so good, and I remembered seeing a recipe for them with cauliflower and—"

"Kyla." I cut her off, touching my finger to her bottom lip. Big mistake. All I want to do now is kiss the hell out of her again. I drop my hand, as if I were being burned, and add, "I love Brussels sprouts and cauliflower. I'm sure whatever you made is delicious. It smells like heaven."

"Okay," she whispers, taking a deep breath. "There's bacon and parmesan cheese in there too."

"I can't wait." And I can't. I'm starved and everything smells amazing.

I watch as she scurries over to the fridge and grabs a salad bowl and dressing. She sets the large bowl beside the entrée and sides before retrieving dinner plates, bowls, and silverware. When she seems to have everything she needs, she waves her hand toward the food. "Grab a plate."

"Ladies first," I state, propping my hip back against the counter.

"But you're my guest."

I shrug. "My mama would smack me upside the head if I made a plate before all the ladies in the room."

The sweetest giggle spills from her lips. "Well, I'd hate to upset Mama. How about we do it together?"

I realize she's talking about making a plate, but that's not where my mind goes. It lands firmly in the middle of a porn, starring none other than Miss Kyla Morgan. Oh, the things I'd love to do. To her. With her. Together.

Forcing the dirty images parading through my brain out of my mind, I grab the two plates, handing her one, and help myself to the chicken. They're stuffed with what looks like spinach and something gooey, most likely cream cheese. I can't wait to dig in.

While I scoop some of the fancy Brussels sprouts onto my plate, Kyla takes one of the smaller pieces of chicken and starts doling out two salads in the bowls. When my plate is full, I glance around for seating.

"We can eat in the dining room, but I thought, maybe, we could just eat in here."

I glance over at the breakfast nook with bench seating and a small table. It looks cozy and perfect to me. Heading for the table, I set my plate and bowl down and return to the counter to help carry drinks.

When we're both situated, we dive into the food she prepared. I almost moan in pleasure when I take my first bite of the stuffed chicken. It's fucking phenomenal. Creamy cheese and tender meat. I'm not sure the spinach really adds much flavor, but it's good, nonetheless.

Glancing around, I notice how formal everything is here. It actually really reminds me of my brother's place, if not a little pricier than his. Kyla definitely shelled out some dough for this place. I can see the dining room from where I sit. It's awfully prim and fancy, and while it fits with the penthouse vibe, it doesn't really fit Kyla. In fact, the table we're sitting at feels a little more like her style. It's a light maple wood which matches the cabinets, but it has a more laid-back feel. As if you'd see a small family sitting around this table, enjoying a cereal breakfast or mac and cheese lunch.

"Did you decorate this place when you bought it?" I ask, hoping I'm not stepping in it by asking a question I should already know the answer to.

She keeps her eyes cast down as she cuts her sprouts and cauliflower into smaller pieces. "No, my father had it decorated for me before he gave me this place."

I watch her until she meets my gaze. "So you didn't get to pick anything out?"

Kyla raises a single shoulder before taking a small bite of vegetables. "It was professionally decorated by the top design firm in the city."

I give the place another onceover. "But do you like it? Is it your style?"

She opens her mouth to reply, but quickly shuts it. Instead, she slowly shakes her head.

I take another bite of my chicken before devouring half the salad. "So, if this place isn't your style, what is?"

Finally, I see a little happiness return to her eyes. Kyla sits up straighter and smiles. "Have you seen those tabletops built from old barnwood?" When I nod, she continues, "I'd love to have one of those with mismatched chairs. Ones that have some scuffs and wear. Life."

I find myself smiling back at her. "Now that I can see. Tell me more."

We spend the next thirty minutes eating and talking, her sharing all of her ideas for redecorating. Funny, when she talks about the master bathroom, a weird bubble of longing fills my gut. The old-fashioned clawfoot tub she wants is exactly the one sitting in my own bathroom at home. Old, rustic, and full of history, much like the rest of my place. I learn in that half hour her style doesn't vary much from my own.

"Oh, I do have something I'd like to discuss with you," she states, carrying the dirty dishes to the sink.

"I can do those. You cooked," I offer.

She waves me off. "No need. I can run the dishwasher later. Let's grab a drink and go sit outside."

While she finishes securing leftovers into containers, I grab two more bottles of beer from the fridge, popping them open. Eventually, she leads me through the living room to a sliding glass door, which opens to an impressive balcony deck with the same spectacular view I saw earlier. I whistle my approval and take one of the Adirondack chairs.

"Yeah, one of my favorite features of this place," Kyla states, after sitting in the chair beside me.

"Impressive."

"Only the best for the Morgans," she says, unable to hide the hint of irritation in her words. Something tells me she's heard that statement a lot growing up.

We sit in silence for a few minutes, both watching the city move and the water glisten below us. "So, what is it you wanted to discuss?" I ask.

"Oh, yes," she replies, sitting up and setting her bottle on the small table between us. "I know I mentioned this to you a few weeks back and you were unable to commit. I understand if you're still unable to, but I'd like to see if you can attend the Fur-ever Home Charity Gala with me."

"The one the shelter is doing?" I ask. Not because we've discussed it before, but because I saw a poster promoting it hanging up at the animal shelter on Sunday.

"Yes," she confirms. "It's two weeks from this Saturday. I'll be working from time to time, but I'd love for you to come as my date."

I mentally run down the schedule my brother left me, and the gala wasn't on it. Probably because he had every intention of me doing his dirty work and breaking up with her last weekend.

"Saturday, right?" I ask, seeking confirmation. Matthew comes home that following day, on Sunday, and then my duty is fulfilled. I'll have posed as my brother for the three required weeks and will, hopefully, be on the first flight out of Boston to head west come Sunday morning.

"Yes."

My eyes meet hers. They're eager and excited, and I can tell she truly wants me to go. Or at least, wants Matthew to go. That thought is sobering.

I clear my throat and try to picture what my brother would do. Not commit, I'm sure. He'd probably work too late and miss most of the event, the one she has been working so hard on. So instead of brushing her off with a noncommitted response, I stun even myself by saying, "I think I can make that work."

Those hazel eyes dance with delight as she beams at me. "That's wonderful. There'll be many business associates there, I'm sure. You'll have plenty of people to talk to. It'll be just like you're at work, but in a tuxedo," she quips with a giggle.

I don't tell her all I need is to talk to her.

"Can't wait."

Chapter Ten

Kyla

We sit out on the balcony for another hour. I tell him all about the gala, and surprisingly, he seems truly interested. He doesn't share much, just listens intently and asks a few questions every now and again. It's weird. I've never been so open and talkative before. Neither one of us even seems to realize our drinks are empty until I yawn and look at my watch.

"I should probably go," he says, standing up and stretching his back.

I can't help but sneak a peek at how well the button-down molds to his arms and chest. When he stretches, the shirt rides up just enough that I catch a glimpse of a strip of dark hair below his belly button. Suddenly, my body is humming, my mouth dry. I'm staring, even after he drops his arms, covering his lower belly with his shirt. All I can think about is exploring that strip of dark hair, discovering where it leads.

Oh, I know exactly *where* it leads...

"You okay?" he asks, breaking through the sudden dirty thoughts filtering through my brain.

When my eyes meet his, I find his full of concern, which makes me blush again. If only he knew where my mind just went.

"I'm good," I assure him, grabbing the empty beer bottles to keep my hands busy.

Matthew opens the door and allows me to enter first. I hear him shut and secure the sliding glass door lock before his heavy boots echo across the hardwood floor. I quickly toss the bottles into the recycling bin and glance at the small stack of dishes from earlier. Those'll wait until tomorrow morning to move to the dishwasher.

Turning around, I find him leaning against the counter directly behind me, watching my every move. His hands are shoved in his pockets, one ankle crossed over the other. He looks casual and so...edible.

My breathing hitches at the thought, and his eyes seem to darken, as if he knows exactly what I'm thinking about. I'm not sure who moves first, but I'm quickly wrapped in his arms, his lips devouring mine. My hands thread into his hair, the strands a touch too long and feel so good between my fingers.

Matthew grips the back of my blouse and pulls me flush against his body. It's hard—*so* hard—and makes me want to climb him like a tree. Even with the height difference, being in his arms is comfortable. Right.

He deepens the kiss, the taste of beer on his tongue. As he slightly adjusts the angle of the kiss, I feel the burn of his stubble against my cheeks and the warmth of wetness flooding the apex of my legs. He leads expertly, and I realize, I'd follow him anywhere if it meant more kisses like this.

His large hands slowly make their way down my lower back to my rear. He manages to grip and lift at the same time, without so much as the slightest break in our connection. When I'm sitting on the kitchen counter, my knees fall open and he steps between them, filling the space with his body. I can feel his erection hard and ready, pressed firmly against the place I need him most.

I gasp, ripping my lips from his and sucking in a huge gulp of air. He uses the break to skim his lips across my jaw and down my neck. My head falls back, granting him complete access, as I close my eyes and just revel in the feel of his warm, wet lips against my sensitive skin.

"I could kiss you all day, every day," he whispers, his breath tickling my collarbone.

"That would make it very hard to get any sort of work done," I tease, even though the idea seems rather inviting.

"It would be a sacrifice, but one I'm willing to make," he states with a smile in his voice.

I wrap my arms around his neck and just hold on tight. Matthew's arms move to my waist as he does the same, the hug seeming to be exactly what we need to help calm our racing heartbeats.

After several minutes of just holding each other close, he finally sighs and says, "I should head home."

I open my mouth to ask him to stay, but nothing comes out. Instead, I find myself nodding in agreement. Matthew and I have become much closer in the last five days, but I don't think I'm ready to take it to the next level. It's as if I'm getting to know him all over again, like each new part I discover. Sleeping with him now may undo all the progress we've made over the last few days, and I'm just not ready for that yet. So instead of asking him to join me in my bedroom and begging him to do all those things I've thought throughout the evening, I nod my head.

Matthew places a kiss on my neck, and I swear I hear him inhale against my skin. A shiver sweeps through my body. He finally releases me and takes a step back. I miss the feel of his presence instantly, especially between my legs, but this is the right thing to do. To take a step away and allow us both to catch our breaths.

"The decorator is supposed to wrap things up by Friday," he starts, shoving his hands back into his pockets. "Maybe we can have dinner Saturday night?"

Instantly, a smile breaks out across my dry lips. "That would be lovely."

He nods and reaches out his hand to help me down. Once both feet are flat on the floor, we walk to the exit. "Did George bring you this evening?"

"No, I drove myself."

I stop at the phone security system positioned by the private elevator and call down to the front security desk to have them retrieve his car. They're incredibly efficient, and I'm sure his fancy vehicle will be waiting at the front entrance when he gets down there.

"Thank you for agreeing to join me for dinner."

"You're an amazing cook, Kyla. Thank you for asking. I had a great time tonight."

My cheeks tinge with embarrassment. "Me too," I whisper, my mind instantly replaying the kiss from just a few minutes ago.

He reaches up and cups my jaw, running his thumb over the apple of my cheek. "Lock up behind me," he instructs, prolonging our departure just a few more moments.

"I will."

Then he kisses me once more. This one is sweet and soft, as if he's savoring the feel of our lips joined together one last time. Unfortunately, our connection only lasts for a few seconds. He pulls away and stands up straight, dropping his hand from my face. "See ya soon."

"Good night, Cowboy."

He quickly smiles at the nickname I've been using, before pressing the call button for the elevator. It opens immediately, since no one has used it since he arrived a few hours ago. Matthew steps inside and presses the descend button. As the door starts to close, I give him a small wave, and then am left standing alone in my foyer.

I almost press the recall button to bring him back up but force myself to just remain where I am. Pressing that button would change everything in a way I'm not ready for. Instead, I return to the kitchen and start turning off the lights. I make sure the balcony door is secured, even though Matthew already did it, and make my way to the stairs.

As I move toward my room, I can still feel the dampness between my legs, another reminder of Matthew's mind-altering kisses. I grab a nightgown from my closet before heading to my en suite bathroom. I quickly change my clothes, wash and moisturize my face, and brush my teeth. When I'm ready for bed, I climb beneath the soft sheets, reaching for my nightstand drawer. I have to dig, but I find the item I'm seeking.

I hold the thick vibrator in my hand, contemplating whether or not to use it. It's been a long time since I've felt the need, but I know there's no way this ache will just...go away. Matthew stirs up something deep inside me, including between my legs. Yes, I'll definitely be using the device this evening.

And thinking about Matthew Wilder.

***

"Good morning, may I help you?" the perky blonde says behind the hostess stand.

"I'm meeting Jerald Morgan," I reply.

I don't have to wait for her to check her computer screen. "Oh, Mr. Morgan arrived just moments ago. If you'll follow me," she coos.

We move through the restaurant to a small table in back. As soon as my dad spots me, he sets his phone down and stands up, a wide smile on his face. I step forward, his arms wrapping around my shoulders. "Sorry to keep you," I say, as he places a kiss on my forehead.

"I just sat down less than two minutes ago," he replies, waving off my comment with his hand. "Have a seat." When I do, he asks, "How was your drive over here?"

"Beautiful." My dad knows I love this part of town. It's one of the oldest sections of Boston, with gorgeous architecture and landscaping. The buildings are massive and ornate, but in a classic and regal way.

He smiles, knowing his choice of restaurant would please me. Even though this place is closer to his residence than mine, he recognizes how much I enjoy the area and schedules luncheons here whenever our schedules will allow, which happens every month or so. I suppose if he actually retires and sells his company, we'll have even more time for random lunches like this one.

"Any big plans this Saturday?" he asks, perusing the menu.

"Not until later. We've been finalizing the gala details," I tell him between sips of ice water.

Our waiter arrives and takes our orders, promising to return with my dad's drink and our bread basket right away.

"Before we get to the gala, talk to me about this young man. I thought maybe you'd bring him to lunch today," he says, the slightest sadness crossing his features.

"He wasn't available this morning," I tell him. The truth is that's an assumption. Since we made plans for later in the day, I assumed he was busy this morning. It's rare that Matthew doesn't work on Saturdays, so I didn't even invite him. With his apartment remodel this week, I knew he was busy.

"Too bad. Maybe soon?"

I give him a nod as the waiter returns with Dad's drink and four warm slices of freshly baked bread. I take a quick drink of my water before grabbing a slice of bread, picking it into smaller bites and dipping it in balsamic and garlic olive oil.

"Tell me about the gala," he invites, listening intently as I go through the plans for the evening. His company purchases a table for the fundraising event and invites his direct support staff and spouses to attend with him. Between his assistant and her husband, the vice president and his wife, the CFO, who's also widowed, and the company lawyer and his flavor of the month, they fill an eight-person table with money and class.

"I'm proud of you, honey. I can't wait to see what this year's event brings in," he says, just as our food is delivered.

I dive into my crab salad, while he cuts into his medium rare prime rib. Between bites, I ask the burning question I've been wanting to ask. "How's the sale of Evolution coming?"

He sets his fork down. "Good. It should be finalized at the end of next week."

My mouth drops open in a very unladylike manner, making me glad I hadn't just taken a bite of food. "Next week? Isn't that rushing it?"

Dad lifts his shoulder as he makes another cut into his meat. "Possibly, but the offer is solid, Kyla. The company who is purchasing it has made a promising deal to keep my support staff in place. That was my biggest concern. I'm not so much worried about Harold, because he's past retirement age, but I don't want Lizabeth and Dominic to worry about losing their jobs," he says, referring to his assistant of ten years, Lizabeth, and the company vice president, Dominic.

"They get to stay on?"

"I've been assured, yes. They want the contracts Evolution has secured, and if that means keeping a few employees on to get those deals, he's willing to make an exception."

"Well, that's good news," I reply, feeling a little better about the sale. I've come to know and love my dad's team as if they were my own family, and the thought of them potentially losing their jobs bothered me greatly.

"It was the only way I'd sell, and they knew it. Harold has decided to retire when I do, which means their team will fill his CFO spot. That makes sense, though, keeping all of the companies under the same financial operator."

I guess he's right. I don't know anything about finance and don't pretend to. I can raise funds like no other, but the actual disbursement of them isn't something I've ever been interested in.

"Well, I'm happy for you. I know this is a big step, and one you didn't take lightly."

He nods in agreement and wipes off his mouth with his cloth napkin. "Of course not. And I've been transparent with my team the entire time. They knew this was a possibility and have appreciated my drive to keep the changes minimal."

"So, golf, huh?" I ask, a knowing grin on my face.

He barks out a laugh. "There's plenty of room for improvement on the course," he replies, finishing up his potato before pushing his plate aside. "You could join me, you know. You're still a member of the club."

I almost roll my eyes, but refrain. My parents have been paying for my country club membership since I was eighteen, insisting I attend outings and dinners with them. After a few times embarrassing them on the course, they agreed to just allow me to attend the dinners. Of course, they offered lessons first, but I wasn't interested. I could barely hold a club right, let alone hit the ball in the direction of the hole. Golf isn't my thing, and I had absolutely no desire to improve my game. "Really?"

Dad laughs. "Your mother insisted, hoping you'd find your love for the game."

"Wasn't happening," I mumbled, knowing he heard my comment.

Mother was very good. She grew up at that very country club, learning from the golf pro on site, and taking additional lessons from a former PGA player in the area. That's actually where she met Dad. He was visiting a friend in college and played eighteen holes. Their small groups bumped into each other on the course and ended up sharing a large dinner table that evening. My parents started dating a week later, and the rest is history.

I glance up and can see the nostalgia in his eyes. He's thinking of her too. "She'd be proud of you," I state, my voice hoarse with emotion.

He blinks a few times and gives me the smallest smile. "I miss her."

"Me too. I'm sure she'd love spending days on end with you on the course or traveling the world."

"She always wanted to go to Venice," he says, averting his eyes. "We never got to go."

I reach over and squeeze his hand. "Then you go. Take her memory with you."

He meets my eyes, his clouded with unshed tears, and nods. "Maybe I will. You could always join me."

When our check is paid, we make our way to the front entrance. I can tell my dad recognizes a few people in the restaurant but doesn't stop to say hello. Instead, he gives them a polite wave and keeps walking until we're standing on the sidewalk.

"Thank you for lunch." I lean in and give him a hug, his arms wrapping around my shoulders and squeezing.

"You're welcome. Thank you for humoring your old man today."

I scoff. "I always love spending time with you," I insist.

"I know, sweetie." He places a kiss on my forehead. "And maybe I'll meet your young man soon?"

This time I don't stop my eye-roll. "Yes, Daddy. In fact, you may meet him at the gala. He's agreed to attend, though that could always change, depending on his work schedule."

He pulls a face. "Don't let him work too hard, you hear? Life passes by too quickly, Kyla. Enjoy it while you can."

I nod, knowing he's once again thinking about Mother and all their unfulfilled promises of travel and time together. "I will," I vow, my heart breaking for him.

"Love you," he whispers before stepping back.

"Love you too."

Then he's gone, slipping into his car, while I get into mine. The whole way home, I rehash his words, about finding my happiness. It's just too bad my true happiness isn't here in Boston. But I won't leave him, not now. I'm content here, and that's all I need.

As I drive, my mind returns to Matthew and our date later. I'm not sure where we're going, but I'm eager to find out.

Chapter Eleven

Mason

I glance around my brother's newly redecorated apartment. It's not my style, but it feels more like my brother than before. Rich cherrywoods and brown leathers. The walls are painted a deep taupe color and there are newly created rafter beams stretched across the living room, dining room, and kitchen. I don't even want to know what all this set him back, especially since they had to bring in a contractor to secure the beams to what's above the ceiling for support.

My phone rings in my pocket, and I'm surprised when I see the name on the display.

"Hello?"

"I believe the remodel is complete?" my brother asks, without greeting.

"Well, good afternoon to you too, brother. How's the weather?" I sass, pacing the living room.

"Do you really care?"

That makes me pause. I almost reply immediately that I don't, but in reality, I do. I don't know if it's living here in his space or seeing him last weekend for the first time in years, but I realize I do want to know. How is he enjoying his trip away? Is he relaxing the way he should? Is that local woman showing him the island, as he indicated?

"Yes," I find myself replying.

Matthew seems to be taken aback by my comment and it takes him a few long seconds to respond. "It's gorgeous. Crystal blue waters and white sandy beaches. The hut I'm staying in is hardly that. It's bigger than my apartment and right smack dab on the water."

"Sounds nice."

"It is," he says, a little more relaxed than moments ago.

I take a seat on his leather couch and kick my feet up on the coffee table, as I've done every night. "Your place here looks great. Your decorator did good."

"She comes highly recommended and cost a small fortune. It better," he retorts with a small laugh.

I can't help but smile. When was the last time I heard my brother laugh?

"You'll definitely like it. It suits your style."

"Good," he states, clearing his throat. "How is everything going?"

"Fine." I open my mouth to tell him about my plans tonight with Kyla but think better of it. Why would he care, especially since he's pushing me to break up with her on his behalf. The last thing he'll want to hear is about how much I'm looking forward to seeing her smile tonight when we go to dinner.

"Listen, I received an email from Jerry. He's ready to sign. I'll be back for it, but he's asked for another meeting next week. I agreed."

Which means one thing, I'll be meeting with the owner of the company my brother is purchasing. I knew this was a possibility, but I was hoping it wouldn't happen.

I sigh. "Are you sure it's wise for me to go in your place?"

"Why not? Can you not handle a dinner with the old man? The deal is already done, Mason. All you need to do is show up in one of my suits and pretend to be interested in his life story."

"What if he asks me questions about your company?"

"He won't. The last time we had dinner, he barely mentioned it. He's lonely, that's all. You'll be fine."

I close my eyes, wishing I didn't have to do this.

"If you're worrying about it, read the information I left you. There's a complete overview of my company, Mason."

I've read it—twice, actually—but that document only gives the basics. It doesn't tell me the day-to-day tasks my brother does, the processes for purchasing and selling a company, or all the work that goes into maintaining a Fortune 500 business. I'm terrified Jerry will see right through me.

When I don't reply, he takes it for my compliance. "What's the status of the third item on your to-do list?"

I'm having dinner with her in a few hours.

My heart starts to beat a little harder in my chest when I think about Kyla. How her whole face lights up when she smiles, and how sexy the little noises she makes are when I kiss her. God, I'm such a dick. I should break it off with her tonight. The more I get to know her, the more I like her, and that's not good for either of us, because at the end of the day—or at the end of this job—I'm going home.

Without her.

"Fine," I find myself saying, my throat thick with regret and lies.

"So you haven't ended things yet, I take it? Not that I care, but just make sure you do it before I get back in two weeks. I don't want any strings left where she's concerned. I'm ready to enjoy all that building has to offer, in terms of the ladies. So many options down in the bar, my friend. Take advantage of it," he suggests, a smile in his voice.

"You're disgusting."

He snorts a cross between laughter and disagreement. "Suit yourself. Have you met Thomas Jones yet? He invites two up to his place at a time. He's usually found in the lounge by seven and returning to his room by eight."

I close my eyes and shake my head. I'm not against casual sex, but how in the hell are we related?

"Anyway, it's late here. I'm headed to bed. Check your email. I sent you the dinner details with the old man."

"Fine."

"Oh, and I noticed you're a little thicker than me in the midsection, so if you need to let out one of my suits, call the front desk. We have a tailor on call."

Jesus, we're the same size, just built slightly different, considering I actually do physical activity all day long and not just sit behind a desk. Though, I can tell my brother still works out a lot, always has. We may have very dissimilar jobs, but we've always enjoyed spending a little time in a gym.

"Thanks," I mumble, checking the time on my watch. I have just over two hours before I meet Kyla.

"All right, I'm headed to bed. Talk to you soon," he says, hanging up without so much as a goodbye.

I click off my phone and toss it on the couch before running my hands through my hair. That phone call was just another example of questioning how we came from the same womb. Yet, as different as we are, I found myself truly enjoying the few minutes we talked. Well, until he brought up Kyla. Mostly because he has zero cares about her, and that bothers me. Not that I want my brother to care about her, but she deserves it. She deserves everything from the man she's dating, and Matthew seems more interested in tossing her aside to move on to his next conquest.

My phone chimes with a text from George, confirming he will be downstairs with the car at six o'clock. That gives us thirty minutes to move through town to get to Kyla's place.

I decided to use George for the evening, so we could enjoy the drive and have a few drinks without worrying about getting behind the wheel. Actually, it was George who helped me prepare for tonight's date night. Knowing very little about Boston, I sought out my trusted driver for suggestions. He seemed shocked at first, probably that I was even concerned about taking Kyla on a unique date instead of the fancy restaurants my brother usually goes on, and offered a few killer ideas.

At first, I was concerned about the booking he suggested, but once I gave my name to the manager and promised a small—not so small—donation, the reservation was set. But I made it willingly, my brother's credit card approved right away. I can't wait to see Kyla's smile when I tell her where we're going.

Well, I don't have long now. Might as well jump in the shower and get ready. This is one night I'm looking forward to.

***

With five minutes to spare, George pulls up in front of Kyla's building. Since I'm early, I opt to go upstairs and knock on the door, something I haven't really done in a while, but it gives it the true official date feel. When the right rear door is opened, I slip out and head for the front entrance.

The same doorman from my last visit is working and smiles as I approach. "Good evening, Mr. Wilder. Miss Morgan is expecting you," he says, leading me to the elevator. He goes through the security process before nodding and sending me on my way.

It doesn't take long before the elevator is stopping on the top floor. The door dings before it opens to the penthouse foyer. I'm able to take about three steps off the car before I'm stopped in my tracks by sheer beauty. Kyla is descending the stairs from the second floor. The moment she sees me, a smile crosses her pink lips.

She walks to me, since I'm suddenly unable to move. "You're early," she says.

"You're beautiful."

Her entire face lights up with my compliment as I reach for her. She's wearing a light purple wrap dress that hits just below her knees and a pair of nude heels. Her brown hair is down in curls that make my fingers tingle to touch, and she's carrying a black sweater. It looks delicate against her soft pale skin, a sight that goes straight to my groin.

"Are you going to tell me yet?" she asks as she steps directly in front of me.

I bend down and kiss her offered cheek, but all on their own, my lips detour to hers. I don't mean for anything but a sweet, chaste kiss, but that's not what happens. The moment my lips meet hers, I want to devour, to claim her as my own and never let her go.

That's a startling revelation.

I pull my mouth from hers with a pop and gaze down at her face. There's the slightest hint of a smile on her lips and her eyelids are still closed. "Well, hello to you too," she quips.

When her eyes finally meet mine, hers are dancing with delight and maybe a little desire. "Are you ready?" I ask.

She takes in my appearance. I'm wearing dark jeans and my boots and paired it with another one of my brother's crisp button-downs. For a second, I considered throwing on a tie, but since I could count on one hand how many times I've worn a tie, I decided against it. They're just not for me. "You look nice."

"You look gorgeous. No one will even know I'm there once I'm standing beside you," I state. The compliment heats up her cheeks a touch and makes her smile, which I realize is my goal for the rest of the night. To make her grin as much as humanly possible.

"Doubt that," she replies, threading her arm through mine.

I guide her to the elevator, which is still waiting on the top floor, and escort her inside. We're both quiet as we move downward and the door opens again, depositing us on the ground floor.

"George is here," she states, noticing my brother's town car sitting in front of the door.

"I thought it'd be nice to have a driver tonight," I reply as we step outside.

"Good evening, Miss Morgan," George greets, offering a wide smile.

"George, lovely to see you this evening," Kyla replies, as she slides into the back seat of the awaiting car.

I nod at my driver as I slip into the back seat, the door shutting securely behind me. "So, are you going to tell me where we're going yet?" she asks, setting her sweater on the seat beside her and buckling the seat belt.

"I am not," I answer, fastening my own belt.

Kyla gives me a withering look that makes me laugh. "Really?"

"Really," I state, reaching over and grabbing her hand. Once our fingers are threaded together, we sit back as George merges into traffic and takes off toward our destination. The partition is up, giving us privacy to talk freely without being overheard. The entire drive, we catch up on things that happened since the last time we spoke, which was last evening, and before I realize it, we're pulling in front of the large building.

She turns and looks out, her eyes wide with shock as realization sets in. "This is Butterfly Meadow."

"It is," I reply, as George opens the door for us to exit.

"Mr. Wilder, so good to have you with us this evening. Miss Morgan," the manager greets as we step up to the front entrance.

"Hello," Kyla replies.

We follow behind the manager, who vowed to personally oversee tonight's date. into the large vestibule filled with butterfly memorabilia. "Right this way," he guides, leading us down the corridor. "The building closed at six o'clock, so you have free rein to view the butterflies and exhibits. Dinner will be served at seven." And with that, he opens the door to their private butterfly garden.

"Dinner?" she asks, stepping inside the large climate-controlled room.

"Dinner," I confirm. The door closes behind us, leaving us alone with hundreds of butterflies.

"Oh," she gasps, gazing at the insects flying and fluttering about. "This is breathtaking."

I know she's referring to the butterfly habitat we're standing in, but that's not where my eyes are trained. I'm staring at her, at the sight before me, and yes, it's breathtaking. "You're stunning," I find myself whispering.

She rewards me with another one of those grins that lights up her face. "I was talking about the butterflies."

"And I was talking about you."

We walk around the garden, reading interesting facts about the different butterfly species. I'm not sure if it's the actual butterflies that are so fascinating or the person I'm with, but I realize quickly I'm truly enjoying my time here. With her.

I catch movement across the room and see a waiter who waves his readiness. "Are you hungry?"

"Starving," she replies, slipping her hand into the crook of my arm and allowing me to lead her to the opposite side of the room.

A small table for two is positioned where we can see the butterflies, but we're not right in the middle of the activity. I hold out Kyla's chair and take the one opposite her once she's seated at the table. "I have your wine, sir, ma'am," the waiter says, pouring a glass of red wine for Kyla. I don't know jack about wines, so I left it up to the caterer to pair a bottle of something nice with tonight's menu. "I'll return with your entrees shortly. Please enjoy the appetizers." He removes the lid off the platter in the center and leaves us to eat in peace.

"Wow, that looks amazing," she half whispers, half groans in delight. The pan is split in half with two options for us to enjoy.

"I hope you like scallops," I say, scooping two from one side of the dish and placing them on her small plate.

"Love them. Is that bacon?" she asks, grabbing her fork.

"Everything's better with bacon." I place a scoop from the other pan, the artichoke and spinach dip, and add a few of the spiced pita chips.

She cuts her scallop into a small bite and slides it through the cheesy butter sauce, grabbing a chunk of bacon as she goes. When she takes a bite, she moans in pleasure, a sound that makes my cock stand up and take notice. "Oh, heaven. These are delicious. I wish you could try one, Cowboy," she says, piercing a piece of food with her fork.

"Me too," I tell her.

"Why did you order them if you have an allergy?"

I shrug and add a big scoop of the dip to my plate. "I've been told they're delicious, so I wanted you to try them."

She seems surprised I'd still order something I couldn't eat but doesn't make a big deal. Instead, she scoops the hot dip onto a chip and holds it out for me. I take the whole thing in my mouth, my lips brushing against her fingers. Fire dances in her eyes, which goes straight to my cock.

We enjoy appetizers and chat until our entrees arrive. I chose a fire-grilled filet mignon with sautéed mushroom sauce and Worcestershire mashed potatoes. There are steamed mixed vegetables and warm, crispy rolls with a sweet cinnamon butter too.

"I don't know what to try first," she says, taking in her plate. "It's like food art."

"Here, try this," I reply, grabbing a small bite of the tangy potatoes on my fork and holding it out for her.

"Mmm," she moans, her lips still wrapped around my fork. "So good. I never would have thought of putting Worcestershire sauce in potatoes."

"Me either," I reply, taking my own bite. "The chef recommended everything."

She cuts into her steak, the meat so tender she could probably use a butter knife. "Delicious."

When our meal is finished, we walk amongst the butterflies once more. After spending another thirty minutes observing the varieties of insects, we head for the exit. Before we reach the door, the manager is there, extending a hand and bidding us farewell. I'll make sure to add a generous tip to the card charge for both him and the waiter.

"How was your evening, Miss Morgan?" George asks the moment we step outside.

"Perfect," she coos, resting her head against my upper arm.

We slip into the back of the car and head toward downtown. Kyla's sitting close—very fucking close. I can feel the heat of her body, smell the sweetness of her perfume, and hear the subtle inhale of her breath. My body is hyperaware of her nearness. All I want to do is take her in my arms and kiss those intoxicating lips.

Kyla shifts in her seat, sliding her bare shin against my leg. The contact goes straight to my groin like a teenager. I reach for the speaker button. "George, would you mind just driving around for a while?"

"No problem, sir."

My intention is to steal a kiss or two, but the moment I turn in her direction, she seems to launch herself at me. Well, as much as she can with a seat belt on. My good intention is thrown right out the window. Her mouth is hot, her touch even hotter.

Suddenly, all bets are off.

Chapter Twelve

Kyla

I have no idea what comes over me. One minute, I'm tucked securely into Matthew's side and the next, I'm practically throwing myself at him in the back seat of the town car like a cat in heat.

My mouth lands on his firm and hard, my leg tossed up and over his thigh. My hands dive for his hair. I want to get closer but am restricted. It isn't until I hear the seat belt release that I even remembered I was wearing it. It's also then I feel myself moving. Without breaking the contact of our mouths, Matthew maneuvers me until I'm straddling his waist. My dress has ridden up but doesn't expose anything, and I'm honestly not sure I'd care if it did.

From this angle, we're able to deepen the kiss. His hands delve into my hair, slightly tugging on the strands as he entwines his fingers within. All that does is make me dig my own fingers deeper into his hair. It's lush and soft, and when I score my nails across his scalp, he groans in pleasure. Speaking of pleasure, I feel it pressed firmly between my thighs at the moment, and all I want to do is wiggle closer to feel that hard length...everywhere.

I have no idea how long we drive around and make out like teenagers, but when I'm completely breathless and out of my mind with need, Matthew breaks the kiss. My eyelids are heavy, but I'm able to crack them open just enough to see the man who's slowly changing my entire world. His eyes are dark and wild, so full of the same desire I feel coursing through my veins.

He moves his right hand, cupping my cheek and dragging his fingers down the side of my throat. Goosebumps pepper my skin at the contact, so intimate. "This dress," he starts, shaking his head when he can't seem to find the right words.

"What about it?" I ask, breathlessly.

"I'm going to have dreams about it for the rest of my life. First seeing you coming down the stairs, and now, watching it ride up your legs," he says, moving his hands to my thighs. He slowly pushes the dress up just a little, his large, warm palms cupping my skin.

I close my eyes and just revel in the feel of his hands. They don't really move any closer to where I ache, which is a little disheartening. "Hey, Cowboy?" I whisper, keeping my eyes shut so I can get through the next part.

"Yes?" His voice is raspy and raw.

"Are you going to touch me?"

When he doesn't reply right away, I feel my heart drop to my toes. Matthew doesn't move, doesn't say a word. His hands hold still on my legs, and I can't help but wonder if I completely misread this situation. Maybe he doesn't want me the way I thought he did.

"Open your eyes, beautiful." His words are direct, yet soft, and when I do as instructed, I find an intensity that steals my breath. "Watch me touch you."

I gaze down to his hands and watch in complete rapture as they finally move. He grazes across my upper thighs, moving toward the apex of my legs. The tips of his fingers sweep across my panties. I'm certain he can feel the soaked material if the way his eyes dilate and his breathing hitches is any indication.

I've wondered what it would be like to have Matthew touch me, and just a few seconds in has already proven better than I've imagined. His touch is firm as he glides across my wet panties. Every time he brushes my clit, it's like I'm electrocuted. I want to pull back from the shocking touch yet wiggle closer at the same time.

His burning gaze locks with mine as he slides his fingers beneath the satin material. I don't even realize I'm holding my breath until he whispers, "Breathe, sweetheart."

I gasp for air as his warm fingers slip between my folds and press firmly against my clit. I cry out and rock my hips, desperate to feel more. He curls his fingers upward, sliding two into my tight body. I can already feel myself tightening around him, my body coiling like a rattlesnake ready to strike.

Matthew swipes his thumb over my bundle of nerves. The combination of his fingers deep inside me and the pressure on my clit sends me flying over the edge of bliss, riding out wave after wave of pure pleasure that rocks my entire body, clear down to my soul.

As the tremors start to subside, all energy seems to leave my body, rendering me boneless and exhausted. Matthew removes his fingers and tries to right my panties, but they no longer fit properly to cover me. I lean forward into his chest, his arms wrapping around me and holding me close.

"That was beautiful," he whispers, running his hand down my back.

"I don't know about that, but it felt pretty amazing," I whisper, grateful he can't see the blush staining my cheeks.

He kisses my forehead, his lips seeming to linger against my skin for several long seconds as he breathes me in. "Most beautiful thing I've ever witnessed to date."

A small smile spreads across my lips. "Just wait until I've regained my strength and return the favor."

I feel him tense beneath me; his arms tighten even farther until it's almost hard to suck air into my lungs. "As great as that sounds, you're tired."

I pull back a little and meet his gaze. "You don't want me to...do that?"

The corner of his lip curls up. "Oh, sweetheart, I've dreamed about you doing *that* all week, but I don't want you to feel required to return the favor. When it happens, it'll be because you can't keep your hands off me. Because you've been fantasizing about having your mouth on me all day. Because there's nothing you want more than to taste me, hard and ready, against your tongue," he says, sliding his thumb over my bottom lip, "knowing what'll happen next will change the course of our lives forever. I'm going to taste you, sweetheart, and then I'm going to make love to you until I'm all you feel and know."

I shiver as a new wave of desire sweeps through my veins. My mouth opens to reply, to tell him I'm ready, but something stops me. Maybe it's the look in his eyes, the one that says he needs to know, without a doubt, I'm one-hundred-percent ready. That I'm his, and not just for the night.

He pulls me back against his chest, my cheek nestled above his heart. It beats wildly, a loud echo that seems to calm my own. After a few minutes, he turns me and starts to set me back down in my seat. My dress is a rumpled mess, and no amount of smoothing it out will fix the wrinkles. Matthew reaches over and grabs my belt, securing me back into the seat.

Our eyes meet right before his lips sweep softly over mine in a slow, tantalizing kiss. Just when I'm about to throw my arms around his neck and return to straddle his lap, he pulls back and smiles. "Thank you for the best night I've ever had."

"I could say the same thing."

He winks before sitting back in his seat and pressing the intercom. "George, we're ready to take Miss Morgan home."

"Of course, sir."

Matthew wraps his arm around my shoulder. It amazes me how well I fit snuggled into his side, my head comfortably resting on his chest. Within fifteen minutes, the car is pulling in front of my building. When the car stops, I release my seat belt and wait for the door to open. Once it does, Matthew slips out and extends his hand, that familiar zip of electricity slides through my fingers when our hands meet.

As I step out, I'm pulled against his side. "George, I'll be back in a few minutes. I'm going to walk Miss Morgan up."

"Good night, George," I state, waving goodbye.

"A pleasure, Miss Morgan, as always. Enjoy your evening."

We step up to the building, the door already standing open. "Good evening, Miss Morgan."

"Evening, Jason," I greet one of the evening-shift men.

He doesn't follow as we make our way to my private elevator and enter my code. As the doors close, Matthew turns and takes my hands in his. "I had a great time tonight."

"Me too," I reply, just as the elevator arrives on the top floor and the door opens with a chime.

We step into my foyer, but Matthew stops before making it too far. "I have a few meetings lined up this week, but I have some free time. I thought I'd meet you at the shelter and take Dolly for a ride again."

I'm instantly smiling. "She'd love that."

"Me too," he replies, stepping closer and eliminating any space between us. "Maybe we can have dinner again this week?"

"And I'd love that."

He smiles, his mouth meeting mine one final time. My body instantly responds in a way it's never done before, and I'm on the verge of asking him to stay.

Matthew pulls back. "I'll talk to you tomorrow."

"I look forward to it."

He steps away and approaches the elevator. "Make sure you lock up behind me," he says.

The alarm system on the elevator will keep the car from moving without my knowledge. Even though we have a manned front desk and the car only moves with a code, it's another level of security to keep it from moving while I have it disengaged. "I will," I confirm, pressing my code into the keypad.

The doors start to close. "Good night, Kyla."

"Night, Cowboy," I reply, his smile cut off by the closing door.

When the car returns to the ground floor, I enter another code and head toward the stairs with a grin on my face and a satisfied hum thumping through my veins. Oh, tonight was definitely one of the best nights I've ever had, if not the greatest. As I get ready for bed, I feel a renewed sense of excitement and can't wait to see him again.

Hopefully soon.

My phone chimes with a text message, and when I glance at the screen, I'm beaming from ear to ear. Since he loves the nickname so much, I changed his contact information in my phone.

Cowboy: *Is breakfast too soon for another date?*

Me: *Absolutely not.*

Cowboy: *See you at 9?*

Me: *I'll be ready.*

And I will. As I climb into bed, a new wave of exhilaration overwhelms me. The sooner I fall asleep, the sooner I'll see Matthew again, and kiss him. I just have to hang on a few more hours.

Easier said than done.

***

I'm downstairs in the lobby fifteen minutes early and am surprised when I see Matthew's car pull up in front of the building just seconds later. Smiling, I head for the entrance, throwing a wave at the security desk as I go.

Just as I step out onto the sidewalk, my breakfast date gets out of the driver's seat. "What are you doing down here?" he asks, coming around to open the passenger door. He's casual in a pair of dark jeans and flannel button-down, his jaw dark with day-old stubble.

"I thought I'd save you a trip up," I tell him, placing my hand on his arm as I approach the open door.

"Yeah, but you robbed me of a good morning kiss," he replies, the corner of his lips curling upward.

I give him a slight shrug. "I guess you'll just have to play catch-up down here."

That slight grin turns into a full-wattage smile. "It would be my pleasure."

Without a care in the world as to who sees, Matthew kisses me, cupping my jaw in his big hands. I can smell the cleanness of his soap and feel the burn of his facial hair against my cheek as his tongue slips inside my mouth. He reluctantly pulls his lips from mine, though keeps my body caged against the car with his own. "Good morning," he mumbles. A ghost of a smile on those full lips.

"It is now," I sass, turning and slipping into the passenger seat of his car.

Matthew's laughter fills the air around us as he closes the door, securing me inside. When he joins me inside the vehicle and pulls onto the road, I take in the view. Tall, gleaming buildings with doormen out front. Young men and women taking dogs for walks. A few women power walking and chatting. It's a nice neighborhood. Classy, yes. Safe, you bet. Where I want to spend the rest of my life?

No.

"So, I thought we'd head over by the shelter and you could suggest somewhere to grab a quick bite," Matthew says, pulling me out of my own head.

"That sounds nice. Since we're so close to the shelter, does this mean we're stopping for a visit?" I ask, excited to head over and see the animals.

I'm rewarded with a warm smile. "I had hoped. Ever since last night, I've been thinking of riding Dolly."

My heart skips a beat. The image of him sitting atop that magnificent horse, so confidently and regal, fills my mind. It's one I can't wait for a repeat performance. Then my brain flashes to everything else that happened last night, before the conversation of Dolly and the shelter happened. "That's what you remember from last night?" I ask, my voice a little breathless.

The moment the car stops at a red light, he turns and pierces me with an intense, dark look. "Not at all, sweetheart. I keep picturing the way you looked coming undone on my fingers. The way you threw your head back and let go. The way your sweet pussy squeezed my fingers and pulsed until you practically collapsed against me. *That's* what I remember most about last night, but since it's not appropriate to walk around with a hard-on in a public place, I've switched my focus to something a little more PG. Like horseback riding."

I stare at him and jump when the car behind us honks. "Oh."

Matthew adjusts himself in his seat and presses down on the gas. We take off like a bullet, moving swiftly through the intersection and down the street. After a few blocks of silence, he finally says, "Yeah, oh." Matthew reaches for my hand and gives it a squeeze. "Don't ever doubt what you do to me, sweetheart."

I find myself smiling as I glance down at his groin, even though it's not funny. He's hard as a rock in his jeans, and my legs clench together as I recall exactly what it felt like when I was straddling his lap last night.

With another squeeze of my hand, we drive toward the shelter. "Take a left at the next light," I instruct as we near our destination. I take it he didn't mention a specific spot for breakfast, he was leaving it up to me to choose, since I know the area well. "Turn into the alley after the jewelry store on the right," I add.

Matthew follows my directions, pulling between the small family-owned jewelry store and the abandoned building which used to house a furniture business. When we reach the back of the building, we pull into the large parking lot, which is already half full. He parks in an available spot close to the small, nondescript building at the back of the lot and shuts off the car. "This looks promising."

"Really?" I ask, glance from the small diner to the man sitting beside me. Matthew Wilder definitely doesn't seem like the type to choose this style of establishment over a five-star restaurant with paparazzi stationed on the sidewalk, but if there's anything I've learned in the last week, it's that Matthew Wilder isn't who I thought he was.

He shrugs. "You haven't led me astray yet."

I give him a grin and reach for my door handle.

"Let me," he proclaims, jumping out and running around to my door to help me out.

With my hand tucked into the crook of his arm, we walk side by side into the run-down diner without a care in the world. Just him and me against the world.

There's no place I'd rather be.

Chapter Thirteen

Mason

As Wednesday finally hits, a sense of dread falls heavy on my chest. My brother's assistant added the details of my dinner meeting with Jerald to my calendar, and even though I've come up with a thousand excuses to cancel, I haven't actually done the deed. Mostly because this meeting is important to my brother and the deal he's made to purchase the company.

I check my watch, having just an hour before I need to get ready for dinner. I consider sending Kyla a quick text, but since I did that before lunch, I should probably lay off. She's volunteering this afternoon at the shelter and is spending time out with Dolly. I'm actually a little jealous. After riding her again this past weekend, I'd welcome any further opportunity to saddle up.

Instead, I grab my keys and the gym bag Matthew keeps in his closet and head downstairs to the gym. Since it's the middle of the afternoon, the large space is practically empty. A man who looks familiar runs on a treadmill off to the side of the room, and after a brief eye contact, he throws me a head nod. Otherwise, he pays me no attention, which is how I like it.

I slip inside the locker room and change into the T-shirt and shorts inside. Fortunately, Matthew and I wear the same size shoes too, and he's got a pair of new Nikes in the bag. I change quickly, using one of the empty lockers to hold my clothes, and return to the gym. The man from earlier is now using the free weights, so I head over to one of the treadmills to keep my distance.

I warm up with a quick two-mile run, something I haven't done in a while. Hell, when was the last time I went for a run? Months. Probably eight or nine of them, actually. When I finish, I'm breathing a little harder than I should be, which is slightly embarrassing, and even though I'm fatigued, the endorphins are coursing through my blood.

I head for the leg press machine next and pick a weight a little too aggressively. The first ten reps aren't too bad, but by the time I'm halfway through the second set, I can definitely feel the burn. My calves and thighs are crying, and when I finally hit ten a second time, I'm more than ready to move on to another machine. Unfortunately, the guy is still lingering by the weights.

"Wilder, haven't seen you in the lounge much lately," he says casually, flexing a bit for the large mirror along the wall.

I slip two forty-pound weights onto the barbell. "Haven't been around much," I confirm, not elaborating any further.

The slightly familiar man moves around the gym for a few more minutes before grabbing a hand towel. "I think I heard Manchester was headed for the sauna. Wasn't he one of the other bidders on that company you're buying?"

I don't respond, mostly because I don't know if this Manchester guy was bidding on the company or not. Instead, I take my own hand towel to mop up the sweat on my face before I wipe down the machines I used with a disinfecting cleaner. But I can't help but wonder what this Manchester guy knows. He wasn't mentioned in the information on the business deal Matthew left me, but I suppose it wouldn't hurt to see what he knows, right?

Tossing the hand towel in the bin, I return to the locker room and strip down naked. I hear the door open behind me, and as I throw a towel around my waist, I see the guy from the gym behind me. "I heard he secured investors to put in a better offer, one Jerald is considering," the mouth says as he strips down to the buff and turns around reaching for a towel to cover his sad little dick.

I'm not sure if this guy is spewing the truth or just trying to get under my skin, but I'm not letting him get to me. I head for the sauna door, leaving the mouth with the tiny dick behind.

Inside the sauna, I'm pleased to only see one man. He's sitting in the corner with his head back against the wall and his eyes closed. I take a seat across from him and just off to the side, not wanting to catch a glimpse at anything peeking from beneath his towel. I've already seen one too many today, that's for damn sure.

Just as I lean back and get comfy, the man across the room opens his eyes. "Wilder," he says politely.

"Manchester," I reply, taking a stab in the dark at who it is.

"Heard you were meeting Jerald tonight," he says, catching my gaze.

"Maybe. That a problem?"

Manchester shrugs his shoulders, his belly protruding over his towel. "Not a problem. I had hopes he'd reconsider my offer to purchase his company, but something tells me I'm barking up the wrong tree. He seems to like you, for whatever reason."

I don't respond, just lean back against the wall and suck in a deep, humid breath.

"Rumor has it you're not even looking to disassemble the company, which I thought was odd. They must have something you really want, like government contracts."

"I'd be an idiot to strip apart something with their stature, wouldn't I? They're a powerhouse in the technology industry, and partnered with the resources available at Wilder Group, we'd be at the top of the game." At least, that's the way I took all that business mumbo jumbo information my brother left me.

Manchester smiles. "Well, for what it's worth, I agree with you. Tearing apart that busines would be a shame. Adding your resources would elevate its status and success. These last two years I've watched you buy up companies and cut them to pieces, selling off what's left. I'm sure it's made you a shit-ton of money over the years, but this was a solid move. I'm proud of you, kid," the older man says with a certain gleam in his eyes. It says he respects my decision—or at least my brother's decision.

I may not really understand what my brother does, but a sense of pride sweeps through my body.

"Thank you," I mumble, closing my eyes and relaxing once more.

No other words are spoken until the guy from the gym comes in and sits beside Manchester. They both offer greetings, the man from the gym instantly diving into talk of business. "Have you heard back from Jerald on your offer?" he asks Manchester, and even though I can feel their eyes on me, I refuse to look.

"Actually, I did. He's comfortable with his current offer, Ted," Manchester replies.

"Interesting," the man—apparently, Ted—from the gym states.

Realizing I'm running out of time before tonight's dinner, I stand up, making sure my towel is secured around my waist. "If you'll excuse me, gentlemen, I have a business meeting to prepare for."

Manchester throws me a wave before turning to Ted to return to discussions of business deals and mergers. All shit I couldn't care less about.

I run through the shower, throw my clothes from earlier back on, and head up to my brother's apartment to get ready. Tonight's dinner calls for a suit and tie and probably a razor. Kyla seems to like the stubble, and since it's my preferred appearance too, I've been pretty lax on shaving. But not tonight. Tonight, I'll need to be on my best behavior and that includes looking the part.

***

At seven on the dot, George pulls up to a fancy restaurant in the heart of downtown Boston. A man in a valet uniform opens my door, greeting me as I slip out of the car. "Good evening, sir, and welcome," he says.

"Thank you," I state, tucking my left hand into my pocket and heading toward the entrance. A doorman greets me with a smile. "Welcome to The Waldorf Restaurant. The hostess is right inside."

Inside, a gorgeous blonde in a fitted white button-down offers me a flirty grin. "Good evening, Mr. Wilder. May I help you?"

"I'm meeting someone," I state, ignoring the fuck-me eyes being cast my way.

"If you'll follow me, your party has already arrived." She turns and heads into the darkened restaurant, a little extra swing in her step that I'm certain is for my benefit.

"Thank you, Malinda," a man says when we stop in front of his table. I may not recognize him, but I'm certain it's Jerald.

"Enjoy your dinner, gentlemen," she coos, placing her hand on my forearm for a few extra seconds before sauntering away.

"Have a seat, Wilder. I took the liberty of ordering you a scotch," the old man say with a polite smile over his tumbler.

I sit down in the chair and grab the glass of amber liquid and take a healthy sip. I've never been a scotch man, but who am I to refuse the good stuff. "Thank you, Jerald. I appreciate the invitation to dinner."

"Well, I've been interested in getting to know the infamous Matthew Wilder," he replies with a grin. "It's been fascinating to see the man outside of the boardroom."

"I do enjoy getting out of the office every now and again," I add, lifting my glass in salute.

"And here I thought a man like you slept at his desk," he teases.

"Who says I sleep?"

That makes him laugh, bringing his own tumbler up in salute and taking a drink.

Our waiter arrives a few seconds later and reports tonight's specials. There's a slow-roasted prime rib with new potatoes and asparagus that catches my attention right away, and after Jerald orders the salmon, I go for the slab of beef. It reminds me of home.

"So, how's life treating you, Wilder?"

Kyla flashes through my mind. To the kisses we've shared and the way her body reacts to my touch. It's been only a handful of days since our date, but she's all I've thought about since. Considering I'm basically just hunkering down in my brother's expensive apartment, I've got plenty of opportunity for my thoughts to drift to her.

"It's going well, thank you, Jerald."

He waves his hand. "My friends call me Jerry."

"Are we friends?"

He takes me in for a few long seconds before responding. "I think so. I don't usually talk about my business with anyone outside of my business, but I've found from the first time you barged into my office and demanded a meeting, I've been drawn to you a little.

You're brutal, to the point, and not someone I'd want to tangle with if the circumstances were different. But I see the other side of you too."

"The other side?" I ask, reaching up and tugging at the crisp tie around my neck.

"The one you hide from the world. The one where you seek control because you secretly crave their approval."

I blink at the older man several times, trying to find the right words. Is he right? Does my brother want approval? In work? I mean, he always made sure he was the best at everything he did and that my parents knew about it. I always assumed he was just that confident, that conceited, but maybe there was more to it.

Our food is delivered to the table, and Jerry and I both dive right in. "How's your prime rib?"

As soon as I swallow, I reply, "Excellent. Your salmon?"

"They have the best here. Caught locally and prepared fresh," he states, piercing his lemon glazed fish with his fork. After a few more bites, he adds, "So tell me about the woman you've been seeing."

I blink across the table, unsure what to say. Matthew told Jerry about Kyla? How much? Considering I'm supposed to break up with her for him, how much could he have shared? And how much do I share? That she's quite possibly the best woman I've ever known? That her smile could light up even the darkest day?

"I take it by that smile, things are going better?" he asks, smirking across the table.

"They have been, yes. She's a wonderful person."

He arches an eyebrow. "Well, I'm happy to hear that. A couple of weeks ago, you weren't certain about the future of your relationship."

I swallow hard, thinking about what my brother could have told Jerry about Kyla. I'm sure it wasn't anything too favorable, which pisses me off. It's replaced by a fresh wave of guilt, however. The realization that I'm tricking her still sits heavily in my gut. I hate lying to her about who I am, but the thought of letting her go almost feels worse. I know I need to come clean, and I will. I just have to figure out the right time to do it.

"She's amazing," I whisper, staring over his shoulder at nothing. "She has the biggest heart of anyone I've ever known."

He gives me a warm smile. "That's wonderful. If you like her, I hope you let her know. Don't leave any room for question." He clears his throat and takes a sip from his water goblet. "You know, my daughter started to date this guy a few months back. Very casual, I guess. She doesn't seem to be in a big hurry to introduce me."

"Maybe she just wants to make sure she sees a future with him before she introduces you to him. Meeting the family is a big deal," I say, finishing up my perfectly prepared slab of beef.

He seems to consider my words. "You may be right. She's had," he starts, stopping to consider his words. "She's had a rough time in the last few years. She tries to be tough and not let me see how the loss of her mother has affected her, but I see it. It breaks my heart. I'm her father and only want the best for her."

"Most fathers do."

"Are you close with your father?" he asks, pushing his plate away.

I think about when the last time I saw my dad was. It's been too long. That thought causes the food I just ingested to sit like lead in my stomach. "I used to be," I tell him honestly. "I went away for a while and haven't seen him and my mom as much as I should."

He nods in understanding as the waiter returns to collect our dishes and offer us dessert. We both decide against it and finish our drinks. "Thank you very much for meeting me for dinner," he says, reaching for the tab before I can grab the folder. He slips his black credit card into the slot. "My treat."

"I am more than willing to cover my portion, Jerald."

"Jerry," he corrects with a smile. When the waiter returns with the credit card slip, Jerry scribbles his name down on the paper and hands it back.

We walk side by side through the restaurant, heading for the exit. As we approach the hostess stand, the blonde from earlier offers me another flirty grin and slips a piece of paper in my hand. I already know what it is, and if the way she's looking at me is any indication, my brother has probably already met her after hours a time or two.

Ignoring her and sliding what is certainly her phone number into my suit pocket, I step outside, pleasantly surprised to have made it through the dinner without any of the worrisome shit I'd expected happening. The valet calls for our rides, leaving us standing on the sidewalk alone.

"It's a shame my daughter is seeing someone. I think you two would make an interesting team," he says with a jovial smile.

I snort out a laugh. "Well, I believe you mean that as a compliment, but I'm not so sure I believe you."

He looks at me as his car is brought around. "You've always been hard on yourself, Wilder, but deep down, I see the goodness inside you."

My heart hammers in my chest. Goodness inside me? I don't feel an ounce anywhere. Not in my head and definitely not in my heart.

Except for the place Kyla has rooted, the happiness she brings me growing every day.

I clear my throat. "I'm not so sure about that," I reply honestly.

Jerald gives me a grin. "I do, Wilder. I see it, and that's why I've agreed to your offer. Even though several have come in, some even more generous than the one we agreed upon, but do you know what? I'm not out to make a fortune. I want to sell for a fair price and know my employees are going to be well cared for. I want someone to take the business I started all those years ago and help it flourish into something even bigger." He meets my eyes. "And you're the man to do it."

I swallow over the lump in my throat and reach out my hand. "Thank you for trusting me."

Jerald returns the hand gesture, his older hand smaller and frailer in my own. "I'll see you a week from this coming Monday," he says, referring to the scheduled meeting at his office to sign the papers for the company.

"I'll see you then."

The older man slips into the opened back seat door, offering me a small wave. I spy George rounding the corner, pulling in behind Jerald's town car. "Hey, Wilder," Jerald says, pulling my attention away from my own driver. When I meet his eyes, he adds, "If anything changes with that woman you're seeing, let me know. I'd love to set you up with my daughter." He laughs and shuts the door, leaving me alone in front of the sidewalk.

"You ready, Mr. Wilder?"

I watch as the older man pulls away, a smile spreads across my lips as he does. I'm not sure the faith he's placed in me—errr, Matthew—is correct, but it makes me smile, nonetheless. "I am, George. Let's go home."

Chapter Fourteen

Kyla

I'm securing the kennel for a new dog we just took in when I feel my phone vibrate in my pocket. My smile is instantaneous when I see his name across the screen.

Cowboy: *Dinner plans tonight?*

Me: *Nothing planned. What did you have in mind?*

Cowboy: *Can you be at my place at six?*

I glance at the time on the top of the screen, having plenty of time to finish up here, run home, and get cleaned up before I need to be to Matthew's.

Me: *I can. Do I need to bring anything?*

Cowboy: *Just you.*

Another grin breaks out across my face as I shoot back a quick confirmation and slip the device back into my pocket.

"A woman smiles like that only when she's thinking of a man."

I turn, startled, and see Debbie standing just off to the side, carrying an older tabby cat. "Oh, I didn't hear you come in," I reply, looking for a topic change. "How's Howard?"

"He's fine," Debbie states, snuggling the fat cat. "He's up to date on all of his immunizations, much to his dismay." Debbie slips the cat into his kennel and makes sure his food and water is full. "Edith says we had three adoptions today."

"We did," I reply eagerly, telling the other volunteer all about the two dogs and one cat that went to their forever homes. I reach into the kennel of the Border Terrier dropped off earlier and sigh. "Hopefully we can send this young lady to a home soon too. She's too sweet."

"That's the new one, right?"

"This is her." I recall the look on the woman's face when she brought the four-year-old dog to us this morning. The woman had been crying, swearing she did everything she could to find the dog a good home, but she was unsuccessful. Her daughter was afraid of the dog, Hattie. She tried everything to help her child overcome her fear, but it was fruitless. After six months, she exhausted all of her resources and felt rehoming the terrier was the best course of action.

"She's a sweet pea, that's for sure."

"I think she'd do well with older kids and lots of room to run. She's spunky, for sure," I add, glancing in the kennel where Hattie rests on a blanket. "I'd take her in a heartbeat, if I had some place for her to play."

Debbie laughs. "You've said that about every single animal to go through here, Ky."

I shrug, knowing she's right. I've said that, but it's true. I'd have taken any and all in need of rescue, including Rocky, the English bulldog with a very grumpy disposition.

"Big plans tonight?"

"I'm heading over to Matthew's for dinner."

"Ohhhh," she singsongs, waggling her eyebrows.

"Stop it," I chastise with a giggle. "You're incorrigible."

"You did talk to him about the gala next Saturday, right?"

"I did," I confirm with a nod. "He's making sure he's off work by six."

"Good. I'd hate for you to get all dolled up and no one be there to appreciate all your hard work."

I sit back, sticking my finger into a kennel and letting a dog nestle against it, and consider her words. I've worked hard on this gala, as have Debbie and Edith. But she's right. What I'm looking forward to most is actually having someone there with me, by my side. Someone to dance with and share in my excitement as the totals from the silent auction items come in. Someone who looks amazing in a tux and knows how to wow a crowd. Yet looks at me like I'm the only one in the room.

Someone like Matthew.

***

I step inside the building and smile at the man holding the door. "Welcome, Miss Morgan. Mr. Wilder is expecting you. I'll escort you," he says, leading me to the elevator and calling for the car.

I take a moment to glance around, observing several men milling around, chatting. They notice me, most offering a small smile or a head nod. As we wait, someone behind me says, "Do you see the ass on that?"

I tense, waves of anxiety rolling off my escort beside me.

"I'd love to get my hands on that thing. I'd leave bite marks on her pale skin. I bet Wilder has tons of fun with that one. The quiet ones are always the wildest."

Before I can even comprehend what's being discussed behind me, the elevator opens, revealing Matthew. He smiles the moment he sees me standing before him, but that easy grin quickly slips from his face. "What's wrong?" he asks, his voice firm and edgy.

"Nothing," I gasp, trying to cover my nervousness with a quick smile.

He steps forward, studying me with a critical eye. I step onto the elevator car and wrap my arms around his waist. "Ready?" he asks, stepping back against the wall, his arm thrown over my shoulder protectively. He mumbles a quick thank-you to the man who was escorting me before the door closes, leaving us alone. "What happened back there?"

"Nothing," I insist, a little too quickly.

He turns me and catches my eye, his gaze intense and serious. "Did one of those guys say something to you?" he asks, seeing right through me.

I shrug. "They just had a few inappropriate comments."

He continues to study me. "About what?" he asks, his jaw tight with tension.

A blush creeps up my neck. "About...my ass."

He seems slightly taken aback by my words, but his shock is quickly replaced by a wolfish grin. He turns me, his eyes cast downward, devouring my rear in the black leggings I threw on after my shower. "Were they talking about how amazing it looks in those pants?"

The corner of my mouth turns upward. "Umm, actually, yes, it was something along those lines." The door opens and we step out together. When we reach his door, I turn to see what's taking him so long to unlock the door, and find his eyes still locked on my backside. Smiling, I ask, "You done?"

His laughing eyes finally look up, meeting mine. Matthew pulls a key from his pocket and lets us into the apartment. As I step through the doorway, he glances down once more. "Nope, not even close."

I kick off my flats and follow my nose to the kitchen. "Wow, it smells amazing in here."

"Thanks. I was going to order something, but found a chuck roast in the freezer, so I thought I'd throw together some Italian beef. There's this bakery down the block that makes fresh bread and when I saw the mini French loaves, I thought they'd be perfect."

I'm smiling as he crosses behind the island and stirs the contents of the slow cooker. "Sounds delicious."

"And I made baked mac and cheese too. It's one of my personal favorites," he says, pulling a foil-covered pan from the oven.

I sit down on the island stool. "I didn't think you knew how to cook."

Something crosses his face as he carefully sets the pan on the trivet. "Well, I guess I've always known, but choose not to do it." He chuckles awkwardly, grabbing a bread knife, and cutting sandwich openings into the fresh bread.

"Well, I think you should do it more often," I reply, taking in the spread he's prepared. "Can I help?"

He nods toward the wine fridge. "Why don't you pick out something that's good with beef and cheese," he says with a wink.

I open the fancy refrigerator and retrieve a sweet white wine. Before I can set it on the counter, Matthew takes the bottle, pulls the opener from the drawer, and removes the cork. "Well, look at you. Much smoother than last time," I reply, grabbing two glasses from the cabinet and referring to the first time he tried to open a bottle and couldn't find the corkscrew remover.

As I pour the glasses, he cages me against the counter and kisses my neck. "Much smoother. Silky smooth, like your skin."

A shiver sweeps through my body, which is suddenly very alive with need. Warmth from his body filters through my clothes, heating my skin with his closeness. "You know, you keep that up and the food will get cold."

His tongue slips out, tasting my skin. "But you'd be very warm."

I mumble a noise and gasp as he nuzzles my ear with his nose.

Suddenly, he pulls back, taking a glass of wine with him as he goes. "But I guess you'll just have to wait until later." Matthew takes a sip from the glass. "That's good."

I swirl my wine before bringing the glass to my lips. "It is, and what happens later?"

He waggles his eyebrows suggestively, making me laugh. "A movie, actually. Get your mind out of the gutter." Matthew sets his glass on the counter and starts making me a plate. When he's piled a sandwich with meat and mozzarella cheese and adds a healthy pile of his baked macaroni and cheese, he hands me the plate and points to the counter.

We sit side by side and eat the delicious food he prepared. It's amazing, actually. One of the best home-cooked meals I've ever had. At first, I didn't think I'd be able to eat all the mac and cheese, but once I started, I couldn't stop until what was on my plate was completely gone.

"Leave your dishes in the sink," he says, coming up behind me as I rinse the remnants off my plate.

"It wouldn't take very long to just wash them now," I reply, reaching for the dish soap.

He turns off the water and takes the soap dispenser from my hand. "True, but it would cut into the time I've set aside for the movie and delay my groping during the scary parts."

I snort out a laugh and turn to face him. "What kind of movie did you get?"

"Scary one. One that'll ensure you curl up at my side and hide against my chest all night."

With an eye-roll, I tell him, "I don't like scary movies."

He gives me another wolfish grin that causes warmth to flood my panties. "I know."

I hit his hard chest playfully.

"Actually, I have a few different ones to choose from. I'll even let you pick."

"Very generous of you, kind sir."

"Come on," he says, taking my hand and pulling me into the living room. It's completely different than it was last week, all warm and cozy, and no longer looks like a simple model home. "This room is stunning."

"It's okay," he replies, taking a seat on the end of the sofa and kicking his feet up on the coffee table. He removed his boots and his feet are bare as he casually relaxes on the couch, and it actually might be my favorite look on him.

"Do you not like it?" I ask, sitting in the middle of the sofa, close to him, but still keeping a respectable distance.

He looks around, taking it in. "I do. It's a hell of a lot better than it was before."

"I agree."

Matthew reaches for the remote and pulls up a movie streaming site. "Here are our choices."

As he flips through the ten or twelve movie options, one jumps out at me right away. "Oh! *The Replacements*. I haven't seen that in forever," I say, tucking my legs beneath me and getting a little more comfortable.

"No?" he asks, selecting the movie. "I don't think I've ever seen it."

"Really? I thought all men watch football movies." I reach for my glass of wine and take a sip. "Especially second chance football movies."

He shrugs and tosses the remote to the other end of the couch. "I must have missed this one. What's it about?"

Matthew puts his arm on the back of the couch, creating a pocket of comfort for me when I curl into his side. "A bunch of cocky professional athletes strike, so they bring in replacement players to fill in for them." He tenses, but only for a fraction of a second. He quickly relaxes, and I wonder if I could have imagined it.

We settle in and watch as Keanu Reeves takes a bunch of has-been players and transforms them into a true team, all while falling in love and getting the girl. I've never really been a fan of sports movies but enjoy them if they have a romantic love story side to them.

By the time Falco throws the winning touchdown to secure the game for his team, I'm completely comfortable, nestled against Matthew and not wanting to ever move. When I glance up, I find him watching me, not the big kiss scene on screen. "Did you enjoy it?"

"Yeah."

"What did you like best?"

"The way he got the girl at the end and kissed the hell out of her." The corner of his lips curling up and his eyes dancing with excitement.

"You weren't even watching that part."

Matthew adjusts me against his side and runs a hand up my outer thigh. "I was watching your reaction to it."

My eyes meet his, hungry and full of desire swirling between them. "And what did you get from my reaction?"

"Well, your eyes widened when he made his move and pulled her into his arms. Then, you held your breath in anticipation for the big kiss," he says, gently turning me until our lips align. "And when their lips finally met," he adds, sliding his hand into my hair and cradling the side of my head, "you sighed in contentment, a smile on these lush lips." The hand slips down my jaw and taps on my bottom lip.

"I'm a sucker for the kiss at the end of the movie." Why does my breath sound so choppy?

"Hmm," he replies, adjusting us so we're lying side by side on the plush sofa. "I think we should reenact the scene."

I wiggle against his broad, warm body, seeking as much contact as possible. "You mean the kiss?"

"Well, to start with. You know as well as I do more happened after that kiss."

I'm already laughing as he gives me a cocky smirk. Feeling a wave of confidence, I slide my hand down his side until I'm cupping his hard length in the palm of my hand. "More? Like this?" I ask, giving him a gentle squeeze. He starts to thicken immediately.

"That's good," he croaks out, his voice gravelly as his hand moves to the apex of my legs. Matthew presses his thumb over my clit, sending shock waves of electricity through my limbs.

Keeping his hand between my legs, he presses his mouth to mine, his tongue sliding along the seam of my lips until I grant him access. The kiss heats up immediately, my hands gripping at anything they can, as his tongue tangles with my own.

I feel his warm fingers graze against my stomach, slowly dancing up my abdomen. "Is this okay?" he asks, tracing the cup of my bra with a finger.

"Definitely okay," I confirm, brushing my palm over his erection. "And this?"

Matthew groans, flexing his hips forward and grinding his hardness into my hand. "More than all right."

Suddenly his mouth is back on mine. He kisses my lips, my jaw, my neck, rendering me completely breathless. Desire swirls in my stomach, as he continues his masterful kiss. He slips his hand into my bra, sliding his fingers against my hard, sensitive nipples and making me gasp.

"I have an idea," he starts, carefully pushing up my shirt. "Maybe we could get rid of this?"

I reach for the hem of his shirt and give it a tug. "Only if you lose yours too."

He gives me a smirk and sits up, raising his arms. Placing my hands on his abs, I let my fingers linger a little longer than I should before I slowly push the material up, dragging my hands against his warm flesh the entire time.

"There," I finally say, pulling the shirt over his head and tossing it onto the floor. I take in the sight of Matthew, shirtless. He's chiseled hard in all the right places with a strip of dark hair that starts at his belly button and disappears into his jeans. His arms are perfection, not too big but with amazing definition. And his chest? Like a sculpted work of art.

"Are you done checking me out?"

"Almost," I respond, trailing my fingers down his abs.

"My turn," he says, lifting my shirt. He takes his time, his eyes devouring every inch he reveals. And where his eyes touch, his hands aren't far behind. When my arms extend up, he pushes my shirt up until it falls on the couch behind me. His eyes find mine once more, a deep desire burning brightly as he says, "There. Now I can look at you while I make you come."

Chapter Fifteen

Mason

God, she's fucking beautiful. Her soft, pale skin is such a contrast to the dark couch, and as I lie her back and settle in beside her, I realize she's my every fantasy come to life.

Trailing my finger from her throat, I let my index finger linger between her breasts. "Are you going to take off my bra?" she asks.

Shaking my head, I reply, "Nope." I give the light blue lace covering her breasts a tug, revealing those two hard nipples I had my hands on earlier. "I'm leaving it on like this." Then, my mouth descends to the left one, my tongue darting out and licking the first tight nub, making her moan. The noise incites me, ensuring I want to hear it over and over again.

Kyla trails her hand over my shoulder, while the other reaches for the fly on my jeans. When I pull back, she gives me an unapproving look. "If you pull back, I won't be able to reach you."

"I think we should set some ground rules," I tell her, swiping my tongue over her nipple again.

Her mouth falls open as she gasps. "What kind of rules?"

"I say we can both touch each other as much as we want," I start.

"I like where this is going," she injects with a grin.

"But our pants stay on."

Kyla looks up at me with question in her eyes. "Well, that's an interesting approach. If we can't take our pants off, how will we..."

She leaves her question hanging open, making me smile like the Cheshire Cat.

"We'll just have to get really creative, love," I whisper before dropping my mouth to her chest, licking and sucking.

"Question," she says, a sound caught between a groan and a gasp. "I can touch you, as long as the pants stay on, right?"

"That's right, sweetheart. The pants stay on," I respond, continually swiping my tongue over her peaked nipple.

Kyla inhales sharply when I replace my tongue with my teeth, her body rocking into mine. She's so damn responsive, I can't help but wonder if I'd be able to get her off without even touching her pussy. I bet I could...

Determined to test out this theory, I focus on her breasts, reveling in the way she writhes and rocks against me. I'm so fixated on her, it startles me when I feel her hand slip into my jeans and grab my cock through my underwear. "What are you doing?" I grit through clenched teeth.

"Well, you said the pants have to stay on, right? You didn't say anything about keeping my hands out of those pants," she says, the sweetest blush creeping up her face. She's wholesome and good, everything I'll never be. I'm the bastard lying to her.

Before I can think too much about it, she strokes my cock, or as much as she can within the confines of my pants. "Jesus," I groan, wishing her soft hand was on the opposite side of my boxers, her warm skin wrapped around my aching dick.

"If you, well, if you keep doing what you were doing, then I'll keep doing this," she whispers shyly, trying to bury her face against my arm.

"I'll keep going, sweetheart, but you aren't going to hide from me. I want to see the pleasure on your face," I state, sliding my thumb over her left nipple.

She responds by moving her hand a little faster along the length of me and throwing her leg over my hip. The movement lines her pussy up with my thigh, which she rolls against, seeking out sweet friction.

I flex my leg toward her. No, not easy with her hand in my pants, but I get the job done. She continues to ride my thigh, while I lick and suck on her glorious nipples. Her hand grips and strokes me to the point where I'm about to blow. "Ky, you better be careful or I'm liable to blow in my pants like a fifteen-year-old."

The grin she gives me is full of sass. "So, you're saying," she starts, moving her hand until her fingers slip inside the opening in the front of my boxers, "if I keep doing this," she continues, stroking her fingers along my cock, "you might get off?"

"No might about it, angel," I groan, rocking into her touch, which also presses my thigh a little harder between her legs.

Kyla gasps, her head falling back and revealing the long column of her neck. I take the opportunity to kiss the hell out of her neck before making my way back down to her chest.

I'm not sure who really pushes who over the edge first, but what happens next is pretty fucking epic. She grinds against my thigh and steels her grip around my cock, jacking me harder. I bite down on her nipple, causing her to erupt like a volcano. Her hand tightens around me, and the combination of that and the sound of her coming in my arms, has my spine tingling moments before I come in my pants.

"Fuck," I groan, riding wave after wave of euphoria, not even caring about the mess I'm making in my jeans.

Kyla gasps for air, while falling limp in my arms. Her hand is still tangled in my boxers, and even though I'm sure it's not very comfortable for her, I kinda like having her touching me that closely. Partner that with her wrapped in my arms, and it's pretty much the best fucking feeling in the world.

"Well, it's not so bad to keep the pants on," she says, a slight smile on her lips.

A laugh rumbles low in my gut as I pull her closer and kiss her forehead. "I happen to agree with you."

We lie together for several long minutes, until I can't take the wet, stickiness in my pants any longer.

"I'll be right back," I tell her, slowly rolling my arm from beneath her.

"I'm just going to stay right here," she whispers, carefully pulling her hand from my pants. I grab my T-shirt and hold it out for her, so she can wipe off her hand. It only takes her a few seconds to do so before she hands me back my used shirt.

With another quick kiss to her forehead, I start to head away from the couch, noticing her eyelids are drooping, as if she's suddenly too exhausted to keep them open.

It takes me a little longer than normal to get out of my dirty pants, and as soon as I do, I decide to jump in the shower. Two minutes and I'll feel a hell of a lot better than I do right now. Actually, I should invite Kyla to join me, but that's probably not the best idea. The moment I see her naked, I won't be able to keep my hands off her, ensuring things progress a little quicker than they should. Not that I don't want her. I want her naked and beneath me more than I want my next breath, but I want to make sure she's ready.

That's why we're pants on until I hear those sweet words from her lips.

It only takes me a few minutes to wash up. I don't really want to get dressed again in jeans, but I'm not a fan of slipping my brother's lounge pants on to go back out there. I throw on my last pair of clean jeans, sans underwear, and button them. I opt to forego the shirt and head back to where I left Kyla.

She's exactly where I left her, lying on her side on the couch. I know I should wake her, to make sure she gets home safe and sound.

But I don't.

Instead, I do the exact opposite.

I slip onto the couch, sliding my arm beneath her neck, and curl around her body. We fit...perfectly. I feel her sigh against my neck as she tosses her arm over my side and snuggles in nice and close. It's the most comfortable position I think I've ever been in.

One I'd love to repeat nightly.

For the rest of my life.

That's a startling thought, yet it doesn't scare me as much as it should. Deciding to ignore every red flag and alarm sounding, I opt to embrace her nice and close and hold on tight.

***

I spend the next week with Kyla every chance I get. We have dinner, snuggle on the couch at either her place or my brother's, and sometimes even wake up cuddled together in the early morning light. But we never take it any farther than that.

My time is running out.

It's Thursday night, leaving me three days before my brother returns and I head back home. But what if I don't head back to Montana right away? What if I send the money I'm being paid to fill in for Matthew, pay off my debts, and hang around Boston for a while? Sounds like a great, easy plan, but I know it's anything but.

Because in order to stay with Kyla, I'd have to tell her the truth.

With every day that passes and my feelings for her grow, that thought terrifies me, but I see no other choice. She needs to know. We'll never be able to move forward until I tell her who I am and why I've lied to her. She's a reasonable person, though. She'll listen, right?

My throat goes dry as dread fills my entire body.

This could very well go badly. She could tell me to get lost, and honestly, who would blame her? She thought she was dating Matthew Wilder. Turns out, she's been hanging out with his financially struggling twin brother. She has let him kiss her senseless, touch her body, and make her come numerous times. She's smiled up at him, her eyes full of laughter and trust.

Totally forgivable, right?

Fuck, I'm a bastard.

I run my hand over my face, hating myself a little more with each passing second.

My phone rings, interrupting my self-loathing. When I grab the device from my pocket, I blanch when I see my brother's name on the screen.

"Hey," I say in way of greeting, pacing the room from one end to the other.

"Mason, how has it been going?"

"Fine," I state, my agitation growing.

"What crawled up your ass?"

"Nothing, Matthew. Nothing at all." The sarcasm is thick, but I can't help it. Right now, I'm pissed as hell, and it's all directed at my brother. The one who got me into this mess.

"Obviously, it's something or you wouldn't be acting like a complete asshole. What is it? Did something happen at the dinner with Jerald?"

I snort out a laugh. "That was over a week ago. You're just now deciding to ask about it?"

"Well, I knew it went well, Mase. I've talked to him since. Is this about your dinner with Jerald?"

I close my eyes. "No. It went fine. For some unknown reason, he seems to like you," I say. "This isn't about Jerald or your precious business deal."

"Then what's this about?"

"Kyla."

That's met with silence on the other end of the line. "Kyla? I assume you're grumpy because you finally fulfilled the third task on your to-do list."

His light demeanor raises the heckles on every nerve ending I have. "No."

"No?" he asks, pausing. "Well, I guess you have a few more days. Might as well let her help you pass the time."

"Jesus, Matthew, do you hear yourself? She's not something to just help pass time like a hobby. She's a beautiful, intelligent woman who doesn't deserve to be lied to and tricked."

I'm met with more silence, so I go on.

"I can't do this anymore. I'm going to tell her."

"Tell her?"

"The truth."

"The fuck you are!" he hollers into the phone line. "Why would you do that?"

"Because I..." I clear my throat. "Because I like her."

More silence.

"A lot."

"You're falling for her." It's a statement, not a question.

"No. Yes. I don't know," I sputter, running my hand through my hair.

"That's a yes," he responds with a chuckle.

"And how would you know anything about falling for someone?"

"Trust me, Mase. I know." I hear a door open, followed by the sounds of the ocean meeting the shore. It's quickly followed by my brother sipping on a drink, most likely something strong and expensive.

Not having the time or energy to dive into whatever in the hell he's talking about, I go on. "I want to come clean with her, Matthew."

"Okay, so say you do that, say you come clean. What do you think the end result will be when you tell her you've been pretending to be me for almost three weeks? Do you think Kyla is just going to laugh at the misunderstanding? And then what? You both ride off into the sunset and live happily ever after? You don't live in Massachusetts," he says, a little too casually.

"I'm well aware of where I live and don't, Matthew. And... I'm not sure what to expect, but I just can't keep doing this. I can't keep lying to her. She deserves better than this," I mumble, closing my eyes and picturing the way she looked this morning, sleeping on my arm in the early sunlight.

Matthew sighs in the phone. "You can't do this, Mase. Not now." There's a hardness in his tone I haven't heard before.

"I have to. I'm done lying to her. We've got that charity gala for her animal shelter this weekend. I'm going to tell her afterward." I start pacing the room once more, my legs carrying me without so much as a thought or care.

"Not acceptable, Mase," my brother argues, his voice hard, leaving no room for argument. "I'm paying you to do a job, and if you tell Kyla about our arrangement, you'll be going against the deal you signed, therefore ensuring the contract is void."

"Matthew, don't do this," I start, but stop when he continues.

"That means you wouldn't receive any of the payment, brother. The money you so desperately need would be gone."

I blink slowly, shocked by what he's saying. "So, if I tell her, you won't pay me the money you promised."

"No, if you tell her, you're breaking the contract *you* signed, leaving me no choice but to not pay you."

"That's bullshit," I holler, my heart pounding angrily in my chest.

"You signed an agreement, Mason. You did this, not me. You could have walked away and not taken the deal, but you didn't."

"Because I felt like I had no choice," I counter.

"You always have a choice, Mason. Always. You tell her the truth and you blow everything."

I close my eyes, knowing he's right. If I tell Kyla what I've done and who I am, I go against the agreement I signed with Matthew. But if I don't tell her, I'm not sure I can live with myself. Either way, I'm screwed.

"Just get through the gala, Mason. I'll be home Sunday and you can fly back to Montana, two hundred thousand dollars richer. Your debt is paid with the bank and you have a small nest egg to help whatever you have planned for the next phase. Forget about Kyla. She'd never understand. She'll never forgive you."

His words repeat over and over, even after I've hung up a few minutes later. I go back and forth so many times, I'm dizzy with exhaustion and indecision. I want to tell her, but if I do, I'm risking losing everything I've been fighting for. I try to chase my problems with scotch, but all that does is make it worse. Now I have a major problem on my hands and I'm drunk.

Could tonight get any worse?

Chapter Sixteen

Kyla

"So tell me all about what's happening with the prince," Amalee says, sipping her second margarita of the night.

I'm all smiles the moment she finally brings up Matthew. We've only been here long enough to order our food, start our second margarita, and devour half the basket of chips and salsa, but it's longer than I thought it would take her to ask about him.

"Smiling's good. Tell me," she demands good-heartedly, a mischievous grin on her face.

"I think I'm falling in love with him." I don't mean for those words to come out of my mouth, but they just...pour from me like a faucet of truth.

Amalee gasps and claps her hands together. "Holy shit, are you serious? I'm so happy for you," she coos, dipping another chip in the homemade salsa.

I take a drink of my cold strawberry margarita and set it down, just as our food is delivered. We wait until the waitress steps away before we resume our conversation. "We've been spending a lot of time together lately," I start, cutting into my chicken enchilada and dousing it with sour cream and guacamole.

"Ohhhh," she sings, wiggling her eyebrows suggestively.

"Not like that," I start, taking a bite of my food. "Well, a little bit like that."

I share a few not-too-intimate details, boasting about the dates we've been on, most of which happen at either his place or mine. I've learned Matthew actually prefers eating in than out, which still shocks me a little, considering how many times we ate in fancy restaurants in the beginning. Maybe that was his way of trying to impress me.

"Do I get to meet him officially this Saturday?" she asks, referring to the upcoming gala. Amalee and Matthew have been to a few events at the same time but have never been introduced.

"Yes. He's agreed to come with me. I'm a little nervous, if I'm being honest. My dad is going to be there too."

"Oh, the boyfriend and the father meeting for the first time? I'm sure it'll be fine. Your dad gets along with everyone. Well, unless it's business related," she adds with a laugh.

I nod slowly, taking another bite of my food. "I'm sure you're right, but still. I just really want them to get along, you know?"

"I do."

We chat about the gala details until we've finished our meal and the plates are collected. Amalee drains her margarita. "So... I met a guy last week," she says, nonchalantly, but I already know this is somewhat of a big deal. My best friend has always been a fan of casual sex. With her high demand profession, Amalee doesn't bother with relationships. Not that she hasn't tried. She has, but the one time she put herself and heart on the line, she was burned badly. Now, she doesn't even try to find someone to spend the rest of her life with. She just finds someone to help warm her bed every now and again, or help scratch an itch, as she puts it so elegantly.

"Really? Tell me more," I encourage, giving her my full attention.

Amalee raises her shoulders indifferently and reaches for her margarita, which is empty. "He's an ADA for the city," she says, averting her eyes. "I've heard of him before, but never met him in a courtroom, since I don't do criminal law. Well, he came in to deliver something to the office next to mine and we shared an elevator."

I'm already smiling. "An elevator ride is like ten seconds, Am."

Now it's her turn to grin. "I know. He invited me to grab a cup of coffee right then and there, so we went back down to the lobby and ordered Starbucks. We haven't been able to meet up again, but...we text. A lot."

Reaching over, I squeeze her hand. "I'm happy for you."

She gives me a casual shoulder lift, but I can see the excitement in her eyes. "Thanks. It's way too early to get too enthusiastic though."

"Maybe, maybe not. You should invite him to the gala on Saturday."

She snorts. "I don't think I'm ready for that yet. Maybe dinner first, then we could tackle a big public charity event."

"Well, I know someone who can get you a last-minute extra ticket," I reply, finishing off my drink.

The check arrives, but I'm not quick enough to get it this time. Amalee slides her credit card inside the black folder. Once the waiter returns, she signs her name on the slip of paper and walks with me out of our favorite Mexican restaurant.

"So, give me a call if you need anything before the gala. I'm not working Saturday and could help with anything that doesn't involve creativity."

I giggle at my friend. She's always been one who needs step-by-step directions. If you tell her to take a stack of flowers and form an arrangement, she breaks out into hives. "Not working?" I ask, shocked.

Amalee rolls her eyes. "Well, let me clarify. I'm not working at the office but have a few things to do in my home office. I'd make myself available to you, if you needed something."

"Thank you," I say, standing on the sidewalk.

"It's still early, you know."

I glance at my watch and notice it's just after eight.

"You could slip over to that fancy apartment complex Matthew lives in and enjoy a night cap, if you know what I mean," she states, elbowing me in the ribs.

I glance around, noticing the man standing beside me is grinning. "Am, everyone knows what you mean," I reply, diverting my eyes as the blush creeps up my neck.

"I think I'm going home to text Callum. Maybe he's into sexting."

The guy beside me laughs but tries to cover it with a cough. I grab my friend's hand and drag her toward the parking lot where our vehicles are before she can say anything else to embarrass me.

"Thanks for dinner," I tell my best friend, pulling her into a hug.

"You're welcome. See you Saturday," she says, throwing me a wave over her shoulder and slipping into her BMW.

When I'm inside my own car, I pull out my cell phone and plug it into the charger. It has plenty of battery left, but it's a habit I'm in, ensuring I always have plenty of juice in case of an emergency. I glance at the screen, a sadness slipping in when I don't see a text from Matthew. He knew I was having dinner with Amalee tonight, but I had kind of hoped he'd invite me over afterward. Or at least text to see how my night was going.

Deciding to take the bull by the horns, I fire off a quick message.

Me: *Just finished up dinner with Amalee.*

When my text goes unanswered, I return my phone to my cup holder and pull out of the lot. I almost turn to head toward Matthew's place, but decide against it. If he hasn't replied, it means he's probably busy. I know he has a big day coming up, with his business deal looming, and could be working.

I will admit, for a man who was very passionately devoted to that particular deal a handful of weeks ago, he's been very lax in the last few. Maybe that's because he has everything where he wants it, which would be good news. I've seen how absorbed my dad would get when he was working to secure a deal, and how consuming work can be the closer it gets to signing. I just hope everything is still on track come Saturday, and no issues arise. The last thing I'd want to see is him too busy to attend the gala.

By the time I reach my building and park, my text message still goes unanswered, so I slip my purse over my shoulder, wave a quick greeting to the evening shift manning the front door, and head upstairs to the penthouse.

Deciding to get comfortable, I change my clothes into a cozy nightshirt and wash the makeup off my face. With my hair pulled up in a ponytail, I move to the kitchen to pour myself a glass of wine and flip on the whole-house stereo system. Ed Sheeran fills the rooms with his soft crooning, and I'm instantly put in a better mood.

The wine helps.

I try not to glance at my phone, but it's fruitless. I must check my device two dozen times over the next thirty minutes, but no response appears. In fact, I go in and make sure I actually sent my original message. When I see it was sent and shows as delivered, I set my phone down on the counter, fill my wine glass with more liquid love, and head for the balcony.

Sipping sweet wine, I watch the traffic below, the cars moving at a steady pace to get to their destination. I end up standing there, leaning against the railing, for nearly an hour, making up stories for those on the sidewalk. Even though I'm too high to see their features, it's an enjoyable way to pass the time, and I don't dwell on whether or not there's a response waiting for me on my phone.

Finally, when I start to yawn and my glass is empty, I head back inside, securing the door behind me as I go. I place my empty glass beside the sink, grab my phone, disable the elevator, and go upstairs to bed. It isn't until I'm settled beneath the plush down comforter that I finally glance at my phone screen.

No reply.

Sighing, I set my phone on the charger beside my bed and snuggle in, where I toss and turn for another hour, until I finally fall into a fitful sleep.

***

I haven't heard from Matthew.

As I let one of the dogs outside to run in the designated area for canines, I can't help but feel that familiar sadness I've tried to keep at bay creeping in. I should give him space, knowing his plate is full with the closure of his deal, but yet, I still want to text him, to see how he is and why he's too busy to respond to a simple message.

Did something happen?

What if he's sick or hurt? He doesn't have family too close by. Would he reach out to his parents or even his twin brother for help if he needed it? A month ago, I would doubt it, but as I get to know him and I've seen the slightly softer side of Matthew Wilder, I believe he would.

Maybe another quick message wouldn't hurt.

He could have just completely gotten sidetracked and forgotten to reply.

I bet that's it.

Grabbing my phone, I fire off a quick text.

Me: *Just wanted to check in and see how you are. Hope your Friday is going well.*

My heart is pounding as I wait to see the bubbles appear, but after ten very long seconds, the message only shows as delivered. Again.

I place my phone into my pocket and step out into the canine pen. It's my day to exercise the dogs, which will also include cleaning up after them, so I'm careful not to step in anything I shouldn't. The Jack Russell Terrier I just let go is running like crazy, tongue hanging, as she enjoys the fresh air and sunshine. Aubrey is a little on the hyper side, not surprising since she's less than two, so we like to let her get some of her running done before we let more dogs out to play. I head over to the water bowl and make sure it's full of fresh water before I take a seat in the wooden chair at the edge of the pen.

After watching her play for fifteen minutes, I grab my phone and check it, only to find my message still unread.

My heart sinks.

The exact same thing happened a few weeks ago. Matthew became too busy and started calling or messaging me less and less. The little things he did to show me he was thinking of me stopped and the dinner dates all but ceased. It wasn't until I showed up on his doorstep for dinner and threw myself at him that I really felt any spark toward him.

Now, that spark is alive and growing.

And it may be coming to an end.

I move to the grassy area, careful of any doggy surprises, and have a seat. Aubrey comes running, jumping on my legs and wanting to play. Being on the ground with her helps lift my spirits, but not much. I still feel the weight of his unspoken replies, a dread that fills my entire soul.

I spend the next few hours with the dogs. Most of them play well together, but the ones that don't will get a little outside time alone. Those are the ones that are just not used to having other dogs around. They tend to be a little more vocal in their displeasure of being out here with others, and until they learn to adjust, we tread lightly with them. We don't force any of them to be with other dogs if they're not ready.

By late afternoon, all of the dogs have been walked, have played in the yard, been fed, and are back in their kennels. Some immediately curl up on their bed for a quick nap. I glance over, knowing my time volunteering today is coming to an end, and spy Hattie giving me the sad eyes. All on their own, my legs carry me over to her kennel and reach for the latch. Hattie's tail starts thumping against the kennel as excitement takes over.

"Shhh, don't tell anyone I'm doing this, okay?" I instruct, grabbing a leash off the nail by where she's kept and slipping it onto her collar. Hattie's tail thumps even louder.

I lead the dog outside for a second time today and release her leash as soon as we're secure in the fenced in area. "There you go," I say, smiling as the pup takes off like a bullet.

She jumps on a ball left in the grass, so I head over and take a seat near where she's playing. Hattie immediately brings the ball to me, crawls on my lap, and starts gnawing at the tough plastic. My hand is on her head, running down her lean body. "You're such a good girl, Hattie." My throat becomes thick with emotion, threatening to choke me. "I'd take you home with me, if I could." I really wish that strict no-pets clause at my penthouse didn't exist.

"You're going to make someone a very happy pet owner, Hattie Girl. I have no doubt you'll be leaving us here soon and have the best owners ever," I whisper, my eyes filling with tears.

Why am I crying? Knowing a dog has the potential for being adopted is a joyous occasion, not a reason to cry. Maybe they're tears of joy. Could be.

I sit there for half an hour, playing with Hattie. I throw the ball and she runs and grabs it, only bringing it back to me with a little extra coaxing. When she does, I make sure to give her extra kudos and encouragement. Yeah, she's definitely going to make someone a happy pet owner someday.

My mood perks up while sitting back here, playing with the dog. I don't even dwell on the fact my phone hasn't vibrated in my pocket the entire time I've been out here. I'm not sure what's sadder: the fact that Matthew hasn't replied or the fact no one else has messaged me either.

Pathetic.

"Can you sit?" I ask Hattie, petting her soft coat. "Sit, Hattie."

She turns her head, as if considering my words, so I reach back and show her how it's done.

She sits easily, holding her pose. "Good girl." Her tail starts to wag enthusiastically.

We go through the command a few more times before I reward her with an ear scratch. "Good job, Hattie. You know how to sit."

The dog drops her rear and sits once more, making me laugh. "Look at you."

She barks in reply, her tail going a mile a minute, until she jumps up and takes off running.

"Wait," I holler, turning to look behind me, ready to get up to retrieve Hattie. Before I can rise, I stop in my tracks, surprised to see a visitor standing there. "What are you doing here?"

Matthew gives me a hesitant grin before he reaches down and scoops up Hattie. "And who is this little guy?" The dog seems all too happy to be shown some attention by the newcomer.

"Girl. Her name is Hattie," I state, trying to keep my voice calm and smooth, even though my heart is tapdancing in my chest.

He doesn't say anything for almost a full minute, eventually taking a seat on the ground beside me. "Mind if I join you?"

I glance his way, noticing the dark shadows under his eyes, as if he didn't get much sleep the night before. His cheeks are covered with a stubble that's thicker than normal, as if he hasn't found time to shave.

My heart trips over itself. A part of me is concerned about his slightly disheveled appearance, but a bigger part of me is damn happy to have him here. At least I know he's not sick or hurt somewhere. Maybe he really has just been busy. He does have a business to run.

All I know is I feel calmer and more relaxed than I have since last night, and that's because of one person.

The man sitting beside me, holding a dog.

There's only one answer to his question.

"I don't mind at all."

Chapter Seventeen

Mason

She's a sight for sore eyes. The balm to heal all that ails me.

As much as I tried to stay away, I just couldn't. I'm drawn to her in a way I've never experienced. Never wanted to. Now, all I can think about is her, even when I shouldn't.

After talking to my brother yesterday, I went back and forth about what to do for hours. Booze didn't help. Ignoring her text message didn't help either. In fact, both just made me feel like shit.

All I wanted to do was text her. Call her. Drive over and see her. I had to shut my phone off to keep from replying, even though I didn't know what I'd say. I was torn between confessing all my dirty secrets and ignoring them. As Friday morning turned into afternoon, I was no closer to finding the answers I was looking for, but one thing was crystal clear.

I wanted to see Kyla.

She had sent a second message, but I opted to not reply, choosing to clean myself up and head over here. The woman who greeted me inside wore a volunteer name badge and directed me out here, a knowing grin on her older face. As I peeked through the window on the door, my heart kicked up a few thousand beats per second.

There she was.

Sitting in the yard, a small dog beside her.

165

She was breathtaking, and all I could think about was figuring out how I can keep her.

The woman, not the dog, though the pooch is pretty fucking cool too.

Seeing her sitting here made me realize one thing: she's worth the risk.

I'm going to tell her who I am and hope for the best. Oh, I know it won't be easy. I'm sure there will be a lot of groveling involved, but after I explain everything, I'm sure she'll be able to see I wasn't out to betray her. In fact, that's the reason I've got to tell her the truth. I don't want to hurt her at all. It's the exact opposite.

I'm falling in love with her.

I clear my throat and scratch behind Hattie's ears. "So, Hattie, huh?"

"Yeah," she says, softly, reaching over and stroking under her chin. "She's only been here a handful of days. I have high hopes on her being adopted very soon."

"She's a cutie," I say, just as Hattie stands on my legs, extends her face toward mine, and gives me a kiss on the chin.

Kyla laughs the sweetest sound. "She is. And apparently, she loves you."

"Don't all women?" I ask goodheartedly, looking at her with mischief dancing in my eyes and a smile on my lips. She doesn't reply, but I can tell she's thinking about something.

"Someone sounds awfully sure of himself," she teases back, reaching over to pet Hattie, even though she's giving her full attention to me at the moment.

After a few long seconds of silence, I finally break into the apology that needs to happen, "So, I got your text messages. I'm sorry I didn't reply back last night. I was working on a few things, and it was late by the time I saw it." Mostly true. I leave out the fact I turned my phone off, because that won't help my case at all. Instead, I give her a piece of the truth. The part where I was home, trying to figure out whether or not to tell her the truth or just cut my losses, like my brother suggested.

The truth is, I *can't*.

I can't walk away from her.

Not yet.

Not until I've laid all the cards out on the table.

Then, we'll see how they fall.

I'm just praying they don't fall, if you know what I mean.

Kyla shrugs and averts her eyes. "It's okay."

I reach over, the dog in my lap thinking it's time to play. She's sadly disappointed when my hand gently grips Kyla's chin, and not hers. "Hey, it's not okay. I'm truly sorry."

She meets my gaze, her eyes relaxing and somewhat smiling. "I understand being busy. Are you still able to go tomorrow night?" she asks, referring to the charity gala.

"I wouldn't miss it for the world," I reply honestly, reaching for her hand and bringing it to my lips.

We sit there for another fifteen minutes, playing with the dog. Kyla fills me in on her dinner with Amalee, and I realize I'm excited to meet her friend. She's attending the event tomorrow night, as is Kyla's father and a few of his employees. Now that one, I'm slightly nervous about. I haven't met the family of someone I've been dating since I was twenty-two and that dad hated me on sight.

Probably because he knew I was planning on sleeping with his daughter later that night.

"So, do you have plans for tonight?" I ask, tossing the ball for Hattie to retrieve.

"No."

"How about dinner at my place? We can order something from that bistro down the block."

"Sounds good. No, Hattie, bring me the ball. Bring it back."

I'm grinning, watching as Kyla tries to persuade the ball from the dog. After a few more tosses, we start to gather up the toys strewn across the penned yard. "I need to put her back in her kennel," Kyla says, scooping up the dog.

"Do you have to?" I ask, realizing how much I like the small terrier dog.

She laughs. "Yeah, I do. We can't leave the dogs out in the yard unattended, especially overnight."

A weird sadness seep into my bones. The thought of Hattie being put back in a cage until she's adopted doesn't sit right with me. Actually, I can picture her running around my ranch in Montana. She's got enough spunk, I'm sure she'd have no problems with the cattle. She'd probably be the boss.

I follow behind as she leashes Hattie and takes her back inside. I spy several dogs and cats, all eager to have a little attention sent their way. I reach fingers through the kennels of the dogs around Hattie, but I find myself gravitating toward the small dog I've just spent the last half hour with. She gives me a look, conveying her dejection at being put back in the kennel, which rips at my heart.

I want her.

"What's your process for adopting one of the animals?" I ask offhandedly, though I'm as serious as a heart attack.

"Well, they'd have to fill out an application and pay a small fee to adopt. Some dog breed adoptions require a home visit, just to see the space a dog would be living in. There would be a meeting in one of the family rooms to make sure the dog and the family jibe. As long as everything on the application checks out and Edith approves, then the family would take the dog or cat home, usually within twenty-four to forty-eight hours."

Kyla makes sure Hattie is secured and her water bowl full, before turning toward the double doors that lead to the front of the shelter. I follow behind, taking one last look at Hattie before I go. The dog lies down on her bed and sighs so loudly I can hear it all the way over here.

"Interesting," I reply, stepping out of the large back area and into the front room.

Kyla heads over to the volunteer at the front desk and fills out a checklist for taking care of the dogs before turning back to me and asking, "You ready?"

I almost ask for an application. Why? I'm not sure. I'm leaving Sunday on a flight back home, and it's not like I can leave a dog with my brother.

Sighing, I reach for her hand. "Ready." As we step out into the gorgeous Boston late afternoon sunshine, I push all thoughts of Hattie and how much I'd like to take her home with me out of my mind. "Want to follow me to my place?"

Kyla hesitates. "Umm, actually, I wouldn't mind stopping by my place to take a quick shower. I love being with the cats and dogs all afternoon but feel like I'm covered in an inch of hair and slobber."

Before I can even think about my words, I'm saying, "You could take a shower at my place."

She seems surprised by my suggestion. Probably because she doesn't have clothes or any of her own things at my brother's apartment. A big part of me wishes it was actually my house she was coming back to, where there might be a drawer or two with her personal effects stored inside.

Jesus, I've only known her a few weeks. How can I possibly be thinking of sharing a living space with her? I casually dated Janea two years ago for almost a year and the thought of moving in together never even crossed my mind. Never. But here I am, ready to clear out space in my dresser for Kyla.

Talk about putting the cart before the horse. The big secret still looms over my head. The last thing I should be thinking about is taking this to the next level with her. Instead, I should focus on coming clean this weekend after the gala. My plan is to bring her back to my brother's place and tell her all about the deal I struck with Matthew.

Money be damned.

I'd rather lose my ranch than lose her. That was what I realized in the wee hours of the morning, when I was *not* sleeping, like the rest of the town.

So, I'm going to tell her everything and pray she understands, because her telling me to hit the road, while a real possibility, scares the hell out of me.

"Oh, well, I guess I could," she says, pulling me from my own thoughts. "I don't really have anything to put on after a shower though." I can see the blush creeping up her neck.

Not wanting to embarrass her, I reply, "You can throw on one of my T-shirts and we can wash your clothes. This way, you have something clean to put back on...whenever you leave." I step closer, invading her personal space and forcing her to look up to see my eyes.

She swallows hard. "I could do that."

Mentally, I give myself a fist pump. Smiling, I pull her into my arms and lightly kiss her lips. Oh, I definitely want to deepen it, pressing her against the nearest hard surface and sliding easily between her legs, but now isn't exactly the right time. Or place. So instead of showing her exactly how I feel with my mouth, I pull back. "Let's go, sweetheart."

We're able to slip into my building without much fanfare, but I can still feel a few sets of eyes follow us to the elevator. I can't help but wonder if any of them were the jackasses who made Kyla feel uncomfortable last week. I know they said something. It was written all over her face, and when I glanced to the man escorting her up, I knew my suspicions were right. Part of me wanted to find those two assholes and force them to apologize for their inappropriate behavior, but something told me it wouldn't mean a damn thing to them. They'd just do it again to the next woman who walked in.

I let us inside the apartment and make sure the door is locked behind us. Kyla sets her purse down on the couch and stands awkwardly by the door, as if uncertain what to do. "Come on, angel. Let's get you a shirt and a shower."

I dig one of my T-shirts out of drawer I'm using while here, as well as a pair of cotton shorts. They'll both be way too big for her, but the shorts have a drawstring, and I'm sure she'd feel more comfortable somewhat covered.

"Use whatever you need in the shower," I tell her, handing over the clothes. "Leave your stuff on the floor and we can throw it in the washer when you're done." I turn to walk away, because if I don't now, I won't at all. I'll climb into that shower stall with her and do very dirty things to her under the water spray. "Oh, do you know what you want from that little bistro place? I can order it while you're getting cleaned up."

"Umm, I'm not too picky. You choose," she replies shyly.

"They have a decent broiled fish with melted garlic and butter sauce. Their steaks are good too, as well as a bacon wrapped pork chop," I tell her, leaning against the doorjamb with my shoulder.

"The fish would be great. Can I get fries instead of the baked potato? I've been craving fries."

"You got it. Come on out when you're all done," I answer, closing the door as I go. Also ignoring the fact she's about to get naked in that very bathroom.

Instead, I turn my focus toward calling in our dinner order. It's the start of the evening rush, so I'm sure there'll be a slight wait for our delivery. I guess that doesn't matter though. As long as she's here—and it helps that her clothes will be trapped in the washing machine, ensuring she can't leave for a while—I'm good.

My order is placed and expected to be delivered within an hour, so while I wait for Kyla to finish her shower, I set the small breakfast table in the corner of the kitchen with plates and silverware. As I grab a bottle of wine from the fridge, I slide it back in its place, opting for a bottle of some fancy beer instead. Did you know my brother has his imported beer delivered weekly with some service? I didn't even know they had alcohol delivery services.

They definitely don't offer this in Casper.

Ten minutes later, I hear the soft sounds of Kyla's feet padding across the hardwood. When I look toward the threshold of the kitchen, I'm absolutely awestruck. She's standing there, bare feet, wearing nothing but one of my T-shirts. It hits mid-thigh and leaves nothing to the imagination. Especially since she's definitely not wearing the shorts I left her. Her hair is piled high on her head in a mess thing, which only seems to make her look even sexier.

"Hey, everything okay?" I ask, my voice a croak through my thick throat.

"Yeah," she replies, stepping into the kitchen. "The shorts were too big, so," she continues, shrugging her shoulders, "I thought I'd just leave them off."

"Good." I clear my throat. "Very good."

Very good? Really, Mason?

"You have something to drink?" she asks, a coy smile on her face as she steps farther into the kitchen. For some reason, I take a step back, needing to keep a little distance between us. I can't seem to think with her all...sexy like that.

"Oh. Yeah. Beer." When she smiles again, I seem to snap out of my stupor. "Or wine. Shit, I'm sorry, I have beer or wine or water. Whatever you want," I state, pointing to the fridge.

Kyla walks over and opens the fridge, slightly bending over as she reaches for a bottle of beer. The hem of the T-shirt creeps up, giving me an unobstructed view of the back of her thighs. Creamy, white, soft thighs.

I groan.

When she turns around, there's a smile playing on her lips. Kyla holds out her bottle for me to open, our fingers grazing as I take the beer and pop it open. I make sure not to touch her when I return the drink, something it appears doesn't slip her notice.

Kyla slowly brings her beer to her lips, maintaining eye contact as she takes a long drink, her throat working rapidly to swallow. My throat, on the other hand, is Sahara dry.

"So," she starts, licking droplets of brew off her bottom lip. "Let's talk about the fact my nipples are poking through this T-shirt."

Chapter Eighteen

Kyla

My heart is pounding in my chest. I don't know what possessed me to try out this new seductress bit, but it seemed like a good idea when I hatched the plan after my shower. Now, I'm wondering if I made a mistake. Matthew seems...tense by my lack of clothes. He keeps moving away, as if the mere sight of me in his T-shirt—and only his T-shirt—is causing him physical pain.

I open my mouth, ready to backpedal and insist my little sexy bit was a mistake, when he reaches forward and grabs the material at my hip.

"Don't take it back."

"What?" I ask, already feeling the heat of his hand near my body.

"I can tell by the look on your face you're about to shut down on me. I'm sorry," he says, stepping forward and invading my personal space. "My brain just couldn't process anything other than the fact you're wearing my shirt and looking sexier than ever before."

Matthew runs his hands up my sides, his eyes devouring me from head to toe. I can feel the shirt creeping up but he doesn't move it enough to discover the fact I'm not wearing any panties. My plan was to try out this whole seductive routine Amalee has bragged about, but it feels so unnatural to me. I've never *not* worn panties, even to bed. It's like an extra layer of protection I've always felt more secure having.

I smile at his compliment, already feeling the slight blush in my cheeks.

"Can I touch you?" he whispers, his voice gravelly.

I nod. When I meet his gaze, there's a raw hunger there, one I've never experienced before. It's actually quite liberating, knowing I brought that look to his face, the one that says he wants to gobble me up for dinner and dessert too.

He seems torn, as if he doesn't really know what he wants to do first. Matthew starts by gripping my waist and doing a little spin and lift move. My butt hits the counter, the shirt riding up a little, the cold hard surface catching my breath. My legs automatically spread, just enough for him to step between. He accepts the invitation, pressing his lean hips between my knees as he leans forward and presses his lips to mine.

The kiss starts slow, his hands coming up to my jaw and framing my face. I can taste the beer on his tongue as it slides into my open mouth, deepening the kiss. My fingers grip his shirt and dance along the hard, muscular planes of his back. I find myself pulling him closer, needing to feel the press of him where I ache the most.

"You are exquisite," he whispers against my lips. He nips at my flesh the way I've come to expect, and I can't help but wonder if he'd nibble *other* places too. "I can't wait to explore your body." He meets my gaze. "But only if you're sure."

"I'm sure," I reply quickly, a little breathlessly.

Matthew presses his erection into the apex of my legs and grinds it, creating the glorious friction. I moan in pleasure, my nails digging into his back and pulling him closer. His mouth takes a leisurely stroll up my neck until it's back on my own lips, branding me with his touch.

He kisses me fiercely, yet slowly, as if he's savoring the taste and feel. His hands are magic. They caress my thighs, on the outside and tops, but never venture between my legs. I almost groan in frustration but refrain when those hands move to my head. One cups my jaw, while the other cradles the back of my head, his fingertips threading into my hair. It makes my every nerve ending tingle with desire and anticipation. I never knew simple touches could feel this dang good.

"I really want to taste you right now," he whispers, lightly dragging his mouth across my chin.

"I *really* want that too."

He pulls back and gazes at me, a wicked smile on his full lips. Matthew reaches down and grips the hem of the T-shirt, his hands hot and heavy on my skin. Just as he goes to move the material, the phone rings. "Shit. That's our food."

A bubble of nervous laughter spills from my lips. "Saved by dinner?"

"Postponed, sweetheart. This is only postponed, unless you're saying stop?" he asks, his voice full of worry, but not because of the prospect of throwing the red light up in regard to having sex. The concern is directed completely at me. As if he's uneasy about me not being ready to proceed.

I make sure to maintain eye contact as I say, "I'm not saying stop, Cowboy. I'm very much saying go."

He stares at me a few long seconds before he grabs me by the waist, lifts, and lowers me to the ground. "Stay here and away from the doorway, Ky. I'll go get our food."

I make sure to keep hidden behind the island, especially since I'm not wearing any pants. I listen as Matthew answers the phone and sends up the food. When he doesn't return to the kitchen, I realize he's waiting at the door. I hear the knock and their muffled words before the door closes again. A few moments later, he returns.

"That smells amazing," I state, as he walks around the island with a large paper bag.

When he glances up, he stops in his tracks. "You look amazing just like that." He sets the bags down on the counter and pulls me against his chest. "Suddenly I'm not hungry for food. I'm hungry for you."

Wrapping my arms around his neck, I lean up on my tiptoes and slide my lips across his stubbly chin. "What a coincidence, I'm hungry for you."

Matthew lifts me against his chest, my legs wrapping around his waist. His hands grip my ass, my bare core pressed to his shirt. I feel him stiffen, his fingers clutch hard. "Kyla?" he asks, his voice hoarse. "Are you wearing panties?"

"No," I reply, giving him a coy grin.

"Fuck," he groans, stretching out that single word as if it had ten syllables.

Suddenly, the bag of food is practically tossed in the refrigerator and we're on the move. With long strides, Matthew carries me easily to his bedroom. When we breach the threshold, he goes effortlessly to the large bed in the middle of the room. It's masculine, with dark wood and rich satin bedding. It looks luxurious and feels even better as he lies me down on top, covering my body with his own.

His kiss is fierce, hard, and full of determination. His tongue delves into my mouth deep, claiming me as his own. I, of course, submit willingly. My hands grip the back of his T-shirt, trying to rip it away. Matthew sits up quickly, grabs the back of the shirt neck and pulls it from his body in one fluid motion. Then he immediately comes down on top of me and resumes his masterful kiss.

I can't seem to stop touching him. Sure, I've seen him and felt his warm skin over hard, muscular planes, but this is different. Maybe it's because there's only a thin barrier of cotton between us, or perhaps it's the fact I'm not wearing any panties and can feel just how much my nearness is affecting him.

"You know," I start, ripping my swollen lips from his. "I could...remove my shirt too."

He meets my gaze and smirks. "I'm trying not to rush this moment, Ky. I know as soon as I get that shirt off, I'm going to be naked and pressing into your sweet body moments later."

"Yes, let's do that," I whisper, his words making me deliriously excited.

Now he rewards me with a wide grin. "Oh, sweet Kyla, we will definitely do that." He goes up on his elbows and shifts his weight. "First, I'm going to have an appetizer."

Matthew positions himself between my legs, and a wave of nervousness sweeps through me. I've only done this twice, both times with a man I dated a few years ago, but it wasn't...good. He seemed to slobber a lot and thrust his finger to the point of discomfort. He never got me off, and I've always wondered if maybe it was me.

The moment I feel his warm breath against my most sensitive area, I almost panic. Not because it's Matthew, but because I'm nervous. The last thing I'd want to do is disappoint him, if there's something wrong with me.

But then I feel the first brush of his tongue across my clit. Fire spreads through my veins as he takes a second swipe, and I find myself wiggling against his face, seeking more. He places his hands against my thighs and gently spreads them farther apart. I don't even have time to get embarrassed about him being down there before his mouth latches on to my clit and sucks. I gasp and rock against his face.

Matthew holds me still and slides his tongue into my core a few times before returning his attention to my clit. With precision, he moves his hand, sliding a single finger into my body. A moan of pleasure rips from my throat, one I wasn't expecting at all, but the combination of his mouth and finger is pure ecstasy.

He continues to move his finger, while licking and sucking on my nub. With each passing second, I'm pushed closer to release. My body starts to tighten, every nerve ending starting and finishing at the exact place his mouth is positioned. When he pulls out his finger, I almost cry out and beg for him to keep going. This feels...amazing. But when he pushes back in, there's a thickness I wasn't expecting. Not just one, but two fingers. He slides them in until he couldn't possibly be any deeper and then curls them upward.

The result is fireworks.

Not the literal ones, but blinding white light explodes behind my eyelids as waves of euphoria steal my breath. I gasp and grind against him, riding out the pleasure coursing through me.

When the tremors finally start to subside, I open my eyes and find his locked on mine, a small satisfying grin on his face. "That was beautiful," he whispers.

My mind tries to process his words, but all I can think about is the difference between the previous oral I received and this one.

Nope, definitely not me.

That's for damn sure.

"What's not you?"

His words startle me. "What?"

"You just said definitely not me. I was asking what wasn't you," he replies, slowly getting up and crouching between my knees.

"Oh." My face burns dark with mortification. I said that out loud? "It was nothing," I stammer, trying to come up with a way to change the subject.

"Hey," he says, leaning forward and holding himself up with one hand. The other goes to my chin, gently turning my face until I meet his gaze. "Tell me."

My heart gallops in my chest as I actually consider answering his question with the truth, because the thought of lying to him doesn't sit well with me. Matthew's a good man. He wouldn't think less of me or make fun of me by my confession.

I open my mouth. At first, nothing comes out, but when I focus on the concern and softness in his eyes, I relax and smile. "First, I didn't mean to say that aloud. I was just...comparing." When his eyes widen, I hurry on. "Not the way you're thinking. Well, I guess a little like that. A man I dated a few years ago did...*that* twice, but it really wasn't very good. He didn't even give me an orgasm. So when you wanted to do it, I was nervous and scared. I was afraid there was something wrong with me, but then you showed me that wasn't the case at all."

His lips curl upward into a mischievous grin. "So, what you're saying is some shmuck you dated couldn't get you off with his mouth on your sweet pussy, but I was able to in like, what, two minutes?"

I roll my eyes. "You don't have to be so proud about it."

He barks out a laugh. "Oh yes I do. I'm damn proud that I made you come with my mouth, and the fact some dick before me couldn't, well, that's just the icing on the cake, sweetheart."

He continues to watch me, but I don't feel as self-conscious as I did earlier. Instead, I feel...sexy. My eyes catch on the impressive bulge in his jeans begging to come out and play. Feeling bolder than ever before, I sit up, pulling my legs together and kneeling before him. Matthew doesn't move, just waits and lets me take the lead.

"May I?" I ask, nodding toward his fly.

He groans and closes his eyes. "I might not survive if you do, but holy hell, do I want you to touch me."

I reach forward and place my palms against his abs. He flexes and tightens against me but doesn't move. I slowly shift my hands down, unfastening the button on his jeans. As I gently release the zipper, I can already see his erection pressed hard beneath his boxers, a small wet spot at the tip that makes my mouth water.

"Can I...take those off?"

"Please do. I think I'm losing circulation below the beltline," he says, a humorous, yet pained grin on his lips.

With a chuckle of my own, I grasp the sides of his jeans and pull them down. When they hit mid-thigh, he shifts off the bed and removes them the rest of the way. He leaves his boxers on, most likely waiting for me to give the go-ahead. When he returns, he sits on the bed and waits for direction.

I crawl to him and gently press on his chest, encouraging him to lie down. Matthew places his arms behind his head casually, but I can tell by the tautness of his body, he's anything but. He watches me closely as I shift myself to his hip and stare down at his boxers. They're the only thing standing in the way now. There's a slight tremble to my fingers as I grab the elastic waistband and give them a tug. Matthew lifts his hips in assistance, remaining in place. When the material reaches his ankles, I toss them on the floor and return to my position at his hips and get my first good look at his hard length.

Oh God.

He's...huge.

Sure, I had anticipated the sheer size of him, having felt it pressed against me and had my hand around it in his pants, but seeing it now, in person, lying on his stomach so big and hard, I had slightly underestimated what we were working with here.

"That's...impressive." My throat is thick and dry.

He chuckles. "You're good for my ego, sweetheart."

I don't reply, just return my gaze to his cock. I take a deep breath and reach for it, loving the way his smooth hardness feels against my palm. I take it completely in my hand and give it a gently squeeze. Matthew groans, and a little bead of wetness gathers on the head of his erection. Suddenly, I need to taste it, taste him. I bend down and swipe my tongue along the head, licking away the moisture.

"Holy fuck," he grits, his abs tightening.

Feeling a new wave of boldness, I hold him firmly in place and lower my mouth around him. I slide my tongue along the seam where the head meets the shaft before slowly working my way down, taking him into my mouth as far as I can. It doesn't seem like it's much, but the sounds erupting from his mouth lets me know he's enjoying it, nonetheless.

I position myself a little more comfortably at his side and start to slide my hand up and down. I return my mouth to the head of his erection, licking away more wetness, and sliding my mouth over his length. I hollow out my cheeks, applying a touch of suction as I begin to move. I swear I can feel him swell beneath my grip as he grunts and rocks his hips. I can tell with each passing second, he's drawing closer and closer to release.

Adjusting my hand, I start to move faster, squeezing just a bit harder. Matthew groans, his hips jerk, as I take him deeper than ever, feeling the tip of his length brush against the back of my throat. My mouth waters, lubricating my hand and helping it slide easier. When I add a little wrist twist, his hips jut up and he reaches for my hand. "Enough."

Trying to process his demand, I sit up and look at him, his eyes feral and intense. "What?" I ask, only releasing his shaft as he removes my hand from his body.

"Enough, sweetheart," he insists, bringing my palm up to his mouth and placing a kiss on my wrist. "I wasn't going to last much longer, and I didn't want to explode in your mouth. I want to be inside your warm, tight body for the first time," he adds, sitting up and reaching for the nightstand drawer. I watch as he pulls a condom out and sets it on the bed. "Lie down, Ky."

I do as instructed, positioning my head in the middle of a pillow. I watch as he rips open the small foil package and sheathes his erection with the protection. He crawls between my spread legs and takes his position at my thighs.

Before he aligns himself up with me, he meets my eyes. "There's still time to back out, if you're not ready."

I look up and hold his gaze. "I'm ready."

With our eyes locked, I feel him adjust his position and press into my body. I don't even realize I'm not breathing until he pauses and cradles my jaw. "Relax, Ky. I've got you."

As he fills me completely, I realize he's right.

He's got my heart entirely.

Chapter Nineteen

Mason

The moment I fill her completely steals the air from my lungs. Not because she's so tight and wet against me—though that's entirely true. It's because when I look down at her, all I feel is love. For her. In just under three weeks, she's wrapped herself around my heart and is embedded there forever.

I give her a few heartbeats to adjust to my size and take a few deep breaths myself. She's so fucking tight and perfect around me, I almost blow it right here and now. Instead, I count to ten and lower my mouth, claiming her lips in a slow, leisurely kiss. When I do, I feel her relax around me just enough that I'm given a little more freedom to move.

And move I do.

I start with measured thrusts, her moans of pleasure spurring me on. I feel the bite of her nails on my shoulders as her ankles hitch over my hips, opening herself wide and allowing me to go even deeper inside her body. My balls are already tightening, the tingle starting at the base of my spine.

But I refuse to come before she does again.

Gripping one of her ankles, I widen her legs a bit more and start to move. Each thrust turns more animalistic, more carnal. I rock my hips, grinding against her clit, and watching as she climbs higher. I feel her starting to squeeze my cock in the best way possible. Going down on an elbow to hold myself up, I take her lips once more, needing to feel the contact.

"Oh God," she gasps against my mouth, her tongue slipping out and tangling with my own.

Just the sound of her voice causes my hips to piston forward. Releasing her lips, I go up on my hand once more and let my body take over. Releasing her ankle, my hand starts at her waist and slips up her side, making a slight detour to cup and fondle her breast. Her nipples are hard and brush against my chest, and that's about the time my brain shuts completely down.

My body is in full control.

Kyla arches her back, pressing into me. Her mouth falls open with a gasp and her pussy starts to tighten. All I can do is feel as her orgasm takes hold, squeezing me so damn fiercely I swear I go blind. I try to ride out her release as long as I can, but it's too much. I'm overwhelmed.

My body thrusts hard as my balls pull tight. My own release is unstoppable, like a freight train running full speed at a brick wall. I grunt as it takes hold, needing to feel her lips against mine as I come harder than I ever have in my entire life. I slide my lips across hers, reveling in the heat of her breath washing over me.

I feel myself sag against her, caging her into the mattress. I know I should move, but I can't seem to make my body and my mind communicate jointly. Kyla nuzzles my neck, taking deep breaths to calm her racing heart.

"Wow, Cowboy," she murmurs, kissing the racing pulse in my neck. "Give me a few minutes and we can do that again."

I bark out a laugh, rotating to my back and taking her with me. Kyla fits snuggly against my chest, her arm curls across my stomach and falls limp against me. I feel more relaxed and in a better place than I have since I arrived in Boston. Sure, it could be in part to the great sex, but I know that's not the real reason.

It's because of Kyla.

She soothes my soul and makes me want to be a better person. She makes me want to make her laugh all day, just to see a smile on her face and hear her amazing giggle. She causes me to think about the future, and I'm damn sure I want her in it.

"I'm going to clean up real fast in the bathroom and get rid of the condom," I tell her, kissing her forehead and sliding out from beneath her. She snuggles into my pillow and closes her eyes. It's hard to leave her lying there alone, all beautiful and freshly sated, but I'm in desperate need of chucking this rubber.

When I get to the bathroom, I toss the condom into the trash and step up to the sink to wash my hands. A quick glance in the mirror confirms the grin I feel pull across my face. I can still taste her on my lips, an intoxicating flavor that already causes my cock to stir to life.

After I've used the bathroom, I grab a washcloth and wet it with warm water before returning to the bedroom. My eyes seek her out immediately, and I find her lying in the exact same position I left her in.

I crouch beside the bed and swipe hair from her cheek. Her beautiful hazel eyes are a bit hazy and unfocused, but she offers me a slight grin. "I brought a washcloth, if you want to clean up quick. Or you can just head to the bathroom."

"I need to use the restroom, so I may just head in there," she replies, sitting up beside me and tossing her legs over the edge of the bed.

I watch, awestruck, as she walks to the bathroom, her beautiful backside on full display. When she reaches the doorway, she glances back. I clear my throat and stand up. "I'm going to go heat up the food."

"Sounds good," she says, flipping on the bathroom light. "I think we worked up a good appetite."

I groan, recalling exactly how we worked it up. "Plus, you're going to need plenty of nutrients for what I have in store for you later."

Her eyes widen and dance with delight. "I look forward to it, Cowboy." She turns and closes the door, leaving me ready and wanting more.

***

It's just before eight, and Kyla is getting ready to leave. She has a full day planned, first with helping oversee the preparations for tonight's gala, and then with her own appointments for getting ready. Tonight's a big night for her, but also for us. I plan to tell her everything after we return from the gala. We plan to go back to her place afterward, which will give us a private place to talk, and I'd rather her be in her own space when I drop the bomb.

I have no idea how it will go. Sure, I know how I pray it will proceed, but if I'm thinking logically, the talk could very easily go the other direction too. I just refuse to dwell on that part.

She comes out of the bedroom, wearing the clean clothes she wore yesterday and a smile on her lips. "Ready to go?" I ask, leaning against the kitchen island.

"I am. The hotel is going to start their setup in about ninety minutes, so I need to make sure I'm there. I want to run home and get cleaned up."

"Hey," I start, taking her in my arms, "I was thinking we could talk tonight when we get back to your place."

She pulls back but doesn't let go of my arms. "Is everything okay?" Worry lines spread across her forehead. I hate the thought of her fretting.

"Yep, fine. Everything's great. Just a few things I wanted to discuss with you," I reply, giving her a big grin. Probably too big, actually. She watches me, taking in my big cheesy—and fake—smile. I wonder if she's going to call me out on it, but she doesn't.

"Okay," she replies, slightly hesitant. "I'll see you at my place at five?"

"Nowhere else I'd rather be, angel."

When she goes up on her tiptoes, I slide my lips across hers, savoring the feel and taste of her. It doesn't last near as long as I'd like, especially since we're nearing the end of my time here. I want to kiss her forever.

"Okay, I better go, or I'll be late."

"Go. I'll see you at five," I reply, taking a step back and slowly dropping my hands. I miss touching her already.

I walk her to the front door, making sure I have the key in my pocket. Taking her hand in mine, I lead her to the elevator and escort her down to the first floor. We ignore anyone milling around the lobby floor or those coming and going from the gym as we pass. We make our way to the parking garage, to where her car waits. Kyla unlocks her driver's door, but before she gets in, I spin her around and press her back against the car.

"One more kiss to get me through the day?" I whisper, slipping my hands into her downed hair.

"Yes, please," she replies, eagerly.

I claim her mouth in a hard kiss, full of passion and desire. If I'm going to be away from her for the next nine hours, I want her to think about me as much as I'll be thinking of her. I pull away, only when I know she's good and breathless, when her lips are swollen and tender.

"Wow," she whispers, gripping the sleeves of my T-shirt.

"Have a good morning, sweetheart. Call if you need any help." I pull back, giving her room to slip inside her vehicle.

"I will, thank you," she replies, sliding easily into the seat and buckling her safety belt. "See you tonight," she adds, reaching for her door.

"Be safe." I help shut the door, closing her off before I can pull her out of the car and kiss her again.

It isn't until she's out of the lot and out of sight that I finally head back inside, my hands shoved in my pockets. A few building tenants wave as I pass, but I try to keep my eyes cast downward to avoid conversation. Fortunately, the elevator is empty when it arrives and whisks me up to my floor just a few seconds later.

Now what?

I guess I can pack a little. I'm taking an overnight bag over to Kyla's when I pick her up for tonight's event, and the rest will be left at my brother's and ready to go tomorrow.

If I actually go.

I'm hoping our talk goes well, and I don't actually have to get on my flight tomorrow. It's not like I'll have the money to go home to Montana and fix the mess I have with my finances. Not if my brother holds true to his threat of not paying me a single dime if I break the contract I signed. I have no reason to believe he won't cut me off without a single cent. Tomorrow, I won't have the finances I need to keep my ranch, but at least I'll have Kyla.

And that's all that matters.

*　*　*

Security inputs the code, and the elevator takes me to the penthouse. I pull on the tie at my neck, wishing I didn't have to wear it, but recognizing it as a key element to the tuxedo I'm wearing. I'm nervous, mostly because I've never attended anything like this. This high society, big money scene has always been Matthew's thing, not mine. Yet, the thought of walking proudly beside Kyla as she celebrates her hard work boosts my spirits and trumps my nervousness.

When the door opens, I step inside. The lights are low and soft music plays through speakers I don't even see. I head into the living area, peeking into the kitchen to see if she's there. When I don't see her, I call out her name. "Kyla?"

"I'll be down in a minute," she hollers from somewhere above me, most likely her bedroom.

Anticipation races through my veins, and I step farther into the room so I can get a better view of her when she makes her descent. She hasn't mentioned anything about her dress, so I have no idea what to expect. I decide to take in the gorgeous view of the river from her penthouse while I wait, anything to try to calm my racing heart.

Movement catches out of the corner of my eye, and when I look up, I swear I stop breathing. There, coming down the steps in a vision of red, is Kyla. Her hair is pinned up in an elegant style that is so fitting and timeless on her. Yet all I want to do is rip out those pins, drive my hands into those lush locks, and kiss her.

I take in the dress once more. It's crimson red and dips down at the cleavage, giving me a tantalizing view of the swells of her breasts. The dress hugs her every curve all the way to the ground, a slit giving me a peek of her leg as she walks. A pair of gold strappy shoes make her legs look a mile long, and all I can think about is seeing them wrapped around my waist.

"Holy shit," I whisper, my legs carrying me toward her before she has even descended the stairs.

She giggles. "I'll take that as a compliment."

The moment she's standing directly in front of me, I place my right hand on her lower back and lean in to kiss her cheek. Only, when my hand meets bare skin, I find myself instantly distracted and needing to see the rest of that dress.

Stepping back, I spin my finger, indicating I'd like to see her turn around. She smiles coyly before doing as instructed and showing me the back of the dress.

"Jeezus, Ky." I gasp, my hand covering my heart.

"You like?"

"Like? I love. You look absolutely stunning. I've never seen anyone look so amazing as you do right now," I answer honestly, committing the image of her right here and now to memory.

Only when I've looked my fill, do I finally take her in my arms and give her the hello kiss I've been thinking of. I place my lips against her warm cheek, careful not to smudge her expertly applied makeup.

"That's it?" she asks, a hint of humor in her sparkling hazel eyes.

"I didn't want to mess up your stuff," I reply, waving a hand around my face as indication of what I'm referring to.

She stretches forward and leans toward my ear. "Just so you know, this lipstick is smudge-proof." When I meet her gaze, she winks at me.

"Challenge accepted, Miss Morgan," I reply, placing my hands on the sides of her head and claiming her lips with my own.

I keep the kiss somewhat PG, even though I'd love to let it run straight to R-rated territory, but I refuse to ruin her night or be the reason she's late. Kyla's put in countless hours, both at the shelter and with event preparation, and I want everything to go off without a hitch.

Taking her hand in mine, I give her a smile. "Ready?"

"Yes," she replies, returning my grin.

"Let's go show you off."

Chapter Twenty

Kyla

As I step inside the ballroom, my heart swells with happiness and pride. There are people milling around, enjoying champagne and checking out the silent auction tables. I'd estimate about half the ticket holders in attendance already, far more than I anticipated would be here so early.

"Drink?" Matthew asks, taking in the gorgeous room.

"Yes, please."

With my hand tucked in the crook of his arm, he leads me past a few familiar faces and toward the bar. When we arrive, I nod hello to the couple standing in front of me and step up when it's our turn. "Champagne, please," I order when the bartender asks.

"And for you, sir?"

"Scotch, neat," Matthew replies, reaching into his pants for a tip.

"Enjoy your evening," the bartender says, setting the glasses on the wood and offering a smile to the next in line.

We turn after Matthew deposits cash into a glass jar at the end of the bar and step deeper into the ballroom. I spy Debbie and Edith talking to last year's big donor and find myself walking that way. "Let's go over there, and I'll introduce you."

"Sounds good."

Matthew guides me around the room until we're standing beside Edith and her husband, Frank, the couple they were talking to before stepping away to get another drink. "Kyla, dear, you outdid yourself this year," Edith croons, leaning in for an air kiss. "It's absolutely stunning."

"Beautiful," Debbie agrees, smiling excitedly.

"Matthew, this is the manager of Boston Cares Shelter, Edith, and her husband, Frank."

"Pleasure," Matthew says, shaking Frank's hand and leaning in to give Edith a kiss on the cheek.

"And this is Debbie and Charlie. Debbie is one of the volunteers and was an amazing asset when we planned tonight's event," I boost, giving Debbie all the kudos she deserves.

"You've all done such a wonderful job. The ballroom looks great," he says, leaning in to kiss Debbie's cheek. When he turns his attention to Charlie, Debbie grabs my attention and fans her face, her eyes wide with delight.

I can't help but giggle, trying my best to hide it behind my champagne glass.

"Matthew, I think I just saw your company's name in the business section of the New York Times," Frank says, pulling him and Charlie into a conversation about finance and business deals.

I turn my attention to the ladies, tuning out to the gentlemen's talk of shop.

"My word, that man looks just as good in a tux as he does in jeans and boots," Debbie whispers so no one hears.

"Agreed," Edith chimes in, tipping her glass toward me in salute.

"Well, if you think he looks good now, you should see him cuddling a puppy," I add, remembering how he looked with Hattie on his lap.

"Aww," they both coo at the same time.

The three of us chat for a few more minutes and watch as donors mill around. Everyone seems to be having a good time.

What's even better, they seem to be hanging around the auction tables and dropping bids on the items listed. The more time they spend over at those tables, the bigger paycheck the shelter will receive at the end of the night.

When the dinner announcement is called, we all start to head toward our table. Our group is positioned near the front where the band will play. Immediately following dinner, Edith will give a welcome speech and explain why donations are so vital to the organization. The slideshow has been playing along one wall, and it's going to be heartwarming to see both the pets we still have to adopt, as well as photographs of the ones who've been adopted by their forever families.

"This is amazing," Matthew whispers in my ear, as we settle into our seats and squeezes my hand beneath the table.

"Thank you," I reply.

Once everyone is seated, waiters start to deliver food to the tables. Salad is the first to arrive, immediately followed by a creamy wild rice soup. Just as my bowl is being swept away to make room for the entrée plate, I feel a presence behind me. Turning, I immediately smile and jump up. "Daddy."

"Hi, princess," he responds, wrapping his arms around me and pulling me into a tight hug. When he pulls back and takes me in, he adds with a soft smile, "You look lovely."

"Thanks," I reply, blushing slightly at my father's compliment. "Daddy, I'd like to introduce you to my date. This is Matthew Wilder."

Matthew quickly turns around and stands, but as he reaches out to shake my dad's hand, the color drains from his face.

"Matthew, what a pleasant surprise. I didn't realize you were dating my daughter," my father says, taking Matthew's hand and giving it a friendly pump.

"Jerald, how are you?" he replies, glancing from Dad to me, a look of confusion on his handsome face.

"Very well. It's a wonderful evening, isn't it?" my dad asks, holding Matthew's gaze.

"It is," Matthew answers, clearing his throat and looking my way. "Kyla did an amazing job on the fundraiser. I'm proud to escort her tonight."

There's a weird tension radiating from him, one that has me looking between the two men. "Do you two know each other?" I find myself asking to no one in particular.

"We've met, yes," Matthew quickly replies.

Before either can elaborate, entrees are delivered to our table, filling the room with delicious scents.

"I'll let you two enjoy your dinner. We'll catch up a little later," Dad says, offering me a tense smile before leaning in and kissing my cheek. "You look beautiful."

"Thanks, Daddy. See you shortly," I reply, watching him step back and head toward the table he purchased. I instantly spy familiar faces and wave hello to my father's most trusted employees.

I feel Matthew's hand press against my lower back, guiding me back to our table. He's silent as we take our seats, his hands instantly starting to cut into his food. I grab my knife and fork and slice into my filet, but my mind is still trying to wrap around the fact that Matthew and my father know each other. I mean, it's a huge business world, but it still seems odd that neither had mentioned it.

Then again, I don't know that I've ever really used Matthew's last name when we discussed the man I've been seeing. So, while it seems odd, I guess it's not unheard of. It's Boston, after all. My father is well known, as is Matthew. They surely run in the same circles, both in business and quite possibly socially, since both often intertwine.

"So, you know my father," I state, taking a small bite of my perfectly seasoned and prepared steak.

"I do," he replies, cutting a much larger bite of his filet mignon.

When he doesn't elaborate, I feel a touch annoyed, but I'm unable to ask more questions because I'm drawn into conversations around the table.

After everyone dines on filet mignon, lobster tail, and steamed vegetables, our plates are collected, and tiramisu is delivered. As dinner wraps up, I realize I'm having a truly great time. I always enjoy our annual gala but having Matthew beside me has made the night truly remarkable. He's so charismatic and easy to talk to, once he loosens up and relaxes. Tonight, I've seen him more relaxed in a social setting than ever before.

By the time the speeches commence, I've all but forgotten about the awkward meeting between my date and my father. All eyes are on Edith as she recounts tales of recent adoptions, of the smiles and tears shed by joining a pet with their forever home. "I'd like to take a quick moment to introduce the hardworking volunteers who help ensure our shelter runs like a well-oiled machine."

She goes through the volunteers and gets to me last. "I want to give a special thank you to Kyla Morgan, who also helped spearhead tonight's fundraising event. We couldn't have done this gala without her extensive knowledge and expertise," she says, waving a hand in my direction.

I smile widely, feeling a blush the same color as my dress creeping up my neck, as everyone gives me and the rest of the volunteers a round of applause.

"I encourage you all to visit the auction tables to see some of the amazing, donated items, and in a few moments, Poppin' Johnny will take the stage and provide musical entertainment for the evening. Dance, have a few drinks, and enjoy our magical event. On behalf of all of us at Boston Cares Shelter, thank you for your support."

Everyone applauds Edith as she steps away from the podium and returns to our table. The delicious desserts are consumed as the band begins to play. The mood is light and cheerful, and as the attendees start to mingle once more, I can't help but finally relax and just enjoy this moment.

"What's that smile for?" Matthew asks, returning mine with a small one of his own.

"It just turned out to be a lovely night," I tell him, as we snatch glasses of champagne from a passing waiter.

"It did," he replies, clicking my glass with his own in toast. "I'm happy to be here with you, Kyla."

"I'm glad you're here too."

Something must flash across my face. "Did you not think I would?"

I shrug, turning my attention for a moment to someone greeting Matthew as he passes. My date doesn't pay the man any attention, however; just keeps his eyes on me. "I guess I was prepared for you to have to work. You're so close to closing another business deal."

He swallows hard and cuts his gaze across the room to where my father and his team are still sitting and laughing. "The deal is almost done, and even if it weren't, even if there were delays and renegotiations that required my time, I'd still be here with you tonight," he says, stepping forward and sliding his thumb across my cheek. "There's nowhere else I'd rather be than by your side, Kyla."

His words are barely above a whisper, but ring loud and clear. I almost open my mouth right there and tell him I'm falling in love with him. Instead, I opt to save that for later. He's wanting to talk tonight, and I can't help but wonder if maybe he's ready to share the same declaration. I see it in his eyes, or at least I think I do. There's definitely something there, something that's been growing with each passing day. I feel it in his touch and in the way he made love to me last night.

He reaches out and brushes his hand against my arm, causing goosebumps to race across my body. "This dress," he starts, shaking his head, "it's going to be the death of me, beautiful. You're a vision."

I lean into his touch, needing to feel closer. Even though my feet are already sore, I go up on my toes. "Wait until you get to peel it off me later, Cowboy." I give him a sassy smile and wink, which makes him groan.

"Devil woman."

I bark out a laugh and sip my champagne, the bubbles tickling my throat. "Just giving you something to look forward to."

He wraps his left hand around my hip and gives it a gentle squeeze. "Oh, sweetheart, I've thought of nothing but how I'm going to get you out of that dress all night."

With a coy smile, I hand off my glass to my date. "Would you mind holding this? I'm going to use the ladies' room."

He takes the glass and leans forward, brushing his lips across my cheek. "I'll be right here, waiting."

I turn and head for the hallway, a little extra swing in my hips. I can feel his eyes on me like a caress, pleased I chose this particular dress for the night, knowing it has him tied up is the icing on the cake.

Hopefully, later this evening, when the dress finally comes off, I'll share the secret I've been carrying. I'll tell him finally that I've fallen in love with him.

Chapter Twenty-One

Mason

I take a sip of my champagne, enjoying the hell out of the view of Kyla walking away. The back of that dress—It's hard-on inducing. I've had trouble keeping myself from getting an erection from the first moment she spun around in her penthouse apartment. I've been thinking of it—and her wearing it—almost nonstop since.

When she's completely out of sight, I turn my attention back to the room. I imagine there are a handful of people here I should know—or who my brother probably knows. Many wave, a few tip their heads as I pass, and I've even witnessed a few glares sent in my direction. At least my brother is consistent with pissing people off. I wouldn't expect anything less.

What I wasn't expecting was seeing Jerald hugging Kyla when I turned around and was introduced to her father. I probably looked like an idiot, standing there with my mouth hanging open and trying to catch up. I clearly missed the part in my brother's packets of information that gave that key piece of information.

My question is why? Why wasn't the connection noted more clearly in the paperwork or even mentioned when Matthew and I were talking about her? Why not just tell me he was dating the daughter of the man whose company he was buying?

Something doesn't settle well in my gut, and as I continue to people-watch while I wait for Kyla's return, the alcohol drops heavy

201

in my stomach with dread. I have a feeling there's a big piece of this puzzle that I'm missing.

Deciding I need something positive to focus on, I turn back to the doorway, hoping to catch the first glimpse of her as she returns to the ballroom. There are many people milling around, but it's one particular person that catches my attention. He's tall and well dressed in an impeccable tuxedo, and the moment his eyes meet mine, my heart skids to a complete stop in my chest.

Matthew.

I instantly turn around and head for a doorway. It leads to a back hallway, one that doesn't have any attendees hanging around. When I know we're alone, I turn and wait for him to join me. Matthew smiles deviously as he approaches, but I don't share his excitement. Actually, I feel like I could throw up. My twin must have snatched a glass of champagne from a passing tray as he made his way through the ballroom and downs half of it before he even gets close to me.

"What the hell are you doing here?" I harshly whisper the moment he's within earshot.

"Good evening, brother. I got back early, and thought I'd take in the gala. I was invited, after all." He takes another sip, a much smaller one this time. "You know, as Kyla's date."

The hairs on the back of my neck all stand up. "That's bullshit," I growl, glancing around to make sure the hallway is still unoccupied.

Matthew finishes his glass of champagne in one final swig. "I'm here to save you from making a mistake."

"A mistake? You don't think walking in here as yourself is a bad idea?" I seethe between gritted teeth.

"I purchased my ticket as Mason Wilder." He smirks that cocky grin I've always known.

My throat is so dry, it feels like there's sand coating it. I step forward, close enough now that I could reach out and touch his chest if I wanted. "All right, Matthew, what's up?" I ask quietly, still careful not to draw any attention, in case someone happens upon the hallway.

"I won't let you tell her and mess up your life. You need this money, Mase."

"So...what? You think us both being here is the solution?"

He gives me a withering look. "Come on, Mason. I'm the owner of a multi-million-dollar business. You think I don't have a plan?"

"Well, get on with it then. Kyla should be back any minute," I argue, waiting to hear the big, fabulous idea the infamous Matthew Wilder has.

"You're going to slip out of here, and I'll finish the night. Go back to my place, get some sleep, and jump on that flight back to Montana tomorrow. The money was deposited into your account this morning, so your debt is clear. You did it, Mase."

I did it. I have the money, I'm able to pay off my debts with the bank, the county, and the local vendors I use for feed and supplies. I'll even have a bit of cash left to make ranch improvements that I've let go over the last few years. It's what I wanted—no, what I needed—and the entire reason I agreed to this farce.

Only there's one problem.

Kyla.

If I go through with his plan, I won't have her. I'll be heading home to Montana without so much as a goodbye, and he'll break her heart before the night is even over. I have no doubt that's his plan. I could tell on day one he has no attachment to her. That was evident when we discussed that third task on his to-do list.

"I can't, Matthew." My heart is trying to beat out of my chest. The thought of walking out the door right now and leaving is killing me. I can't leave her, not like this.

"You have to," he demands, stepping closer, our chests practically touching now. "This is the only way. Kyla won't understand."

I open my mouth to argue, but I'm stopped before I can even utter a word.

"What won't I understand?"

Kyla.

My wide eyes glance over my brother's shoulder and meet hers. There's a touch of confusion mixed with the contentment I see when our gazes meet. She seems to relax. I just wish I could do the same. I can't. Things are about to blow up in a way I couldn't have predicted, couldn't have prepared for.

"Ky," I whisper, my voice barely above a whisper. I'm rewarded with a small smile, but it's short lived when our view of each other becomes blocked.

Matthew turns around.

"Hello, Kyla," he says, crossing his arms casually in front of his chest, one hand still holding the delicate champagne flute.

Her eyes widen, almost comically. If it were any other situation, I might find her reaction to seeing me and my twin together amusing, but there is nothing funny about this. If anything, it has disaster written all over it with a capital D. "Hello," she murmurs, her mouth hanging open as she looks from my brother to me.

"Kyla," I start, but no additional words seem to come to life. I have no idea what to say.

My brother takes the opportunity to fill in the silence with words, ones I despise and wish held no truth. "Kyla, I believe you've met my brother."

She looks back and forth between me and Matthew, trying to understand. She paints a smile on her lips and extends a hand to my twin. "Yes, I can see that. You must be Mason," she says, extending her dainty hand in his direction.

My stomach drops into my shoes.

Matthew offers her a grin, one that starts slow until it reaches its full wattage. Women love that beam and have always reacted to it.

I hate that smile.

I hate what is happening.

I hate what I've done.

"Actually," he starts, taking her hand in his and holding it. "I'm Matthew."

I hear her gasp of shock. I'll hear that sound for the rest of my life. She looks my way, her wide gaze searching mine for answers. There's only one thing to do now, and that's tell her everything. And pray. Pray she sticks around and listens long enough to understand why I did what I did.

Stepping around Matthew, I gently grab her upper arm and guide her a few steps away from my brother. She continues to look at me, expectantly, waiting for me to explain. Taking a deep breath, I finally confess the words I've been trying to figure out how to say all day.

"I'm not Matthew. I'm Mason."

Kyla doesn't say a word, doesn't so much as react actually, except for a blink.

From here, the words just pour from my lips like gasoline on an open flame. "I had planned to talk to you about this later tonight, but it appears there's a need for this conversation sooner, rather than later. Can we go somewhere to talk?"

Before I even have the request out, she's already shaking her head. "No, I think I need to hear this now."

I want to argue, but I can see by the look in her eyes, she's not going to relent. "All right," I concede, taking a deep breath. "For the last three weeks, I've been pretending to be my brother." I'm going to vomit, I know it.

"Why?"

This is where it gets bad. "I needed money to help my ranch, and Matthew here offered it to me. I had to pretend to be him for three weeks, overseeing a few different tasks during my time here." Fuck, this sucks. There's no way to *not* hurt her. "I was actually supposed to break up with you for him, but I couldn't."

"Why?" she asks, her eyes filling with tears.

"Because I started to fall for you."

The wetness gathering in her eyes falls onto her delicate cheek, marring her prefect skin with pain. The vision will forever be embedded in my mind, the one of her crying as I rip both our hearts out with my deceitfulness.

"I was supposed to let you go, but that first night, the one where you came to my brother's place for dinner, I couldn't do it. You kissed me, and I felt...alive. For the first time in my life, I felt content and happy and wanted more. I didn't tell you, even though I wanted to, because I didn't know how. I had signed a contract with Matthew, one that said I'd lose all the money he promised me if I said a word. I didn't want to risk it," I confess, loathing myself more with each word I say.

"The problem is, the more time I spent with you, the more I started to fall for you. I realized I wasn't going to be able to go through with it. I couldn't fulfill the terms of his contract. I decided to tell you everything because it was the right thing to do and because," I take a deep breath, maintain eye contact, and finish, "I fell in love with you."

The tears fall in earnest now, her sniffles the only sound in the deserted hallway. The sound rips my heart clean from my chest and fills it with pain. I want to turn, to yell at my brother, but I don't. I can't take my eyes off her, but also I know it's not his fault. Not really. It's mine. I shouldn't have accepted the deal. I should have found another way to figure out my financial difficulties. I should have done more.

I'm about to tell her just that, when another voice interrupts my thoughts.

"There you are, honey." It's Kyla's father, Jerald. "Is everything all right?" he asks, coming up beside her and kissing her cheek. It's only then he seems to take in the carnage around him. "What's going on?" he demands, finally noticing his daughter's tears.

Jerald turns to me, to find out why the hell his daughter is crying, when he spies my twin brother standing there.

"Jerry, good to see you again," my brother says, extending a hand as if nothing out of the ordinary is happening.

"Matthew?" he asks, obviously confused at seeing my twin and me together.

"Yes, sir. I'm sure you're wondering what the heck is going on here, and I assure you, we have it handled," my brother replies formally.

He draws his eyebrows in confusion. "What is being handled?" he asks, skeptically.

"Why don't you join me in the ballroom for a drink, and we'll let them chat," Matthew instructs, placing an arm over Kyla's father's shoulder and trying to turn him around.

"Actually," Jerald states, moving out of Matthew's grasp, "I think I'd like to stay. My daughter is crying, and that's not acceptable. I'm sure you'll understand."

When Jerald returns to his daughter's side, he turns his gaze to me. It's hostile, as if he knows I'm the reason for the tears. "Someone better fill me in now," he demands, his tone leaving no room for question.

"It seems Matthew has a twin brother, Daddy," Kyla states, sniffling. She turns her gaze to mine. It's hard and full of pain. "Mason, right?"

I swallow over the lump of emotion lodged firmly in my throat. "Yes, I'm Mason Wilder, sir."

"Mason here has been pretending to be his brother Matthew for the last three weeks. Apparently, they had a little deal to swap places for a while, but there was a little problem with their plan: Me." The tears have now dried up, her eyes turning fierce and dark.

"What do you mean?" he asks, searching her eyes for answers.

"Mason was supposed to break up with me, Daddy, but he didn't. He pretended to be his brother and continued to...date me." She swallows hard at her admission but holds her voice and her gaze steady.

Jerald appears surprised, his dark eyes turning to me. "Why?" he asks, truly curious.

"He says it was because he developed feelings for me, isn't that right, Mason?" she asks, turning cool eyes my direction.

"That's correct," I answer, even though it's painful to do.

He looks over his shoulder to my brother and asks the question I don't think anyone is prepared for. "Does this have to do with Wilder Group and Evolution?"

I blink a few times, trying to understand what he's asking. I glance at my brother, doing what I can to get a read from him, but he's as cool and calm as ever. In fact, he just seems to relax even more, which only pisses me off further.

The question must register with Kyla though. Like a lightbulb going off, she gasps and turns wide eyes to Matthew. "You're the buyer?"

"I am," my brother informs.

"You didn't know?" Jerald asks his daughter, who merely shakes her head. "Matthew's Wilder Group was the business I settled on to purchase Evolution. I've met with him a few times over the last few months, along with his team several times to prepare the deal."

Kyla looks from her father to my brother until suddenly, realization sets in. "Oh God!" she bellows, turning huge, hurt eyes to Matthew. "That's why you pursued me." It's an accusation, not a question.

It's as if the lightbulb turns on in my own brain too, and I finally realize why his relationship with Kyla was so off. "You didn't," I harshly whisper, my eyes glued to that of my twin.

"I had to ensure the deal went through," he replies in a business-like tone, as if using someone is just an everyday part of his world.

I'm in disgust over what he's done. He wasn't interested in Kyla, not really. He used her as a tool to ensure he got the business he wanted.

"You used me," she whispers, the tears forming in her eyes once more as she stares at Matthew.

He doesn't reply.

"I need to get out of here," she demands, swiping at a tear angrily.

"I'll take you home," I quickly insist, taking a step toward her.

My words are cut off by her hands held up, halting my steps. "No. You're not welcome."

I want to argue, to insist we go back to her place to talk, but she doesn't give me the opportunity.

Kyla stops directly in front of me and meets my gaze. "You lied to me. From the very beginning, you lied." Her eyes brim with tears once more. "It hurts, knowing I was a pawn in your brother's quest to get his hands on my father's business, but do you know what hurts more than that?"

I don't think I want to know.

"Your betrayal hurts most of all," she whispers, the tears spilling from her gorgeous eyes once more as she chokes up. "It hurts because you knew the truth and never said a word. You allowed me to fall in love with you, which I guess was my mistake. I fell in love with someone who doesn't exist."

She turns to her dad, not allowing me to get a single word in. And what would I say anyway? Sorry seems like such a pointless, useless word at this point. "I'm going to head out. Can you make an excuse with Edith, please? Tell her I'm sick," she asks her father, wiping away tears and steeling her back.

"I will, but you're going with me. I'll have my car brought around," he replies, taking her hand and leading her away.

"Kyla," I blurt out, not wanting to see her walk away, realizing if she does, it'll be forever. "Please."

She stops but doesn't turn around, at least not right away. After a few very long seconds, she glances over her shoulder. Her eyes are firm and hold a resolve I wasn't prepared to see, because it means whatever I'm about to say won't mean a damn thing. Not anymore. The damage is done.

"Goodbye, Mason. I wish you luck with your ranch."

Kyla turns around and walks away, taking my heart with her. She reaches the end of the corridor and rounds the corner without so much as a glance back. Pain radiates through my entire body, my soul crushed into a thousand pieces.

But it's my fault.

I did this.

To her.

And to me.

I have no idea how long I stand there, staring off at the last place I saw the woman I've fallen in love with, willing her to come back so we can talk about this. Yet, knowing in my heart it's over. There's no coming back from this, even though the will and drive is there. I lied to her, plain and simple. This is exactly what I was afraid would happen, and maybe even, deep down, knew would happen all along. Maybe if I'd had told her sooner things would be different now. But fear is a powerful thing. It keeps you from doing what's right, even when you know in your heart you should.

I knew, but I didn't act.

That's on me.

I'll have to live with that pain and the hurt my actions caused for the rest of my life.

At least I'll be able to wallow in my misery alone.

"Why'd you do it?" I find myself asking the only man still standing in the hallway.

Matthew sighs. "I needed the potential insurance to make sure the deal went through."

Sighing, I lean against the wall and close my eyes, my body suddenly extremely drained.

"Well, let's take a moment to give thanks that an intent to sell contract was drafted and signed. Otherwise, I'd be a little worried about the sale not going through on Monday," my twin says, pulling me out of my own head.

I stand tall and turn to face him. We look the same, only a few minor differences that most wouldn't even notice. But I notice. I see them all. "I don't even know you anymore. A man who became so consumed with business and less about individuals. You've hurt people, Matthew, and don't even seem to care. I can't live like that. If there's one thing I've learned in the last few weeks, it's that I'd rather have friendships and laughter surrounding me. Money is nice, but at the end of the day, it doesn't keep you warm at night. Love does. You'll never understand, and that makes me sad for you."

I walk past him, heading for the exit.

"Mason," he says, his words causing my legs to stop. "You and I, we're just built differently. Always have been."

I turn to face my brother. "Maybe, but we don't have to be. We choose the roads we're on, Matthew. If we wanted to have a better relationship, we could, despite our differences. Believe it or not, even after knowing what I know now, after seeing you in action, I miss my brother. Maybe it's just a pipe dream or wishful thinking, but I miss him. The boy I grew up with, played with, and dreamed with about what our lives would be like as adults. I never thought there would be a divide. For all the things that make us unalike, I never saw us this far off course."

I take a deep breath, wondering where all that came from. But do you know what? I don't care. I said what's been building for years and have no regrets now.

He stands still, his matching brown eyes boring into me.

"You know where I live, Matthew. Take a few days off every now and again and visit. If you want, I'll do the same." I head the rest of the way down the hall, ready to turn the corner when I add, "Oh, and go visit our parents."

Then I leave. I walk straight out of the hotel and down the block. With my hands shoved into my pockets, I ignore the way my feet hurt in my fancy black leather shoes until I reach the end of the block. There, I wave at a passing taxi and jump in as soon as he stops. Sure, I could head to the valet and find George, but I'm done being Matthew.

From now on, I'm Mason.

Heartbroken rancher from Casper, Montana.

The man who lost his heart to a gorgeous woman with intoxicating hazel eyes on a lie.

And I'll have to live with what I've done for the rest of my life.

Chapter Twenty-Two

Kyla

Longest night ever.

My eyelids are heavy and gritty as I indulge on my second cup of coffee of the morning, but when you're going on only four hours of sleep, desperate times call for desperate measures.

The elevator dinging grabs my attention. I don't get up, because I know who it is. When Dad left last night, it was with the understanding he'd be back in the morning to talk. I was pretty tight-lipped on my ride home, mostly because I was still trying to process the information I obtained just a short time before.

Matthew...or Mason, as it would happen to be.

What a mess.

Now that I think back, I can see when the swap happened. I may not have seen it before, but from the outside looking in, it's clear. After that lunch with Amalee, where I worried Matthew and I weren't connecting, she advised me to kiss him. We had kissed before, but it was so very different than the one we shared that night. Before, it was nice, but somewhat clinical. There was never any...spark, and it never went any farther than a polite kiss.

Gratefully.

Now, the thought of engaging in any sort of sexual anything with the real Matthew is nauseating. Not because he's not attractive, but because of what I felt with his brother. I already feel dirty enough, but the thought of sleeping with both Wilder brothers would have really put me over the edge.

Before my mind is able to replay everything I shared with Mason, my father joins me in the kitchen. "Good morning," he greets, coming over to kiss my forehead.

"Hi."

Dad goes over to the coffee pot and makes himself a cup. "How'd you sleep?"

I shrug but don't give him an answer.

As he brings his black coffee over to the table, he says, "Edith will probably check on you today. She was concerned about your sudden illness."

I glance over at where my cell phone is resting on the counter. It's off, however. I didn't want the temptation of calling Mason. That's why I didn't take it upstairs with me when I finally went to bed. "I'll be sure to reach out to her soon to let her know I'm fine."

He sits across from me and takes a sip. "Are you? Fine?"

Again, I shrug. "I will be."

We didn't talk much last night, when my father's driver brought us back to my place, but he understood the gist of it. Matthew and Mason are twins and swapped places three weeks ago. The man I've been spending all my time with, getting to know, and steadily falling in love with was, in fact, Mason Wilder.

And I never knew.

Looking back, I should have, but didn't. There's a big difference between Matthew and Mason. No, not in appearance, but in personality. Matthew is very by-the-book. A businessman to a fault, with no personal ties to anyone or anything. Mason, on the other hand, is gentler, kinder, and full of personality. It took a bit to get to see it, but it was there.

"Tell me what you need, Kyla." Dad sips his coffee, keeping his gaze on me.

I'm sure I look a fright too. I showered this morning, but that was as far as it went. No makeup, hair pulled back in a ponytail, a hoodie sweatshirt, and sweatpants I had to dig out of the back of the closet. "I guess I just need time. I think I've come to terms with the fact they deceived me, but I just can't understand why. For a business deal? For money?"

He sets his cup down on the table and relaxes into his seat. "Kyla, I've always known you haven't wanted anything to do with the business. Even though a part of me wished I could turn it over to my only child, I learned early on it just wasn't in your blood the way it was mine.

"Over the years, I've built a good foundation. I've made contacts all over the world, some of them eventually earning me additional ways to grow my company. I did that a decade ago when I secured government contracts. Those alone are priceless, Ky. Anyone in the industry would kill to get their hands on those deals."

"That's why Matthew wanted Evolution so badly," I conclude, taking my own sip of coffee.

"At first, yes. I think he saw what my company had and wanted it for his own. But something else happened over the last several months, honey. I saw him change. Sure, Matthew Wilder is still a ruthless, cutthroat businessman, but as I was meeting with him, I saw the approval he craved. It's nothing he'd let the world see, but it was there. He slowly understood why the people of Evolution were so vital to its success."

He sits up straighter and holds my gaze. "Did you know, he didn't fight me once when I said my team must stay on during the transition period? Never once balked about having to merge his team and my

216

own, and do you know why?" I shake my head, listening intently. "Because he believed our two companies were stronger together. He didn't really want a hostile takeover, as I might have suspected in the beginning. He really did want what was best for Evolution. For Dominic and Lizabeth. For the hundreds of employees we employ. That's why I agreed to sell him the company. Matthew Wilder isn't the greedy, condescending man he's portrayed in the media. He's better than that. He just refuses to let anyone see it."

I absorb his words, trying to wrap my head around what he's saying.

"What he did with you, pursuing and dating you, was wrong, no doubt. Paying his brother to fly to Boston and pretend to be him is almost inexcusable, especially since you were involved, but I don't believe he really did it to hurt you. I think he did it because he felt pushed, and maybe a little trapped. He needed reassurance he could close this deal as quickly as possible."

"That's no excuse to lie to someone, Daddy."

"No, no it's not. He was dishonest, plain and simple, and I think the best step forward is to tear up the contract tomorrow. There are a dozen companies ready and willing to purchase Evolution and probably even pay more than Wilder was. I've had a few reach out to me lately, trying to swindle their own negotiation under the table. I bet Harold would even stay on a little longer to help," he says, referring to his CFO who is retiring post change-over.

"No," I find myself saying. "Don't do that." I don't know why I'm even consider saying what I'm about to confess, but I guess my father's words, his observation regarding Matthew stuck with me. "I don't think you should cancel the deal with Wilder Group."

"You don't?" he asks, genuine surprise filtering across his face.

I shake my head. "No. You chose him for a reason. You put your entire faith and trust in him and his company before you found out about Mason and what they did. I don't think you'd be truly happy with anyone else taking your business, Daddy."

"That wouldn't matter. There's a principal here, honey. He wronged you."

"He did, but you yourself said, you don't think he did it to hurt me."

"But he *did* hurt you."

I sag a little in my chair and give him a small smile. "No, he didn't. It stinks that he was only dating me to make sure he got your company, but he's not who hurt me, Daddy."

"Mason."

I nod.

"You really fell in love with him," he says without a trace of question.

"I did."

He reaches across the table, takes my hand within his, and sighs. "What he did was wrong too. We know it, but he does too. I saw it in his eyes. The hurt, the anguish, the love."

I'm already shaking my head in disagreement. "You don't do that to someone you love, Daddy."

"No, no you don't, but what if you fell in love along the way? What if you had a job to do, whether it was right or wrong, and over the course of completing the job, you started to fall? I've only met Mason once, over dinner last week, but do you know what I learned during that hour and a half we ate and chatted?"

Suddenly, it dawns on me that last week's client dinner was actually a meal shared with my dad. I can't believe it. I close my eyes and shake my head in disbelief. When I open them, he's still watching me, waiting for me to answer. "What did you learn?"

"Mason Wilder is a decent man, sweetheart. He's a man who made a big mistake, but I have no doubt he's a good person."

What do you say to that? I want to argue, but what's the point?

"Can I ask you something?" he asks, holding my gaze. When I nod, he goes on. "What do you want?"

"What do you mean?" I ask, confused by his question.

"What do you want from this life, Kyla? Are you happy, living here and volunteering at the shelter?"

"I love the shelter," I argue immediately.

"I know you do," he says, smiling. "It showed last night. I can tell by the way you light up every time you share a story about an adoption or something one of the animals did that day. You were born to work with animals, honey. It's your calling, but that's not really what I meant. Are you happy here? In Boston?"

I open my mouth to insist I am, but nothing comes out. The city has never really felt like a home to me. It's comfortable and close to the ones I love, which is a big part of why I've stayed.

"That's what I thought," he says, shaking his head and looking away. "This is my fault."

"What is?" I ask.

"You stayed here for me."

"That's not true," I argue, but he won't let me continue.

Dad holds up his hand so he can explain. "It is true. I knew it in my heart the day I handed over the keys to this place. Oh, you thought it was lovely and was impressed with the security measures, but it wasn't what you really wanted. You've never really enjoyed the city life or having tall, steel buildings surrounding you. So, tell me the truth, Kyla. If you could live anywhere in the world, where would it be?"

I want to lie, to insist I love my home and the city, but I know he'd see right through me. And it would be wrong of me to lie to him, especially when the whole reason I've been upset is because I was deceived.

Closing my eyes, I picture myself living out of the city, in a wide-open space with room to run. A yard with dogs napping under the shade trees and chickens around the barn. And horses. There would definitely be a horse or two and cows. Lots and lots of cows. There would also be a cowboy fixing a broken fence board, his ballcap low on his face to shield the hot sun and his T-shirt molded to his body from sweat. He feels my eyes on him and turns around, awarding me with a panty-melting grin that promises dirty things later that night.

Mason.

I don't even realize I'm crying until a napkin is placed against my palm. Bringing it to my eyes, I hold it there to mop up the moisture, but it's well saturated quickly.

"Kyla?" my dad whispers, drawing my attention. "I want you to be happy. If that's here, great. If not, then I want you to sprout wings and fly."

"But what if it takes me away from you?"

He smiles proudly. "Did you forget I'm about to sell my company? I was rather financially stable before, but this time tomorrow, I'll be set for life. And the next one and the next one after that too," he says, chuckling. "My point is, I can travel anywhere I want, and if that means flying to Timbuktu several times a year to visit my only daughter, then it's a flight I'm willing to take."

"That's not fair to you. This is your home," I argue, the tears burning beneath my eyelids.

"I can make a home wherever. I want to travel more and see the world through fresh eyes and can hang my hat up anywhere, honey. Even in Montana."

My eyes fly up to meet his. Where his are full of humor, mine reflect shock. "What?"

"Just saying," he says, taking another sip of hot coffee. "I think I'd love to visit Montana, actually. Maybe even purchase some land near a cattle ranch, buy some Levi's and some cowboy boots. I might actually enjoy that." Dad smiles over the rim of his cup. "Listen, Kyla, I want you to be happy and only you can decide what...or *who* makes you happy. I know he hurt you. Maybe you can forgive him, maybe not. That's for you to figure out," he says, finishing off his beverage.

I stand up as he does, leaving my cup on the table. "Thank you, Daddy," I whisper as I pull him into a hug.

"I'd do anything for you, honey, but only you hold the key to your own happiness. Take some time and figure out what that might be. Maybe you can go and do some traveling of your own," he adds with a wink. He places a kiss on my forehead and turns toward the elevator.

Before the door closes to whisk him away, he turns back to me and adds, "I love you, Kyla. Be happy."

When the door closes, I'm left alone with my thoughts and conflicted heart.

I'm still angry. The pain is too raw. I can't even think about a future, let alone consider what that might entail—or who. Right now, I just need to relax and take a nap, and maybe then, I'll be able to think about what I really want and whether or not it's obtainable.

I place my cup in the sink and head for the stairs, wishing the ache in my chest would just stop, at least for a little while. But I'm guessing I'll be carrying that particular pain for the rest of my life. All

I can do is pray it subsides enough to get through the day without continually thinking of him.

Easier said than done.

***

By Monday morning, I'm more than ready to get out of my penthouse. I need fresh air and sunshine and fewer walls closing in on me. It was good to use yesterday as a day of relaxation and reflection. Sure, there were tears. A lot of them actually. Just when I thought I couldn't cry any more, they'd just start to fall all over again.

Midafternoon, I went downstairs to grab something to eat. That's when I found Mason's bag sitting along the wall. I knew what it contained, and while I tried my hardest to ignore its presence in my residence, I ended up opening the bag and pulling a T-shirt out. Only then did I return to my bedroom, remove my own pajamas and slip his shirt over my head. The cool cotton did nothing to soothe my achy heart, but it did help me fall asleep. I ended up wearing it the rest of the day.

And the night too.

Now, I need something that's just mine. Something that will help bridge the pain in my chest and the confusion in my head with some normalcy. After pulling into the small parking lot behind the shelter, I already feel my mood shifting. Even when I pull open the door and come face to face with Edith's concerned gaze, I still feel better.

"Good morning," I chirp, pasting on a big smile.

"Morning. Feeling better?" she asks, her critical eyes searching me from head to toe.

"Yes, thank you," I reply, bypassing the front desk and heading for the back room. I can already hear the dogs barking.

"You sure?" she asks.

I pause before heading inside to start today's volunteer task sheet. When I meet her gaze, I give her a small smile. "I will be."

Pushing through the door, I stand there for a few minutes and just take in the scene. Some of the pups sit there, watching me, while others are spinning excited little circles in their kennels. I head over and grab the clipboard, ready to start, when something catches my eye.

Hattie's name is crossed off.

My eyes fly to her kennel, only to find it empty. I don't even know why my eyes start to burn. I mean, it wasn't like I knew young Hattie very long, but the thought of her being adopted brings on a wave of melancholy. I should be happy. This is a good thing, right? This is the goal of every animal we have at Boston Cares Shelter.

The door behind me opens and Edith walks in.

"Where's Hattie?" I ask, trying to figure out why I'm so sad to see the small terrier gone.

"Adopted. Yesterday, actually. She was super delighted, and the new owner passed all the application processes. They went home yesterday afternoon," she says happily.

"I've never known you to release a pet before the twenty-four to forty-eight hour waiting period," I say through a throat clogged with emotion.

"Well, I make an exception every now and again, and since it was their second in-person visit together, I went ahead and approved her adoption. Plus, the owner made a considerable donation to the shelter," Edith adds with a chuckle.

I hear about half of what she says as she goes over today's list, but my focus keeps returning to the empty kennel. I don't know why I'm so saddened by Hattie's departure, but I am. I didn't even know her very well. I mean, she'd only been here a week before she was taken to her forever home, but her exit feels like a bullet hole-sized wound in my chest.

Maybe it was because the last time I saw her, she was curled up on Mason's lap, playing with a ball. It could be the correlation connecting that particular dog to a time when my heart wasn't broken, and things made sense. She was a link to Mason, or the man I once knew as Matthew. Before the gala and everything unraveled like a ball of string. When I was still happy and in love.

Now they're both gone.

Chapter Twenty-Three

Mason

4 weeks later

I'm headed to the barn to check on a new calf as the sun starts to creep up over the tree line. My faithful companion is at my side, ready to take charge in the barn and let the animals know she's there.

I work through morning chores peacefully, with no complications. Once I have them completed, I head to the chicken pen I've been rebuilding and finish repainting the old coop. The old structure was in good shape, just needed a little TLC. I've already replaced the run fencing, including adding a top to ensure hawks and other predators can't get them. At least they can't while they're in the run, but outside the protective fenced in area is another story. Hopefully having some other animals around will keep the hunters at bay.

I've been home a month. Leaving Boston was the easiest, yet hardest thing I've ever done. I was ready to get the hell out of there but hated the thought of actually leaving. Mostly I hated leaving Kyla, but I knew I needed to go, to give her time to think. To come to terms with what my brother and I had done, if she would ever really be able to do it. I just want her to be happy, with or without me. Of course, I'd rather it be with me, but if that's not in the cards, I'll be okay.

I almost went to her penthouse that Sunday morning. I wanted to explain once more, to tell her pretending to be Matthew was the most difficult lie I've ever told. I wish I would have told my brother to take a flying leap off a tall building, but since there's no way to redo the past, I just have to live with the damage I've done.

Every single day I've wanted to call her. I've picked up that phone and pulled up her contact. One night, in a desperate attempt to stop the hurt in my chest, I even clicked send. Before the call could connect, I touched the end button and slammed the device onto the counter.

What would I say to her anyway? I'm sorry still doesn't feel like enough and the right words have yet to come, even four weeks later.

Matthew closed his business deal that Monday after everything blew up. Honestly, I'm surprised. I would have thought Jerald would have told my twin to shove the deal straight up his ass without any Vaseline. I think Matthew was even a little surprised by the outcome. Pleased as hell, but a bit shocked.

I've actually talked to Matthew more in the last month than I have the last two years. Even though he's crazy busy with the transition at Evolution, he's called me weekly to check in, seemingly somewhat interested in how the operation is running at the ranch. In fact, he even offered a few key pieces of financial advice that I took and implemented immediately. We may not be the best of friends, but we're at least cordial and are working on bridging the crater between us. My brother even promised to come out and see me before the end of the year.

I actually hope that happens.

By the time the bright blue sky starts to darken and the horizon streaks with vivid oranges and reds, I have everything completed that I wanted to get done. I let out a whistle and start to head toward the house. It's been a long day and a shower is in my very near future. Then I'll be able to make a sandwich, grab a beer, and enjoy them both on the front porch. When the walls start to close in, usually late at night when I can't sleep, that's where I find my solace.

Just as I round the side of the barn and head for the back door, a pair of headlights flash through the trees along the lane. I stop in my tracks and watch the vehicle approach, not recognizing the headlights. This late in the evening, I don't have too many visitors, so I definitely take notice of an unusual vehicle heading my way.

When the lights finally stop near the house, I take a few steps in that direction. The dog at my feet starts to bark, running a few feet ahead and standing between me and the unwanted visitor.

The car shuts off, and when the driver's side door opens, someone steps out into the night air. I hold my hand up to my forehead to help see until the headlights finally turn off. It's just dark enough I can't see specifics or a face, just a short stature. It's a woman.

The dog barks again, spinning in circles. "Hat, enough!" I holler.

"Hattie?"

I know that whispered voice. I hear it nightly, when I'm sitting on the porch and the wind blows through the trees. It's hauntingly beautiful, but right now, I'm a little worried about my mental status. It's probably not good when you're hearing the voice of the woman you love, who just so happens to live thousands of miles away.

The dog takes off like a bullet, charging toward the visitor, and I'm on the move. The woman drops to her knees in the dirt driveway and Hattie is all over her. My pup is barking and spinning and showering the new arrival with kisses.

"Hattie, enough," I demand as I approach the car.

"It's okay," the woman says, petting my dog behind the ears.

The moment the moonlight hits her face, the most beautiful hazel eyes reflect back at me, stealing my ability to breath. "Kyla?"

She stands up, dusting off her hands. "Hi, Mason," she answers softly.

Stepping forward yet again, bringing me within reaching distance of her, I try to wrap my head around her sudden appearance in Montana. "What are you doing here? Are you all right?" I ask, worry gripping at my chest.

"I'm f-fine," she insists, seeming to stutter a bit with her words.

I want to step forward and take her in my arms, but I don't. I can't. I don't know why she's here, but I do know she's not mine to touch. However, I can look, and look I do. Even under the dark of nightfall, I can tell she's beautiful. The most stunning vision I've had since I was in Boston. She's wearing an oversized T-shirt and jeans. Yep, a pair of basic blue jeans that hug her legs to perfection. On her feet are a pair of cowboy boots with a rounded toe. I've never seen her in anything like she's wearing, and it's sexy as fuck.

"I was hoping, maybe, we could talk," she finally says, her voice laced with nerves.

"Sure," I answer quickly, afraid she'll up and leave. "Do you want to come inside?"

"Umm, okay."

I step back and slowly make my way to the front door, which is closer. Usually, after a long day outside, I'd use the back one so I don't track dust, dirt, and cowshit through the house. But the front entrance is closer, and all I can think about at this moment is getting her inside.

We step up on the front porch, and I reach for the screened doorknob. "Actually, would it be okay if we sit out here? It's such a beautiful night, and your view is breathtaking."

I nod and wait for her to take a seat. There are only two options on this side of the wraparound porch: the left side of the swing or the right. Kyla chooses the right, leaving me the open space beside her. I sit down, careful not to let my outer thigh touch her leg. Out of habit, I start to rock, letting my long legs move the swing at a slow and steady pace. Hattie drops at my feet and sighs, like she does most nights.

After a few minutes, she finally speaks. "I'm sure you're wondering what I'm doing here."

"Well, the thought has crossed my mind," I reply, a very slight smile causing my lips to curl up for the first time in a while.

I catch her own grin out of the corner of my eye, and my heart feels just a touch lighter. She clears her throat and leans her head back against the top of the swing back. She looks up, and I wish we could see the stars. Unfortunately, from this vantage point, you can't see the stars, even on the brightest nights. Since the back porch is uncovered, that's where I go to see a starry night.

"I've had a lot of time to think over the last few weeks," she starts, continuing to keep her gaze on the ceiling. "About what happened."

I don't know if I should say something or just let her talk, but the need to open my mouth is too strong. "I've been thinking about it too. A lot, actually."

She sits up and turns her head, meeting my gaze for the first time since we sat on the swing. She still doesn't say anything. Those wheels in her beautiful head must be spinning a thousand miles a second. The worry remains that she'll just get up and leave, never to be heard from or seen again.

I can't let that happen.

Needing to bridge the line of communication, I ask, "How did you find me?"

"Matthew."

That answer is unexpected and like a punch in the gut. All air seems to leave my lungs in one quick whoosh.

"I called him last week and asked him to meet with me. I had a few things I needed to say."

I nod slowly, trying to anticipate whatever she's about to say.

"I needed to look him in the eye when I told him I was disappointed in him. He actually sat there and listened to me get it all off my chest."

"Wh-where did you meet him?" I don't know why I ask that. Okay, fine I do. The thought of Kyla meeting Matthew at his place or hers makes me a little ragey, which is stupid because she was his before she was mine.

"At the coffee shop near the shelter. It was midmorning and fairly empty. It was actually kind of comical seeing him in one of his black power suits, sitting in a booth with ripped red vinyl seats," she says with a grin, kicking at a small clump of dirt on the porch.

I can picture it now, and the image is pretty funny. "I'm sure it was good for him to step out of his comfort zone."

She turns and meets my gaze. "He said he's been talking to you."

"He has," I confirm. "We're both making an attempt. We talk every week. On Sunday, mostly, when he's working from home." After a few seconds, I ask, "I heard the deal between your dad and him went through as planned."

Kyla nods. "It did. Dad was going to terminate it, but I told him not to. Ultimately, Matthew was the one my dad felt comfortable enough with to sell his company to. My father made his choice before everything went down, and I believe it was the right one for him. I don't like what Matthew did, but I'm not the judge or the jury."

I swallow over the thickness in my throat. "That's big of you, Ky. You could have very easily made sure that deal fell through, leaving my brother without the company he was coveting. Eye for an eye, if you will."

She keeps her eyes trained down. "I must have gone back and forth for an entire day, but ultimately, I just didn't want to carry the hurt and anger with me, and it was what my father said about looking past your brother's flaws and seeing the decent he hides from the world."

I can't help but snort a laugh. "My brother? Decent?"

"Believe me, I didn't really want to see it either, but I do think it's there. He just keeps it well concealed behind a no-nonsense demeanor and very thick skin."

I nod, wondering if there's a chance she'll forgive me as easily as she did my brother, and maybe, just maybe, it has something to do with why she's here tonight. A man can hope, right? I'd rather think of that than the alternative. That she's here to speak her piece so she can move on with her life. I'm not sure I could handle it if she does.

"I don't consider him a friend, but I don't hate him either. In fact, I'm a little grateful to him," she says, her sweet voice soft.

That catches me by surprise. "You are?"

She nods and shifts in the swing, meeting my gaze head on. "I am. He brought me you," she whispers so quietly, I almost didn't hear her. In fact, after a few long seconds of silence, I wonder if I imagined it, but as I continue to search her hazel eyes, I see a light I haven't witnessed in four long weeks. "I understand why you did what you did."

"You do?"

Kyla nods. "I'm sure it wasn't an easy decision to make. I know you mentioned that night your ranch was in trouble, but Matthew explained it in a little more detail, and I finally started to understand. You felt trapped and out of options."

She takes another deep breath. "What you did, it may not have been the right thing to do, but I understand. You weren't out to hurt me."

I feel the ball of tension in my body seem to subtly relax. "When we were in high school, Matthew was dating this girl. It was probably his first real relationship and they were together for about two years before I noticed his indirect change. He was pulling away from her, from me, and aligning himself for the next phase of his life.

"He came to me one night, asking for help. He wanted to break up with Suzanna, the girl he was dating, but didn't have the balls to do it. So, he asked me to swap places with him and do it for him. I refused, of course. No way was I going to break up with his girlfriend for him, but he knew how to play me. Matthew had photos of the girl I was interested in. She was naked, and he told me he was going to send it to all his friends if I didn't swap places with him.

"I tried to call his bluff, but I knew in my heart he'd do it. That girl, she was the class valedictorian and senior class president. I have no clue how he got his hands on them, but I couldn't let him ruin her like that. Her dad was a preacher, her mom a teacher. She was a good person, and I didn't want to see that tarnished.

"So I did it. I went out with Suzanna that Friday night and broke up with her in my brother's car in the parking lot of the fucking movie theatre. She cried so fucking hard," I confess, shaking my head as the memories flood back like a broken dam. "I felt dirty and horrible, but I did it, so Bethani Feltman wouldn't have her reputation ruined by my evil twin."

232

I sigh and sag against the swing, not even realizing my feet stopped moving and we were sitting still. "I went home and found him in his room with the head cheerleader. He barely waited until I broke his girlfriend's heart for him before he was screwing someone else. It was the first and only time I ever punched my brother in the face. I vowed to never swap places with him again. We had done it a few times when we were little, but never to actually hurt anyone. I never wanted to hurt anyone," I repeat.

Kyla reaches over and squeezes my hand. "I'm sorry you went through that. I'm sure it wasn't easy on you."

"The worst. The only positive was a few months later, Matthew went off to college and Bethani did too. The photos were never distributed, but the real damage was done. I carried a lot of resentment and anger toward my brother and it severed our relationship. Over the last decade, we've barely had one.

"And then he called me up almost two months ago. I was desperate again and out of options. I didn't want to do it, Ky, I swear to you," I insist. "I just didn't know what else to do."

She moves her hand, slipping it beneath mine and entwining our fingers together. It's the first time I've touched her in four long weeks, and the connection is like a balm to the gaping hole in my soul. It calms the storm inside me and brings peace to my battered heart.

Kyla holds my eyes and gives me a small smile. "Mason, I forgive you."

Chapter Twenty-Four

Kyla

I feel just as free saying those words to Mason as I did when I spoke to Matthew. Only this time, there's a lot more emotion at play. I feel compassion for what he went through, both as a younger man and as an adult, as well as pride. I'm proud of the man he became, that his heart remained gold and true. He could have easily turned cold like his brother, but that's not who Mason is.

Ever since I met with Matthew and got Mason's address, I've been anxious to come here and see him. I realized two weeks ago that while I was hurt by the way everything transpired, I knew in my heart Mason wasn't being malicious. If anything, he was acting out of his budding feelings for me.

"Thank you," he whispers, releasing a huge puff of air. "I never meant to hurt you, Kyla. I'm so fucking sorry for betraying your trust and faith."

"I know you are. I realized it wasn't actually that hard to forgive you, Mason. Once I thought about it, it was pretty easy."

"It was?" he asks, seeming confused.

"Yes, because that's what you do when you love someone."

My words strike him like a bolt of electricity. His eyes widen in shock momentarily before the most handsome grin spreads across his face. "You do?"

"Yes," I reply, as he releases my hand and pulls me into his arms. They're warm and familiar and feel oh so right.

"Good, because I love you too."

Then he kisses me tenderly and slowly, like he's cherishing the feel of our lips connecting. It's a beautiful moment, full of hope and redemption, love and elation.

When he pulls back, his eyes reflect contentment. "Do you want to go inside? I was just about to make a sandwich."

I glance out at the quiet Montana night, taking a moment to soak in the serene view. It's peaceful and beautiful, and I can't help but wonder if this is the view I'll be taking in for the rest of my life. "Well, as much as I'd enjoy just sitting here and relaxing, I'm actually quite hungry."

Mason stands, causing Hattie to jump up, her tail wagging in excitement. "Let's go inside and I'll show you my home." He helps me up, takes my hand, and guides me to the front entrance. "Come on, Hattie. Time to eat."

As we step through the threshold, I say, "I can't believe you adopted her, or that Edith kept it from me. She never mentioned who purchased her."

"I asked her not to, if possible. I didn't want to cause you more grief," he replies, coming up behind me and letting the screened door slam shut. "I missed my Sunday morning flight home, but was able to catch one later that afternoon, with Hattie in tow."

I glance down at the happy pup. "She seems to be very content here."

Mason toes off his slide-on cowboy boots. "She rules the roost, don't you, Hattie girl?" Then he takes a few steps forward into a living room. "This is my place."

I glance around at the homey space, loving the classic mismatched furnishings and the old woodwork trim. "I love it," I state honestly.

We move through the house as he shows me room after room in the old farmhouse. I can tell he's taken decent care of it, but it could still use a little work. As we reach the kitchen, Mason heads over to where Hattie waits by her food bowl. He tosses a cup of food in the empty dish and fills the other with fresh water.

Then he moves to the fridge and opens the door. "I don't have too much available right now, but there's some lunch meat and fresh veggies in here," he says, turning toward me. "I can go to the market tomorrow." A look of panic crosses his face. "Wait, you're not leaving right away, are you?"

I'm already moving in his direction. When I reach him, I press my hands to his chest, the steady beat of his heart beneath my fingers. "I guess I didn't really make myself clear," I say, stepping into his personal space and pressing my body against his. "I'm not going anywhere, unless you want me to."

Mason wraps his hands around my side, letting them trail slowly down to my butt. "If I had it my way, you'd never leave. Ever."

I shrug. "Well, that actually works well for me. I'm in the process of selling my penthouse and am looking for a new place to live."

"Really?" he asks, his eyes wide with delight. "I just happen to have a room."

"That's convenient. Though, I don't really like sleeping alone. I hope that room comes with a roommate."

He flashes me a wide grin. "Oh, there's definitely a roommate. He'd love nothing more than to hold you close every night, sweetheart."

"Then it's settled. Maybe later we can go out and get my bags in the trunk of my rented SUV."

"Why wait?" he asks.

I move my hands up and wrap them around his neck, pressing my chest against his. "Like I said, I'm hungry."

"I'll make us sandwiches," he insists, yet to pull his body away from mine.

Giving him a coy grin, I whisper, "I'm not hungry for food, Cowboy."

His eyes flash with desire, and I can feel his erection growing against my stomach. "Funny, I'm starved too, and not for food."

Then he kisses me, hard and full of desire. It's like a homecoming, of sorts. A meeting of two souls who've craved one another and have found its other half in each other.

"Ky?" he whispers, nipping at my swollen lips with his teeth. "Are you wearing my T-shirt?"

I feel the blush creep up my neck. "Oh, uh, yes. I've been...wearing it."

His eyes hold humor and a new wave of need. "That's sexy as fuck."

"When I found your bag at my apartment, I just wanted to feel close to you for a bit. That turned into a night, then two, and before long, I'd been wearing it nightly for almost a month." His eyes flash. "I've washed it, of course."

Mason swipes his lips across mine in a gentle kiss. "Come on, Ky. Let me show you how much I love you," he whispers, picking me up in his arms and carrying me off toward the hallway stairs.

This moment may not be our beginning, but it's definitely the start of something special. I don't know where our road may lead, but I know we're at least traveling along the same course. We're together, growing and building. It'll take time, but as long as we're both willing to put in the work, we should be able to make a fulfilling and lasting life together.

Who would have thought I'd fall in love with my boyfriend's twin brother?

Not me, that's for sure.

But that swap was the best thing to ever happen to me.

It brought me Mason.

My cowboy.

Epilogue

Mason

1 year later

I hear the back door slam and smile.

I've been out working for the last hour and just waiting for Kyla to make her appearance. My girl's definitely not a morning person, but she's trying. I'm up before the sun and ready to hit the barn, but I hang around long enough to wake her up and share a cup of coffee and some breakfast. Then, when she goes upstairs to get ready, I head out and get to work.

Once she's dressed for the day—usually in a pair of sexy Levi's and some cowboy boots—she, Hattie, and Edward, our lab puppy, come out to start their chores. She's in charge of the chickens, of feeding, water, and collecting their eggs. She even convinced me to get a few more roosters and incubating our own eggs. She'll have another batch hatching any day now.

I pretend to keep myself busy in the barn, but my eyes are on her the entire time. I watch the way she moves, and how she talks to each chicken as she takes care of them. We still keep Edward out of the chicken run, only because he's still so young and thinks he needs to play with the birds, but Hattie goes inside and keeps watch.

After she fills their watering buckets with fresh water, she exits the run and leaves the gate open. Slowly the chickens start to come out, pecking at the ground and searching for bugs to eat, and Kyla and the dogs head for the barn.

I grab her saddle and make my way to the first horse stall. Kyla's extremely predicable, and I already know she's going to want to go for a ride after she completes her morning chores.

"Hey," she says, approaching the stall. The moment she sees her horse, she grins. "Morning, Dolly." Kyla reaches in and pets her horse's nose.

Shortly after moving here, Kyla was talking to Edith about the shelter and learned Dolly was still there. The shelter manager was stressed, worrying about not being able to find a new home for the mare as quickly as she thought they would. After their phone call, Kyla was full of melancholy and worried about the future of the horse.

That's when I had the idea.

We have a huge barn here, one that I was slowly getting back into tip-top shape and had plenty of room. It didn't take much convincing on either part to decide to purchase the gorgeous mare in Boston and have her shipped to Montana. Believe it or not, it was actually Matthew who helped put me in contact with a gentleman out east who was willing to make the trip. A week later, Dolly arrived at our ranch and has been here ever since.

Usually, Kyla would prefer to saddle up the horse on her own, but I've noticed lately she's been a little more fatigued than normal. So instead of giving me a hard time for prepping the mare for a ride, she gives all her attention to the animal itself. When I have everything secure, I turn to the woman I love and get ready to help her mount.

"Thank you," she says, settling into the saddle. "You coming?"

My cock twitches in my pants at the unintentional innuendo. "Yep. Give me a few minutes to get Samson ready," I reply, referring to my horse. We got him about three months after Dolly in an estate sale from a nearby ranch.

I was able to use the money I was paid from Matthew and pay off all the debt I owed on the ranch. What was left was used on the grounds and to slowly start to bring in more animals. The beef market turned around, with prices skyrocketing when many smaller ranches started to flounder. When cattle numbers started to drop, demand began to rise, along with the prices. I knew it would happen and was grateful I was able to stick it out until it did.

While Kyla walks Dolly around the paddock, I saddle up Samson, a fresh wave of nerves starting to set in. The dogs are out with Ky, leaving me alone in the barn with my horse and the ring burning a hole in my pocket. I've been planning this day for what feels like forever. In reality, it's been a little more than a month since I picked up the custom engagement ring made by a local jeweler in Casper.

Glancing around, I realize this is it. The moment that could potentially change the rest of life. It would tie Kyla and me together forever, until death us do part. Equal parts excitement and edginess, I mount my horse and head out to find my love.

"Come on, let's head over to the western pasture and check the fences," I tell her when I approach.

"Sounds good," she replies, turning Dolly to head off to the trail.

I follow behind, enjoying the view of her sitting atop the horse and also trying to figure out what in the hell I'm going to say. Everything I've been planning for weeks seems to just evaporate from my mind, as if I haven't been stressing and obsessing about these words. By the time we get to our favorite pasture, my heart is threatening to jump right out of my chest. Once we reach the small cluster of trees that gathers near the pond. I quickly dismount, leading Samson over to a smaller tree and tying him up. Once he's secure, I move to Kyla, anxious to help her down. Not because she needs the help, but so I can put my hands on her.

"Thank you," she giggles, as my hands slowly slide up her sides.

"Anything to get my hands on you," I tell her honestly.

Once Dolly is secured to another tree, I take Kyla's hand and walk her toward the water where the dogs are already swimming. They love walking the property with us, especially when we come out here where they can swim in the small pond.

"Let's go for a walk," I say, pulling her away from the water's edge. "I have something I want to show you."

***

Kyla

I'm nervous. I've been trying for two days to figure out how to have this conversation with Mason, and it appears the perfect opportunity has presented itself. He loves this pond, much like I do. It's probably my favorite place on the ranch, with the exception of the front porch. My hope is that it'll relax him enough to not take my news like a bomb tossed in his lap.

"Let's go for a walk," he says, pulling me away from the water's edge. "I have something I want to show you."

We head for the cluster of trees I love, weaving into the middle until we reach a small clearing. That's when I look up and notice the platform. "What's that?" I ask, gazing skyward as he leads me beneath it.

"Come see," he instructs, pointing to the wooden ladder. As I place my hands on the rung above me, he adds, "They're safe and secure, I promise."

I smile, already knowing that. Mason would never let me climb a ladder he wasn't sure was secure. As I breach the flooring, I grab on to the railing and hoist myself up and take a look around. We're not super high, but enough I can see into the trees and the pond off in the distance.

I wonder what we're doing up here and when he could have done this. I know he goes off with the ranch hands alone a lot, but I would have thought he'd tell me he was building a structure back here.

When I turn around, I'm surprised to find him on the floor. Not sitting but kneeling on one knee and holding something in his hand. "Mase?" I ask, confused at what's going on.

"Kyla," he starts, meeting my questioning gaze with one full of anticipation and love.

That's when it hits me.

"Oh my God!" I bellow, my hands coming up to cover my mouth.

He chuckles and reaches out for a hand. I slowly bring my shaking left one down and place it in his. First thing he does is kiss the top of it before returning his eyes to mine. "Sweetheart, I've thought of this day so many times over the last year. I've thought about how we started and how far we've come together since you showed up here. Every day, I fall more in love with you and look forward to each day that follows. I want to continue to build our life together, and maybe someday, when we're ready, fill this treehouse with kids. I know it's not much now, just a floor, but it's a good base and a solid foundation. I want to build it all with you. I want to spend the rest of my life with you." He takes a deep breath. "Kyla Morgan, will you marry me?"

He blurs slightly through my unshed tears. I nod, knowing there's only one answer to his question. "Yes."

Mason slides a ring on my finger and jumps to his feet, taking me in his arms. His kiss is full of an overwhelming sense of happiness and passion, and all I want to do is strip him down and show him just how much I love him.

But I can't.

Not yet.

I pull my lips from his and suck in a gasp of air. "Mason, actually I have something I need to tell you."

He looks worried as he takes in my words, his critical eyes scanning me from head to toe. "Is everything okay?"

I clear my throat and smile. "Yes, I think so. I'm hoping things will be very okay," I reply nervously. I pull back and put a little space between us. He lets me go, but I can tell he doesn't like it. I take a deep, cleansing breath and let it out. I've wondered how I'd say these words to him. Do I just say it, like ripping off a Band-Aid, or do I give him some sweet words, like he did with his proposal?

Maybe a spot in between...

"I'm pregnant."

Oops!

That's not at all how I was going to do it. So much for finding the sweet spot in between.

"What?" he gasps, his eyes wide with shock.

"I just found out two days ago. My period was late and so I took a home test. It was positive."

"You're pregnant?" he asks, trying to wrap his head around what he's heard.

"I am."

He blinks a few times before a smile sweeps across his handsome face. Mason lets out a whoop before taking me in his arms and spinning around. I laugh, my feet dangling above the ground, until he suddenly stops and sets me down. "Shit, Ky, I'm sorry. I probably shouldn't have done that."

"It's okay," I reply, sniffling. Suddenly, I'm all teary-eyed again, my emotions completely overcoming me.

He pushes back, his eyes dropping to my stomach. I feel his hands gently caress the flat skin. "This is the best day ever," he whispers, before taking me in his arms once more and placing a kiss on my lips.

"It is."

"I can't believe we're going to have a baby," he says, almost absently. "I'm going to have to hurry up."

"Hurry up?"

"Well, first I need to get you down the aisle. I want to marry you as quickly as we can arrange it. And then I need to get these walls done."

I bark out a laugh. "I don't think the baby will be able to climb into a treehouse for a few years, Mason."

"No, probably not, but I still want to finish this place so it's ready to go." He offers me a smile. "We're having a baby."

"We are," I confirm once more, placing my own hand on my belly.

"I can't wait to watch you grow with our child, Ky. Thank you. You've given me two gifts today."

"Thank you for loving me," I reply, wrapping my arms around his waist and settling my cheek against his chest.

"Easiest thing I've ever done, sweetheart. Loving you is the greatest part of my life." He glances down and grins in contentment. "And now, we get to share that with a baby. I'm truly blessed."

We both are.

Blessed beyond imagination and it's only the beginning.

THE END

Don't miss a single reveal, release, or sale! Sign up for my newsletter.

http://www.laceyblackbooks.com/newsletter

Books Also by Lacey Black

Rivers Edge series

Trust Me, Rivers Edge book 1 (Maddox and Avery) – FREE at all retailers
Fight Me, Rivers Edge book 2 (Jake and Erin)
Expect Me, Rivers Edge book 3 (Travis and Josselyn)
Promise Me: A Novella, Rivers Edge book 3.5 (Jase and Holly)
Protect Me, Rivers Edge book 4 (Nate and Lia)
Boss Me, Rivers Edge book 5 (Will and Carmen)
Trust Us: A Rivers Edge Christmas Novella (Maddox and Avery)
~ This novella was originally part of the Christmas Miracles Anthology
BOX SET – contains all 5 novels, 2 novellas, and a BONUS short story
With Me, A Rivers Edge Christmas Novella (Brooklyn and Becker)

Bound Together series

Submerged, Bound Together book 1 (Blake and Carly)
Profited, Bound Together book 2 (Reid and Dani)
Entwined, Bound Together book 3 (Luke and Sidney)

Summer Sisters series

My Kinda Kisses, Summer Sisters book 1 (Jaime and Ryan)

My Kinda Night, Summer Sisters book 2 (Payton and Dean)
My Kinda Song, Summer Sisters book 3 (Abby and Levi)
My Kinda Mess, Summer Sisters book 4 (Lexi and Linkin)
My Kinda Player, Summer Sisters book 5 (AJ and Sawyer)
My Kinda Player, Summer Sisters book 6 (Meghan and Nick)
My Kinda Wedding, A Summer Sisters Novella book 7 (Meghan and Nick)

Rockland Falls series

Love and Pancakes, Rockland Falls book 1
Love and Lingerie, Rockland Falls book 2
Love and Landscape, Rockland Falls book 3
Love and Neckties, Rockland Falls book 4

Standalone

Music Notes, a sexy contemporary romance standalone
A Place To Call Home, a Memorial Day novella
Exes and Ho Ho Ho's, a sexy contemporary romance standalone novella
Pants on Fire, a sexy contemporary romance standalone
Double Dog Dare You, a new standalone
Grip, A Driven World Novel

Co-Written with *NYT Bestselling* Author, Kaylee Ryan

It's Not Over, Fair Lakes book 1
Just Getting Started, Fair Lakes book 2

Lacey Black

Can't Get Enough, Fair Lakes book 3
Fair Lakes Box Set
Boy Trouble, The All American Boy Series
Home To You, a second-chance novella

Acknowledgments

First, THANK YOU to Ruth Cardello for the opportunity to write in this world! I had the most fun diving into the Bachelor Tower and adding my own twist to an amazing series. Thank you to your behind the scenes team, and to your loyal readers for welcoming me into the Cardello book family. And a special thank you to the other authors writing in the world – it's been a wonderful experience!

A huge thank you to the best editing team there is – Kara Hildebrand, Sandra Shipman, Joanne Thompson, and Karen Hrdlicka.

Thank you Melissa Gill for another amazing cover design. Thank you Gel with Tempting Illustrations for gorgeous images and teasers. Thank you Brenda with Formatting Done Wright for making the book pretty. Thank you to the team at Give Me Books for helping promote this book.

Thank you Kaylee Ryan, Holly Collins, Lacey's Ladies, and my ARC team for your support.

To my husband and kids, thank you for always standing by my side and forgiving me when I submerge myself into my book world. It's not easy, but we make it work together.

To all the bloggers and readers, thank you, thank you, thank you. I hope you enjoy this story as much as I loved writing it.

About the Author

Lacey Black is a Midwestern girl with a passion for reading, writing, and shopping. She carries her e-reader with her everywhere she goes so she never misses an opportunity to read a few pages. Always looking for a happily ever after, Lacey is passionate about contemporary romance novels and enjoys it further when you mix in a little suspense. She resides in a small town in Illinois with her husband, two children, and three rowdy chickens. Lacey loves watching NASCAR races, shooting guns, and should only consume one mixed drink because she's a lightweight.

Email: laceyblackwrites@gmail.com
Facebook: https://www.facebook.com/authorlaceyblack
Twitter: https://twitter.com/AuthLaceyBlack
Website: www.laceyblackbooks.com

Sign up for my newsletter so you don't miss a single sale, reveal, or release!
http://www.laceyblackbooks.com/newsletter

Printed in Great Britain
by Amazon